MW01385822

Molly Stroud-Smith

DEAD BABIES

The first baby was born dead.

He had a head full of black hair and weighed just a little over eight pounds.

They named him Isaac Thomas Rutherford.

Sometimes Doreen thinks he was the lucky one.

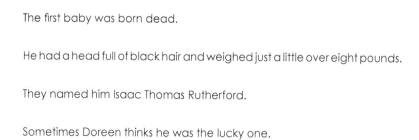

She locked the kids in the car again last night. In the dark. She could hear the baby's screams echoing off the concrete walls of the garage from inside the house. She ran the shower to drown out the sound. Delilah insisted that it was too hot but dared not whine. Doreen snapped at her to shut up as she scrubbed and scrubbed the child's body.

Watching faces pass at church after the sermon has ended and while she's waiting out the crowd so that she can collect the children from the nursery, she recognizes almost everyone. She smiles weakly and straightens her bangs.

When she sees her sister-in-law she feels the expression on her own face turn into something pleading.

Reaching out to touch the arm of her husband's sister she begs, "Pray for me."

September 2000

It's raining again when the alarm goes off. It's raining for the fourth day in a row. This weather makes everything more difficult. Getting the children to the bus, running errands with three toddlers, taking them in and out of the car, carrying umbrellas and worrying about rain gear. Avoiding getting mud and mess on the carpets. An already taxing day becomes more so with all this rain.

But Doreen knows it's not right to complain. God must have his reasons. He knows what He's doing after all and it is not for her to question. She should be humbled and grateful not bitter. Before her feet hit the floor she asks His forgiveness.

Forgive me Lord for being such an ingrate.

She goes to the basement and does fifty sit-ups and twenty-five pushups and jumps rope and jogs on the spot.

She goes upstairs to shower.

When she hears Gracie begin to stir, the hairs on the back of her neck become erect. She feels herself cringe. She feels something inside of her curdle and squeeze. She hopes the baby will fall back to sleep.

She dresses quietly while her husband snores. The blankets are pulled up to his chin and the daylight is beginning to creep in, allowing her to see a tiny line of drool seeping from the side of his mouth. Repulsion chokes her. The thought of him coming at her with his stiffness and his need makes her throat close.

Reverend Smiley has told them many times before that God created sex for pleasure. To be enjoyed between a man and his wife. To reject her husband would be to reject God. So she has learned to be gracious and giving despite herself.

Gracie is still fussing and soon will wake Faith if she isn't tended to.

Doreen tries to smile when she enters the girls' bedroom. She tries to feel enthusiastic to see her baby. To rejoice in her bright eyes and her tiny clinging arms. She is stung by the aroma of piss.

She scoops Gracie up quickly, checking on Faith who is still taking the deep breaths of slumber. The baby is fussy. She is rubbing fluids into Doreen's clean shirt. Saliva and mucus. She smells like rot.

As she fusses Doreen shushes her, jostles her, talks in high pitched tones and tries to soothe, but fails. The baby's crankiness only seems to intensify as she carries her down the stairs.

By the time they get to the kitchen she is at a moderate whimper, winding into a cry.

Doreen lays her on the couch so she can arrange a bottle and warm it in the microwave but the baby gets up immediately and follows her into the kitchen. Her noise becomes a full cry.

Doreen sighs and lets the child cling to her leg while she continues to prepare the bottle. Before the microwave has even beeped Delilah is standing in the kitchen doorway holding her brother's hand.

The baby takes the bottle and quiets and Doreen orders the other two down to the rec. room so she can begin to prepare for the day ahead. Breakfasts and lunches and back packs and outfits and rain coats and rubber boots.

And so it all begins again.

Thank you God for another glorious day.

When Tom has left for work, to go do business in the city, and the older two children have been put on the bus with soggy clothing and damp hair, Doreen takes Faith and Jacob and Grace Isabella into town to the playgroup.

She drinks a coffee and talks to the other mothers and the daycare providers and the Early Childhood Educators who run the program. She talks about diaper rash and letter formation and fussy eating habits. She talks about good deals on toothpaste and spaghetti sauce and toilet paper. She talks about parent-teacher interviews and safe parks. She talks about Kraft Dinner and Mini-Go yogurt and whole milk.

Jacob and Faith run around and ride tricycles and climb ladders. Faith pushes a doll around in a plastic baby stroller. She jabs at any other little girls who come near her, warning them, "Mine!" Doreen interferes the first few times but then gives up. Several mothers give Faith disapproving looks. Doreen doesn't blame them really. Faith is an abrasive child.

Jacob, in contrast, shares with the other boys who are playing with the same train set as him. At snack time he doles out some of his own cubed cheese so that his baby sister can have extra. He drinks his juice and wipes his pink mouth with a napkin. This small gesture makes Doreen smile.

The baby clings to her for most of the morning while the other children play. She whines and moisture comes out of her nose and mouth. She still smells like something slightly sour.

Faith and Jacob make art with paint and cookie cutters. Doreen helps each of them print their names. They're both exceptional at it. She's been teaching them at home since they could hold crayons in their pudgy hands. Even Gracie can already recognize the letter G and sometimes A and C.

Eden is another story altogether. Doreen wonders sometimes if she didn't eat enough protein during her pregnancy with Eden. If she neglected to consume enough folic acid. She is sure the blame is somehow hers.

One of the teachers says, "Wow Faith! Look at you printing like a big girl!" She turns to Doreen and says, "That's fantastic." Doreen smiles politely.

She finds it difficult to feel endearment toward Faith, and of course, she knows this is wrong. It is a mother's duty to love her children.

With Jacob it is so much easier. His dirty blonde hair and dark brown eyes. His little man's voice. His manners, his vocabulary. He is the easiest one to love.

He smells like dirt and grass, unlike the girls who have always managed to smell like something bodily.

At home Doreen makes lunch. She feeds the three younger children and gives Grace a bottle of water to take for her nap. Only water in the bottle for sleeping. Anything else will rot her teeth. She's fifteen months now and will have to give up the bottle soon.

Thank God there's not another one who needs it.

She hasn't gotten pregnant again yet. Every month when she starts to bleed she thanks Him. *Thank you lord for deciding that our family blessings are plentiful enough. Thank you God for my empty womb. You are so gracious Lord. Thank you.*

Tom would kill her if he knew. If he ever heard it out loud Doreen knows that Tom would not approve of this prayer. He would tell her she was ungrateful and blasphemous. She whispers the prayer inside her head. Whispers it on the toilet while clots of blood drop from her body. *Thank you Lord.*

The baby naps and Doreen does her best to keep Faith awake while Jacob snuggles under a blanket on the couch. Jacob can doze but if Faith falls asleep she'll be awake until midnight and Doreen will lose patience and sleep. It's very important that she gets her sleep and that the children are all in bed by eight. Especially if Tom wants at her. She hates hearing the children in the background while he grunts and pants and pushes.

Doreen does puzzles with Faith and colours with her and plays a game of Trouble.

Faith gets frustrated when her red pieces are sent backward on the game board to start all over again. She becomes agitated and unmanageable, eventually flying into a tantrum. Doreen tries to stifle it but once it begins it's too late. It only escalates, snapping Jacob out of his grogginess and causing his eyes to widen.

Doreen loses patience quickly. She slaps the child in the face hard, leaving an angry welt on the cheek and her own hand stinging. The child only stops her racket for a second and then returns to it with heightened ferocity, assaulting Doreen's ears with the intensity of her pitch.

Doreen slaps the child again and shakes her. Jacob pulls the blanket up over his head.

Scooping Faith up under her arm as she kicks and screams and takes punches at her mother, Doreen carries the anguished toddler to the bathroom where she will lock her. She knows she shouldn't. Tom wouldn't like it. Tom would say it's not right. And so would her mother-in-law.

Martha has caught Doreen before, with the children confined and she was not happy although she did not confront Doreen about it. Doreen could see it in her eyes for weeks afterwards and knows the incident was passed in whispers and tongue clucks amongst the members of her husband's family.

No, Martha would not approve, but if Doreen does not get away from this creature she will kill it. She will snap its neck like it's a crippled kitten.

She deposits her daughter in the bathtub but the child follows her out and is at the door before Doreen has a chance to shut it and lock away the noise. Faith reaches the doorway and braces it with her chubby hands, clinging to it as Doreen tries to pull her loose so that she can close the door. There is snot coming out of the child's face. It is running onto her lips and bubbling out of her nose and Doreen gags at the sight of it. It's yellow and thick. Between the child's open screaming lips and teeth are strands of saliva, some of it clear, some of it white and frothy.

Doreen pulls her hard, freeing her from the doorframe, and puts her fully clothed body into the bath tub, the child fighting her all the way. She turns the water on cold, full blast, and the shock makes Faith release her mother's arms and freeze in the downpour, giving Doreen time to reach the door, close it, and lock it.

When she emerges from the hallway and into the kitchen, her sleeves soaked with frigid tap water, Doreen becomes aware of Gracie's cries from upstairs. She feels herself begin to break apart.

She can't go. She can't go from one screaming child who is now pounding on the bathroom door in something that can only be described as exacerbated panic, to go to another one who has been woken by the commotion and will now be needy and will demand to be coddled and will want to smudge herself all over her mother's body.

She goes to the basement, to the laundry room. She turns on both machines with no clothes in them. She puts her hands over her ears and sinks down onto the concrete floor, her back against the cool washer which vibrates as it fills with water. Tom would be angry that she is wasting water and electricity. She closes her eyes and hums.

She prays, *Forgive me Lord, oh gracious God, forgive me.*

After she has met Delilah and Eden at the bus and brought them in for a snack and after she has looked through their backpacks and washed out their lunch containers and hung up their coats and sent them down to the rec. room, after all of that she can begin to prepare supper. She skins chicken and peels potatoes and whisks gravy and boils corn and tosses salad.

When supper is ready the children become obnoxious in their desire to eat but they must wait for Tom who is late more often than not. No matter how their bellies grumble and ache they must not eat without him.

At six forty-five Doreen calls Delilah up from the rec. room and hands her a sleeve of soda crackers and some juice boxes. Delilah says, "Thank you Mom," as she balances it all in her seven year old arms. She is so responsible. So grown up and helpful.

Doreen watches her walk down the basement steps to her siblings and feels a pang of something unpleasant pinch at her insides. She knows she isn't fair to Delilah. She knows the girl is beyond her years in duty and sacrifice. And yet she never complains. Delilah is a good girl.

Doreen justifies her treatment of her eldest daughter by telling herself that she is only preparing her for the job of being a wife. When it's Delilah's turn she will have long ago realized that life is about surrender. She will be prepared for all that family life affords a woman.

Tom finally gets home a bit after seven. He is damp when he comes in.

Doreen calls the children up and they scream, "Daddy!" running up the stairs and jumping all over Tom before he even has his coat off. He is patient with them to begin with. He pulls Jacob up into his arms and then Gracie. He ruffles Eden's hair and gives Delilah a quick squeeze. Faith clings to him the entire time. Wraps herself around his leg and moves with him as he comes into the kitchen and pulls out his chair.

Doreen puts the food on the table, none of it as good as it would have been an hour ago, and knows Tom will comment. Knows it won't be satisfactory.

"How was your day?" she asks him.

"Fine," he tells her.

He sits and pulls Faith up onto his lap. "What's up with you girlie?" he asks her. Looking at her face he sees the red welt left earlier by her mother's open hand. Doreen watches his face turn dark. "What happened to your face?" He looks up at Doreen, "What happened Doreen?"

"She was having a tantrum. She wouldn't stop. You know how it is with her."

"I thought we discussed this. Never in the face."

"Spare the rod, spoil the child," Doreen reminds him.

"Use the wooden spoon next time," he tells her, "on the butt or the leg."

"I'll remember."

"I hate your hair like that," he says as he lowers Faith from his lap. The child tries to hold onto him. She makes demanding noises. She whines.

"Let go of Daddy Faith," he tells her, "or I'll get that spoon." The child covers her bottom with both hands and Tom laughs a little.

He turns to Doreen and says, "Your hair."

Tom hates her hair pulled back. Her ears are too big. It's difficult, with the children, to keep it nice. Her hair gets in the way while she's caring for them. She forgot to pull the elastic out before he got home.

She goes to the mirror, pulls her hair out of the make-shift bun she had it in and rakes her fingers through it a few times before returning to the table to eat supper with her family.

"The chicken's cold," Tom informs her.

When Jacob barely eats anything on his plate and Grace Isabella spends most of her time at the table stuffing corn kernels into her mashed pota-toes, Tom looks perturbed.

"How come you're not eating boy?" he says to Jacob, "You should be starving."

Jacob shrugs, he says, "I'm full," in his soft, little man voice.

"Full?" Tom belches. "How can you be full, you've barely eaten a thing. Did Mommy give you snacks before supper again?"

Jacob nods. Tom looks at his wife, "For the love of Christ Doreen."

"Tom!" she snaps. Doreen hates that expression or any other expression that takes the Lord's name in vain, but Tom insists on using that one in particular. Out of some sort of habit she supposes, although he only uses it around the house and never in the company of family or friends.

"Well that's a pretty stupid thing to do don't you think? Feed the kids before supper?"

"You were late. They get hungry."

"We only had a few Daddy," Delilah tells him.

"Stay out of this Dee. This is just Mommy not using her brain as usual."

Delilah looks down at her plate.

Beside her, Eden too hangs her head. Her blonde hair touches her mashed potatoes.

"I won't do it next time. I'll let them wait."

"Yes you will," Tom says.

When Tom finishes his supper he sits in front of Gracie and force feeds her a few large spoonfuls of mashed potato and corn. She fusses and spits and eventually is excused.

But Jacob has to sit. Jacob has to eat. He is forced to remain at the table after everyone else is gone. He is threatened with the spoon. Little tears run down his eyes as he gags on his cold congealed food but continues to shovel it into his own unwilling mouth. Tom assures him again and again that if he doesn't finish every morsel he's going to get that wooden spoon across his butt. Tom reminds him repeatedly that this is what happens when bad boys eat snacks before supper.

Doreen, watching this, feels her throat drying and constricting.

She looks at Tom who wears a smug expression, his eyes holding all the arrogance of a high school jock, and she feels a film crawl over her skin and leave her clammy.

By the time Jacob is finished and she is done cleaning up and loading the dishwasher, it is long after the eight o'clock bedtime she strives for with the children. Tom has retired to the couch with his feet up. They stink. She can smell them from the doorway.

"I'm taking the kids up to get ready for bed," she tells him. He yawns.

As she's turning away from him to begin the stressful and tedious task of putting five children to bed, her husband calls her name. "Doreen." She turns back to look at him, he tells her, "take a shower."

She feels her heart stop for a minute and then start back up with a thud. He wants her clean.

She braces herself for the night ahead.

When the kids are finally asleep and she has washed and he comes for her she reminds herself, once again, of Reverend Smiley's words. She reminds herself that to forsake her husband is to forsake God.

She reminds herself that she long ago learned the price of forsaking God.

She rolls her eyes back into her skull like an epileptic and holds her breath.

In the morning it begins again.

Doreen wakes up damp between her legs, and prays that God will continue to spare her. No more babies. *Please God, no more babies.*

She prepares everyone for their day, sees Tom off, sees the older girls off, tends to Faith and Jacob and Grace all day. She cooks lunch and supper and cleans up after both.

She spends a frustrating amount of time at the kitchen table doing Kindergarten homework with Eden, whose brain is something porous and slow. But the child does not complain. She tries her best. Doreen can clearly see that she is making an effort and yet this makes the task of trying to explain things to her no less agonizing.

She bathes the children and reads to them and tucks them into bed. She listens to Gracie scream in her crib for a good half hour before she finally tapers off into a snivel and falls asleep hic-upping. Tom tells her, halfway into the tantrum, to go get her, quiet her down, he doesn't want to listen to it anymore. But Doreen can't bring herself to go into the room. She can already feel her hands squeezing around the child's throat, and the gratifying and permanent silence that would be the result.

Faith is unbearable throughout the day, every day that week and for the weeks that finish out September. She is demanding and difficult and makes an hourly habit of throwing herself around and expelling great gusts of noise. She oozes things constantly. Tears and everything that tears perpetuate. The fluids that repulse and disgust Doreen.

She asks Tom again, begs him this time, to please let her send Faith to Jr. Kindergarten. But he refuses her and tells her not to bring it up again.

"But she's so difficult! Please Tom, it's only every other day. I need the break from her."

Tom looks up from his newspaper and says, "What kind of a mother are you if you can't handle your own child? We didn't have these kids so that the system could raise them. She stays home with you. Period."

"She's really advanced Tom. She's bored at home. Stacey from the play-group said..."

Tom cuts her off, "Did you misunderstand something I just said?" he asks.

Doreen hangs her head.

"I didn't think so. Dismissed," Tom says, and goes back to his paper.

Dismissed. He actually says this to her.

Her brain becomes a soup that is spitting and bubbling and getting ready to boil. Bad thoughts come to her. Wrong thoughts. Violence tugs at her imagination. But she tells herself that she has no right to be angry at Tom. No right at all to think the thoughts that she does, to picture his face bashed-in and bloody. Tom was the one who saved her from a life of loneliness and despair. Tom was the man who accepted her and was willing to love her even after what happened. After she had been so badly damaged and dirtied. Tom was her saviour.

He never hits her. He provides well for the family. Doreen should never even dream of complaining.

A wife is to submit herself graciously to the servant leadership of her husband even as the church willingly submits to the headship of Christ.

Once again she asks the Lord to forgive her for her insolence. *Forgive me Father, sinner that I am. Forgive and humble me Lord. Amen.*

They still come to her in her dreams.

Even after all these years have passed their bodies still press into hers, their hands still grope and slap and dig into her flesh. She can feel the heat of their breath, smell the stench of cigarettes and alcohol and evil as it is expelled from somewhere deep inside each of them and onto her exposed flesh. She wakes in the night panting and clutching at herself, surprised to find that her clothes are still intact around her and not ripped and hanging from her bruised body.

Tom sometimes stirs, the movement of his limbs waking her. Other times he is startled into wakefulness with the force of her thrashing, the volume of her gasps.

"For the love of Christ Doreen," he says, "go back to sleep."

But she never can go back to sleep. She lays for hours staring at the walls, feeling semen splashed and caked on her face and neck. On her stomach and thighs and buttocks. Her nostrils burn with the scent of cum and urine.

She prays for release from the memory of those boys but knows she'll never have it.

The memory is her ongoing punishment and a reminder of what it means to live an unholy life.

The memory is God's way of reminding her.

Thank you Heavenly Father, for your guidance.

October, 2000

Doreen thanks God for the day ahead and steps out of bed, grabs something loose fitting to work out in and heads downstairs and through the kitchen to begin yet another day.

She smells dog shit.

The puppy whines and licks at her bare feet, which makes her instinctively kick at it. It yelps when a quick jab makes contact with its nose.

Tom decided two weeks ago that it was a good idea for the children to have a pet. He had a dog growing up, a black Lab named Blackie. Tom has, for some reason, suddenly remembered Blackie with a vengeance and has conjured a long standing belief that children benefit from the responsibility of pet ownership. Tom has all kinds of fond memories of Blackie that have, without an obvious trigger, come recently to the surface of his brain. He has some old photos previously stashed away in a damp box and seemingly unimportant, that last week he brought up from the basement to show to Doreen and the kids.

The children of course were over the moon about the idea. Tom had them so riled up about the prospect alone that Doreen had been having to peel them off the walls to get them going in the mornings. For days their mouths seemed incapable of uttering any words that did not concern the new puppy that Daddy was promising to bring home.

Doreen had not been as excited.

Puppies are a lot of work and she knew exactly where that work was going to fall. Not on any of the children, save perhaps for Delilah from time to time, and certainly not on Tom. This puppy would be one more task for Doreen to tend to. One more chore, one more stress factor. She knew it but she did not broach the topic with Tom. He had made up his mind without ever consulting her and had enlisted the children in his eager army of six against one without bothering to call a vote.

Of course, the puppy was every bit the pain in the ass Doreen had known it would be, perhaps even more so. It needed to be let out every hour and twice during the night. She had only just gotten Gracie sleeping through the night a few months back and it was the first time in eight years that she herself had been, on dreamless nights, getting a solid sleep. Now she was getting up for a puppy. For more urine and feces. Standing in the chilly night waiting for it to defecate.

This morning it has shit on the floor and seems not to have a clue that it has done anything wrong. It is now demanding of her like the kids do. Swarming her and slobbering on her and needing something although she isn't sure what. Constantly needing something.

Doreen picks up the poop and cleans and disinfects the carpet but only after she has taken the puppy outside so that it can once again make waste.

On her way down to the basement she hears Gracie begin to wind up from her crib upstairs. She can tell it's going to escalate rapidly this morning and that if she doesn't make it up the stairs in short order, Faith will be awake too. And Doreen prizes every second that Faith remains asleep.

She is forced to forfeit her workout. She feels resentment plow through her veins as she lifts the baby roughly from her crib. She puts her mouth close the child's ear and whispers through clenched teeth, "Stop it."

Something in her tone causes Gracie to react. She stops crying and looks at Doreen with wide frightened eyes.

And another day begins.

Thank you Lord for the blessings of the day I am about to embark on. Thank you. Amen.

It is Thanksgiving weekend.

Jacob turned three years old on the second of October which was a Monday. The puppy arrived the next day. They celebrated Jacob's birthday with a homemade cake and a stack of glitter glued cards and a trip to the dollar store in town. And of course with the puppy. The children wanted to call it "Cupcake" because of its correspondence with Jacob's birthday, but Tom said no. The puppy would be called Champ.

Then Tom had informed Doreen that Jacob's birthday would be celebrated again this weekend, along with his family, on the same day as the Thanksgiving celebration which Doreen would be hosting. Tom told her she would have to make another cake. One big enough to feed his mother, four of his seven sisters, and their husbands and children as well.

It is Sunday morning and Doreen has woken up extra early in order to try to get more cleaning done before church. The house will have to be immaculate in order for her to avoid the ridicule and snide comments of her husband's ruthless sisters. They've never liked Doreen. The only one that's even remotely nice to her is his youngest sister, who still allows herself to be called Suzie, but Doreen questions her sincerity. She pictures Suzie smiling sympathetically and then turning around and delighting, with the rest of her sisters, in some error Doreen has made.

And she always seems to be making mistakes Doreen does. She just can't seem to get anything right.

The puppy shows no signs of understanding the concept of house training. It stops whenever it needs to and does its business wherever it pleases. Doreen grinds its nose into the carpet until it yelps and throws it outside, but it only comes back to the door immediately and whines and barks until it is let back in. The animal reminds her of Faith.

Doreen scrubs and vacuums and scours and bleaches. She knows it is all in vain. The children will destroy everything she has done as soon as their demanding little feet hit the floor.

Doreen is feeling on edge. Her appetite is gone and she can feel her blood sugar plummeting as she exerts herself moving furniture around so that she can clean underneath it. When she finally hears Gracie's uncompromising racket coming from upstairs, there is a persistent buzzing in her ears and her hands are shaking. Her knees feel as if they might buckle underneath her.

On the floor in the kitchen, squatting to scour the cupboard under the sink, the intensity of bleach odor accosting her nostrils, Doreen goes to stand up so that she can head upstairs to snatch Gracie from her crib before she disturbs anyone else. When she stands she comes face to face with Tom who is holding a sulky Grace in his arms.

He doesn't look pleased.

"What are you doing?"

"I'm cleaning. There is a lot that needs to be done for this dinner."

Tom hands the baby to her. Gracie protests, holding her arms out pleadingly toward her father, wiggling her body in attempt to escape Doreen's grip.

"I want the kids in nice clothes today Doreen, not in the rags you've been carting them around in lately. It's Thanksgiving alright."

As Tom walks away Gracie becomes more agitated, more seemingly frantic to not be left behind with her mother.

Doreen squeezes her arms and says, "Stop it now," but the child only continues to make noise and repeat, "Daaa-daaaa" as her face once again begins to expel things.

Doreen, irritated and overwhelmed with all there is to be done, and feeling like she might pass out, tugs the high chair from its spot against the wall and plunks the baby down into it. She feels the impact of ass meeting seat and sees Gracie's neck snap back with the force. The baby cries harder than it was already doing.

Doreen straps the baby into the chair. At almost sixteen months she is able to wiggle free, she is able to push aside the tray. She is able to crawl down from the chair and once again attach her body to her mother's.

White noise begins sloshing around in Doreen's ears, reaching intermittent peaks that deafen her. She wants to beat this child into a coma. She wants it to stop making noise, to stop being wet and reeking of excrement. She wants the noise in her head to stop.

She goes to the garage. The baby follows her, crying and throwing herself around. Demanding and insisting.

In the garage is a Rubbermaid tote full of outdoor toys. There are skipping ropes. Long, and rubber with hard plastic handles. Doreen grabs as many of them as she can. She is blind now with rage and dizziness and the overwhelming urge for all of it to just end. Right now. For all of this living to finally be over with.

Reverend Smiley has spent an uncountable number of sermons explaining and preparing them for The Rapture. Doreen wants her gracious Lord to bring the Rapture down upon her. Right this second.

The baby is now inconsolable, beyond hysterical. The garage is chilly. The rubber ropes in her hand are cold. She is sweating. Her head is damp and sticky. The baby will not shut up.

Doreen grabs Gracie. She rips her pajama pants down her legs causing the child's noise to taper momentarily as she stares at her mother in shocked confusion. Doreen rips the rancid diaper from her baby's body. The weight of it in her hands is disgusting. The smell is putrid. She throws it across the garage, as far from herself as she can manage, and yet the odor still attacks her nostrils, burning and biting at the inside of her nose. The baby begins to howl again.

Looking around in a state of intoxication Doreen sees the bars of Tom's work shelves. The metal shelves are stacked with tool boxes and golf clubs and hunting gear. She drags Grace by her tiny arm, ripping her across the concrete floor, scuffing her bare feet as she pulls her. She can feel the floor resisting the little feet, rubbing against them, tearing skin she's sure.

She slaps the baby's body up against the frame of Tom's shelf. She holds her in place with one hand while she untangles a skipping rope with the other. Doreen's body works instinctively. Her hands move as if they are separate from her and are not dependent on her brain for instruction. Strength has ravished her.

She pins Gracie hard against the skeleton of the shelf and begins to wrap the rope around her body starting in the middle. The baby wails. The noise echoes and vibrates all around them.

The unrelenting fucking noise.

Doreen wraps and wraps and wraps rope around the body. She pins the arms and disables the legs. She coils rope tightly around the child so it's as if a snake were suffocating it, preparing to ingest it.

The child is at last restrained. It pisses. Yellow, pungent fluid pours out of the middle of its body and runs down its legs, staining the garage floor.

Now for the noise.

Doreen looks around again, finds a rag. Its original colour is beige but it is streaked with something dirty, something oily. She wraps it around the child's face, muffling, at last, the sound. She ties it tight at the back of the head. The eyes are wide with terror.

And yet, it continues to scream.

Doreen is on her hands and knees scrubbing when Tom comes into the kitchen. The other children have been ordered down to the basement and told not to come up no matter what. Delilah has been warned of the consequences of letting any of her siblings upstairs. Delilah has asked about Gracie and been told to shush. Delilah has been plenty warned.

"Where are the kids?"

She hears his voice but makes no connection with the words coming out of him. She scrubs. Bleach splashes up into her face. She can feel the penis of one of those boys. It is forcing itself into the back of her throat. The sting of bleach on her tongue, as she licks it from her lips, is soothing.

Tom's voice comes out of his mouth again but all she hears is noise. Always so much noise.

She can see Tom in her peripheral vision. He is moving about. He is doing things.

She hears doors opening, feels gusts of cool autumn air. She scrubs and scrubs and scrubs.

Suddenly Tom is in front of her with the baby. The baby is naked from the waist down and she is red in places and her face is dripping.

Tom is screaming at Doreen, making a great deal of noise, his mouth opening and closing and spitting.

Delilah is there suddenly and Doreen feels a quick stab of anger at her oldest daughter for disobeying her. She points her finger toward Delilah and tries to open her mouth to reprimand her but is overwhelmed by the smell of bleach.

The room turns gray starting at the edges. The grayness turns black and bleeds into the middle of the room, blankets everything. Doreen feels her head hit tile.

Quiet.

Thank you oh wondrous God, for the quiet.

———————————

Doreen floats on a calm ocean of something that allows no noise, no confusion, no heartache.

From between her legs, through a slippery and co-operative opening in her body, the doctor pulls a small human.

A boy.

He is bluish-purple and silent.

He is covered in blood and something else that is white and curdled. The room smells strongly of her insides.

The face is perfect, each feature so very exact, flawless.

He is so quiet. So still.

She holds the infant against her breast and feels the weight of him there. Such a beautiful silent baby. An only child. Immaculate in his soundlessness.

Doreen smiles.

"So Doreen, explain to me why you think we are here."

The counselor is female and older and quite attractive. She has long straight hair the colour of coffee. She has a delicate nose and jaw line. Her lips are slick with something Vaseline-like.

When Doreen arrived the woman introduced herself as Lisa Griffin and told Doreen to please call her Lisa.

The sentence she has just uttered to Doreen, the first in their actual session, comes across as condescending. *Why do you think we are here?* Doreen is reminded of high school, sitting across from a perturbed principal, someone wiser and more aware than her. Someone with superior intelligence and innate knowledge of rules and what happens when they are broken.

Not only is she being asked to explain herself, but to explain what she *thinks* is the reason for her actions. Not what she *knows*, but what she *thinks,* implying that Doreen's version of events is simply her own and does not necessarily correspond with reality.

Tom's sisters laugh from hidden places around the pale yellow room. Once again Doreen is the family idiot.

"Doreen?"

"My husband and our minister thought it would be beneficial."

"Okay. And why do you think they thought that?"

Doreen stares at her hands in shame. She can picture the baby's half naked body, the terrified eyes, the frayed skin of the stubby toes. She can't bring herself to meet eyes with this woman. She mutters and twitches and says, "um," a lot as she goes into her guarded explanation of why she is here.

She tells the counselor that she was having some trouble at home. Some stress with the kids. She had a bad day. She hadn't eaten much, she passed out on the kitchen floor, had to go to the hospital. Tom and Reverend Smiley had decided the situation was best kept within the family and the church and dealt with promptly. And that's why she *thinks* she is here.

She provides this summary while simultaneously trying to figure out how much of the truth she is allowed to tell. This woman was recommended by Reverend Smiley specifically because of her church affiliations and analogous beliefs. Doreen has been told that she has helped many members of the congregation with a variety of situations. Although Doreen has never personally spoken to her, and surprisingly does not find even remote familiarity in her face, Lisa Griffin is a member of her church.

She is one of them. Although this should make Doreen feel better, it for some reason has the opposite effect.

In her re-telling Doreen leaves out the part about tying Gracie to a steel shelf in the garage and muzzling her with a dirty rag.

Tom told her to be careful. To remember that many things are family matters and that all therapists have certain obligations whether they are church affiliated or not. That the last thing they needed was Children's Aid involvement, some atheist government smart-asses telling them how to raise their kids.

"Would it be fair to say that you had a little bit of a melt-down Doreen?"

Doreen nods. Although she's not sure the "little bit" part is completely accurate.

"So then," the counselor shifts in her seat, poises her pen over her note pad, "in your assessment of the situation, what was it that brought this on?"

She wants this hour to be over with. The clock says only ten minutes of it have passed.

She shrugs at the therapist. "I don't know. I guess I get stressed out sometimes with all the kids."

"The kids. Yes. How many children do you have again," she looks through her notes, lifting pages, "six?"

"Yes. Six. But one is dead. So five."

The counselor pauses for a minute but Doreen doesn't see the expression on her face because she refuses to look directly at her. She can see her hand moving as she again writes something in her note pad.

"And you stay at home with the kids?"

Doreen nods.

"And you're finding that a little stressful sometimes are you?"

"It's a decision that Tom and I made before we got married. That he would work and I would stay home with the kids. Tom wanted lots of kids."

"How about you Doreen? How did you feel about having lots of kids?"

Doreen picks at a fingernail. She tears away a bit of cuticle. A small balloon of blood erupts at the point where skin meets nail.

"I think I wanted them too. At the time."

The counselor pauses again, writes something down, then asks, "At the time? Can you explain what you mean by that Doreen? At the time."

Doreen feels as if she is somehow being tricked. Like a trap is being set and that if she opens her mouth, her stupid, error-prone mouth and lets the wrong words trickle out, there will be no recovering from what it might cause.

She sighs heavily. She mulls over her words, examines them before she allows them to be born.

She says, "I wanted a big family yes. Tom and I both did. But I guess," she stops and looks up from her now bleeding cuticle and into the face of her counselor, into the eyes of this 'Lisa'. She says, "It's just I sometimes find it to be a lot of work."

The counselor nods, "It *is* a lot of work. Mothering is extremely taxing Doreen, and you have *five* children. You're not the only one who has ever felt worn out or frustrated by your kids."

Doreen stares into her eyes, struck by these words. Nothing comes into her head to say, she just stares, wide-eyed and surprised.

The counselor writes something.

For a brief second Doreen feels lighter. Something inside her shifts and gives way and she squeezes her injured finger in attempt to assist her blood in clotting.

Then, just like that, defeat smothers her again when this Lisa looks up from her notes, puts her pen on her clipboard and says, "That being said of course, each and every child is God's greatest blessing. Motherhood is God's gift to you and one that you must work every day to uphold."

Doreen lets her finger go. Blood oozes from her torn flesh, red and warm.

> **Children, from the moment of conception, are a blessing and heritage from the Lord.**

Forgive me Father, for I have sinned.

On the way home in the car Tom grills her about the session. He wants to know what they talked about, how much Doreen shared of their personal lives and that she kept quiet about anything she had done, physically, to the children.

Doreen answers his questions feeling the flatness of her own voice. She nods and says yes, no, and I'm not sure. She tells him she feels tired and groggy and would really like to go home and lie down.

He continues with questions and for what feels like the hundredth time says, "Remember, all I told the doctors was that you'd been under some stress and you fainted."

"Yes Tom. I know. I remember."

Anti-anxiety pills, the doctor had suggested, *a little something to calm your nerves.* Of course not, Tom had said, the body is the temple of Christ.

As the garage door lifts, the sound of its gears grinding together in exertion wakes Doreen from a sleep she didn't realize she'd been in.

Inside the garage she opens her eyes. There is Tom's utility shelf, a framework of cold gray metal. Skipping ropes still lay in a pile beside it. Gracie's unrelenting screams come back to her, blaring so loud in her memory that she has to shake herself to escape them.

Tom comes around to her side of the vehicle and opens her door, a gesture she has not been on the receiving end of since they first began dating. Somebody else's lifetime ago.

He takes her arm and helps her out of the car, guides her toward the back door of the house. She feels warmth where their arms are entwined. She stops and looks at him. He has a full mouth that may have been inviting at one time, back before he began to spit demands from it constantly.

"Are you happy that we had so many babies," she asks her husband.

"What? What are you talking about right now?" He looks instantly frustrated.

"This life we chose, does it make you happy?"

"Come on Doreen. Knock it off."

Doreen looks down at her husband's shoes, scuffed and old.

He gives her a gentle tug. "Come on," he tells her, guiding her toward the house.

She feels so weary and weak. Exhausted. Trying to explain herself for an entire hour without revealing anything that Tom had warned her not to has left her drained and needing desperately to rest.

She knows there will be no rest.

The door to the house laughs at her. She dreads going in. She wishes she could pass out again now, flutter to the ground and bang her head on something hard and sharp.

Inside the children await. Not only the children, but Martha. Sent to 'help'. To observe and instruct and pass judgment and report back.

"I don't feel well Tom," she says as he turns the knob of the door that will lead them into their mudroom.

"Well you better snap out of it," he tells her and she squeezes her eyes shut as he pushes the door open and the first thing she hears is Gracie's ear-splitting blast ricocheting off the walls of their home.

The house is pungent with the smells of the supper they had hastily eaten before leaving to drive into town for her appointment. Tom's mother had made cabbage rolls, something Doreen could never perfect. Something Tom had told her, after six months of marriage, to give up even bothering with. "There's no point Doreen. If I want cabbage rolls I'll just go visit my mom or one of my sisters."

Now the air is thick with tomato sauce and ground beef and garlic and spices despite the fact that three hours have passed since they ate. It's almost exactly eight o'clock.

Gracie's screams are coming from upstairs and Martha has the rest of the children on the couch, cuddled together in front of a large, brightly illustrated book. The children remain beside her, stay snug on the couch next to their grandmother even when their parents enter the adjoining room. Only the dog moves, barreling toward Tom who bends down and fluffs the thing's ears repeating its name in a voice he does not use for anything else.

Tom goes to his mother and leans down and kisses her cheek. "Hey Mom," he says. "How were they?"

He unbuttons his coat while Doreen stands mannequin-like near the kitchen table, watching. Watching these people like a program on TV. For a minute she questions who any of them even are.

Martha talks. Doreen makes sense of random words. Bath. Faith. Homework. Puppy. Crying. Sleep.

The voices of Tom and his mother and the children fade in and out and her head now feels full of something spongy and fibrous. Something that blocks anything that makes sense from coming or going. A material so obstructive that it will not allow her brain to signal her body to move.

Maybe if she just stands there. Maybe if she stays very still, this strange scene in front of her will evaporate and she will be a young woman standing on the threshold of her life with a million choices laid out before her. With the wind howling in her ears, assuring her of her freedom. Maybe if she just stands still enough.

And then she hears it. A voice that she does not recognize, but that is somehow familiar. It is a deep voice, a male voice. It sounds like God.

She looks around at first, expecting a new person in the room. A physical body. There isn't one. Only the kids and Martha and Tom.

This voice is coming from inside her somehow. From deep in her skull.

It begins as something soft and quiet and gradually becomes more pronounced. It says things she has never heard anyone say before. It assures her of what is right and good. It tells her where freedom lies. She listens intently at once appalled and enticed by what this voice, strange yet comforting, is suggesting.

She feels her coat being tugged from her shoulders and the voice dissolves instantly. Vanishes.

Now it's Tom's ugly voice demanding of her again. She's been standing still for too long, what's wrong with her just standing there like that? She should take her boots off. She should help her mother-in-law put the children to bed now that Gracie has stopped crying. She should take a shower.

She nods and begins to move and all around her small humans and furry things swarm and seem to multiply. There are just so many of them, and she is only one person. She tries to move without tripping over one of their outstretched limbs. She feels claustrophobic and fearful of being made to fall over, of losing her balance and falling into this sea of living things.

Her head is full of cotton and incoherent whispers.

Then she sees the boy child. He reaches out to her, touches her arm. His little fingers are warm. Tiny circles of heat are left on her skin by his gentle imprints. She looks down at him. His dark eyes, his silent mouth.

Isaac.

She steadies herself, reaches down into the crowd of limbs and heads and eyeballs, and she pulls the boy up into her arms. Plucks him from his siblings. Saves him from the swarm.

The realness of his weight against her chest clears away the fog in her brain. His small sleepy voice says, "Mommy," and the whispers in her head stop.

He is a beautiful cherub-faced little boy with bangs that need to be cut and he smells like tree bark and corn stalks. She buries her face into his small neck, inhaling him.

"Jacob," Doreen says, and feels her chest lighten as she exhales a breath she didn't realize she'd been holding.

Oh gracious God in Heaven, thank you for this little boy. Thank you God. Amen.

Doreen wakes up clear-headed. The thick material that had been lodged in her skull the night before has disintegrated. The whispers have been silenced.

She wakes, un-routinely, to sun and quiet and an empty space beside her. She knows immediately that she has slept through her morning obligations. Panic seizes her.

She jumps from the disheveled king size bed and throws on her robe. She sprints downstairs, fearful of the quiet and the stillness of the walls around her. Her throat constricts with the unfamiliarity of a silent, unmoving home.

Downstairs the sun has filled the kitchen and the living room, pouring in through windows and sliding glass doors, illuminating cleanliness. There is not a visible speck of dust on anything, not a dish in the sink, not a toy in need of being stowed away. Surfaces are gleaming and her nostrils fill with the scent of lemon. There is not a crumb anywhere.

It is so quiet.

On the counter is a note from Martha. She has taken Delilah and Eden to school, she has the other three children with her, the puppy is tied up in the yard. Doreen is instructed to enjoy some peace and quiet, to enjoy her day. Martha will return to greet the children at the bus and make supper.

In the eight years since Delilah was born, this has not happened. Not once has Doreen had an entire day to herself.

She fills the kettle and sets it on the burner, turning the dial to high. She puts a teabag into a large ceramic mug, gets out a spoon and sets it on the counter. She goes into the living room and turns on the radio. Christian rock seeps through the speakers as she looks for something she can straighten or wipe. There is nothing.

She returns to the kitchen as the kettle begins to boil, screaming at her like a famished infant. She pours her tea, steeps it, removes the tea bag and splashes the steaming beverage with skim milk.

Back in the living room she stands with her tea in front of the sliding glass doors, taking tentative sips, making quiet slurping sounds. She stares out at their property; trees with a spattering of red, brown and yellow clinging to their branches. Bushes still green but no longer vibrant. Dead leaves immaculately raked into fat piles and waiting for Tom to bag.

A bird flutters past. Her hot mug warms her hands. Her stomach growls. A woman on the radio sings about the glory of God and the sanctity of

Heaven. Doreen thinks about the Rapture and Heaven and wonders if this is what it will be like. Silent and still. Looking out onto a beautiful piece of land without actually having to inhabit it.

When the Rapture comes Earth will turn to Hell, and the believers will be lifted up into the arms of God. Heaven will be eternal for all of those who have abided by His rules. Sinners will be left to suffer His wrath. Doreen prays she will be among the Saints, hopes that she has repented sufficiently for her sins. She hopes that she will one day be standing somewhere silent and still without obligation to move or speak. That she has earned this promised eternity of uninterrupted peace.

That she will hold Isaac in her arms again.

Reverend Smiley has assured her that in the afterlife the baby would be waiting and Doreen would understand then, the reason for God's decisions. And he would be hers. Raven haired and silent. Flawless baby boy.

Doreen makes oatmeal and slices bananas into it. She sits at the table and eats and finishes her tea. She goes upstairs, into the master bedroom, and makes the bed. She goes into the children's' rooms to tidy and make beds but it has already been done. Looking around at all that Martha has managed to accomplish with what appears to be efficiency and ease, Doreen feels the familiar cloak of inadequacy come to blanket her. She is just not good at much.

When she was a little girl she was reminded daily of how inept, at practically everything, she was. Explanations for her shortcomings were demanded while a belt loomed overhead. If she had no answer, if her brain froze and her mouth stayed slack, leather met skin with a sharp snap and sting. Her skin would welt and blister. She learned to say that she was bad, that she was wrong, that she was stupid and naughty and dumb. If she hated herself enough and could express it in time, she might be spared the bite of leather and buckle.

Her father showed her leniency because she was a girl. Her brothers wounds would bleed and scab and burn for days, sometimes scarring permanently.

And here she is, decades later, still so damn inadequate. Incapable of running a household, of doing her hair, of making cabbage rolls.

She thinks about the Rapture again.

For God did not appoint us to wrath, but to obtain salvation through our Lord Jesus Christ.

Oh, God in Heaven, I am ready for the Rapture whenever you see fit. Lift me up Lord, into your gracious and all-knowing arms. I am ready Lord. Amen.

———————————————

Doreen spends the day attempting to pass the hours, the long drawn out minutes, the excruciating seconds of being alone with her thoughts.

She reads her Bible. Pages and pages of scripture until her eyes burn.

She sings hymns and sways, eyes closed, holding herself in the bright empty living room. Cradling her own body she tries to feel Jesus embracing her. She tries to find connection with spirit. Longs for it. She tells herself that she feels it. She feels Jesus in the room rocking her, holding her up, feeding her with His love. She so desperately needs his acceptance, but in the core of herself she feels unnervingly disconnected. Distanced. Almost numb.

She is so easily penetrated by things that take her by force and dirty her, yet it seems that when she looks to be opened up and filled she remains hungry and vacant.

She calls out to Jesus, to God. She begs to feel the Holy presence, to be in His company and not so sickeningly hollow.

She feels nothing.

She is stuffed in a dark closet waiting for her father to decide how many lashes with the belt will be necessary to cleanse her of her sins, of the unforgivable mistake of being who she is.

After lunch she goes outside and releases the puppy from its chain, but only after cleaning up piles and piles of excrement. The thing jumps all over her tearing into her shins with untrimmed claws, leaving dirt and moisture on her pants. It licks at her hands and this makes her stomach clench in protest. The wet thick tongue is like something slithering, uninvited, across her. She pops the animal on the nose. It lets out a sharp startled whine.

She takes it for a walk and it empties its bowels again, not once, but twice. It urinates every five steps. It crosses in front of her, tangling itself in its leash and when she unwraps in from the mess it does the same thing all over again. It barks at birds and squirrels and falling leaves. It steps in front of her and stops, then jerks its body into motion again spastically. The entire time she is walking it she feels as if she must stay on guard or she will be tripped and likely trampled by the idiotic thing. She consciously wonders what it is that people enjoy about dogs.

When she gets it back home the paws are filthy and wet and she does not want it on the carpets. It has a strong smell now, something like body odor and dirt and innards. Meaty and rank. She feels her gag reflex begin to quake as she sets down some food and water for it, as the whole time it is jumping up almost knocking the bowls out of her hands.

She goes inside and makes another tea and wonders what she used to do with her time all those lifetimes ago. What did she do with the hours of her day when she wasn't caring for a thousand invalid-like human beings?

She worked. That took up eight hours of her day five days a week. She had a gym membership. She was heavily involved in the church. She sometimes got her nails done and went shopping. She went to work functions when they arose. She took photographs of things. Churches and flowers and clouds and statues. She read. On dreamless nights she slept in long uninterrupted stretches.

Now it is still only two o'clock and the silence of the house is bearing down on her. Jesus is nowhere to be found and that dog is nothing but an annoyance.

She stands in front of the radio now, listening to a folk-y male voice sing, *I have felt a little bit stronger, a little bit stronger with you, I can last quite a bit longer, eternally longer with you.*

It becomes somewhat unpalatable.

She goes to the dial, reaches out, touches it. She never touches the dial on the radio. It stays put. It never moves. She discovers on the outside edges of the dial the only dust remaining in the entire house after Martha's un-witnessed cleaning rampage. Her fingers smudge the thick layer of dead skin, leaving imprints in it. She inhales the ashy substance as it scatters. She has the strong urge to eat it, to lick the dust from her fingertips.

Tom says this is the only station they need to listen to. Tom says this is all the children's precious Christian ears should be exposed to. Tom says.

Doreen turns the dial.

New sounds explode through the speakers. Beats and guitars and raspy voices. She spins it and spins it, listening to snippets as they spatter and burst, violating her puritanical living room. She wonders if Jesus is anywhere now.

She hears something catchy, an interesting rhythm, an energetic male voice. She tunes it in. She listens, feeling some sort of excitement gurgling around in her depths, something she can't really give name to, spitting and frothing in her guts and threatening to erupt from her esophagus.

The male voice sings of a girl who cried so much that she drowned the world. He sings that she looks very sad in pictures but that he loves it when she smiles.

Listening to this strange concoction of sounds she goes to the bathroom mirror. She pulls back her long dark hair. Her ears are massive. Tom is right. She is disgusting. She is ugly. She is lucky anyone wanted to marry her at all. Gracie has her ears. Her big ugly Dumbo ears, making the child even more revolting, more difficult to tolerate. Pour homely Gracie. Tom calls her Yoda. She giggles dumbly, not knowing yet, still blissfully ignorant to the fact that this feature will make her harder to love.

Doreen goes back to the kitchen and takes some scissors from the drawer. The song is different now. No more crying girls drowning the world, as God did in the days of Noah, but now a man who describes himself as bent and scared. He's asking for help, from who she isn't sure. A woman perhaps. Someone beautiful.

Doreen feels like the songs are speaking to her. Maybe Jesus has entered the room. Her body feels alive and full of something electric. Bursts of light and energy. It is not entirely a pleasant feeling however. It borders on irritating, taking jabs at her and threatening to knock her over, just like that fucking dog with its insane convulsions underfoot.

She goes to the bathroom mirror. She pulls back her ugly black hair and looks at those ears of hers. The flash of a different face comes to her. Crew cut, acne, sadistic grin. She remembers the feeling of hands pulling hard on the roots of her scalp, tugging her hair matted with earth and river water. The motion, back and forth, the sharp jab against the back of her throat, the smell of body. Of mushrooms and sweat.

She grabs a huge chunk of her hair with one hand, holds it tight, and with the other hand she lifts the scissors. The blades gleam in the light of the bathroom, sparkling in the mirror. She opens them, rests them against the strands that she is holding, and begins to close them. Her hair resists. It is thick and the scissors are dull. She opens the scissors again and closes them. Pieces of hair begin to fall away. Black debris flutters into the white sink, dirtying it, blemishing the shiny porcelain that Martha has surely slaved over.

She opens and closes the scissors again and again and again, the action getting easier with each motion. More hair falls and flies and scatters and makes her cough. A woman is singing on the radio now. She hears a voice but no lyrics. She tries to feel Jesus but becomes confident that he has abandoned her. He is just not there.

Another chunk of hair. More opening and closing of the scissors. She hacks and tugs and carves, getting so lost in her task that she cuts herself in several spots including the top of one of her massive ears. It stings and bleeds but she carries on. In a frenzy of motion and determination she whips her scissor- wielding hands around cutting and cutting and cutting.

At last she stops.

There is not much else to chop away. Her hair now ends above her ears in jagged black chunks.

She breathes out a labored exhalation and lets her hand and the scissors fall into the sink. A man's voice is singing again. This time about

Californication. Doreen does not know what that is, but she has a feeling it would not be okay with Jesus. Or Tom.

She looks long and hard at the ugly bitch in the mirror. Those ears are gargantuan. They are a mistake. An abomination. The pediatrician had actually begun talking to them about pinning Gracie's back, but Tom said no. Tom said that God makes no mistakes. And yet he insists that Doreen cover the ears God gave to her. With her hair and with her hands, never allowing certain things to make contact with her eardrums.

She will have to clean this up now.

Fear strikes her.

There will be no hiding this. The act of terrorism she has inflicted upon herself is absolutely blatant.

She looks at the massacre again.

Sharp bits of severed hair dig into her neck and chest.

She smiles at herself.

She prays.

Oh thank you Lord. For these perfect ears. For never making mistakes. You humble me Lord. Amen.

When Martha walks in the door with the children her eyes balloon open and become huge saucers of black pupil. The children gasp, all except for Gracie who is asleep on her grandmother's shoulder.

Delilah says, "Oh Mommy!" and looks as if she's about to cry. She wraps her arms around Eden as if consoling her younger sister in a time of tragedy.

Doreen touches her ears.

"Okay." Martha says, and begins to move in a way that indicates she has a plan of action. "Okay," she says again, "it'll be fine."

Tom's reaction, when he returns from work hours later, is much worse. There is yelling. The children are escorted out of the room. Doreen is escorted upstairs. She sits on the bed and pulls her knees up to her chest and buries her head into them, hiding herself from Tom.

He flies around the room and makes angry gestures with his hands and arms. Things are thrown. Things crash around her.

She hears the voice again. The deep male voice from the night before. It says something vulgar. It curses in her ears. It comforts and unnerves her.

Eventually Tom's energy is spent. Doreen lifts her head to meet his eyes and they are bulging from their sockets, red and vein filled. She has no idea what colour her husband's eyes are although she thinks they may have been blue at one time. His mouth is covered in spit. Tom is very displeased.

"What in God's name could you possibly be smiling about right now?" she hears him say. She didn't know she was smiling. She reaches up to touch her own mouth and finds that it is true. Tom is right. Her lips are curled upward and her teeth are bared. She touches her cheeks and feels that they are full and rounded. Her entire face reeks of joy.

"I'm sorry," she tells her husband, but the smile remains. Beyond her control her face continues to exude happiness.

Now Tom will have no choice but to look at her big ugly ears. She pictures his erect penis deflating, turning soft and mushy, becoming nothing more than a useless flabby hose.

Smoke seems to be coming off of him. Doreen cannot force herself to look upset. She wants to repent but she can't. She is a sinner.

Finally he throws his hands up in the air and leaves the room. The door slams, making Doreen jump.

Oh humble Lord. Oh Heavenly Father and Saviour. Tom is very angry I'm afraid. Very angry Lord. Amen.

Lisa Griffin appears sincere when, at the commencement of the next therapy session, she tells Doreen that she likes what she's done with her hair. Doreen touches the back of her head and looks down. She sits. She does not acknowledge the compliment.

Martha had stayed with the kids the day following Doreen's episode, so that she could go to the salon and have her hair evened out and styled. The young girl cutting it seemed frightened, like she thought Doreen may have escaped from somewhere remote and heavily guarded. Of course, she hadn't escaped at all, but rather was still under Tom's direct instruction, as was the reason for her appointment.

Because of the enormous chunks Doreen had liberated from her head and the helter-skelter way she had done so, the end result, even in the hands of a professional, was a hair-do so absolutely short that there was no way to describe it other than boyish. She looked like a boy. One with very big ears.

"How has your week been?" Lisa is asking. Doreen isn't sure how to answer this question appropriately considering everything that has happened. She thinks a minute before speaking.

"My mother-in-law has been staying. Helping me out with the kids."

"Has that been good? Do you feel a bit less stressed?"

"She's a very good homemaker. Better than I am."

"I'm sure you're a very effective homemaker Doreen. You've just hit a rough patch."

Doreen had not been fishing for this reassurance and feels insulted slightly by its deliverance. She says nothing.

Lisa Griffin writes something down, takes a minute to lift pages and review notes, and then looks up and smiles. Her teeth are very white, perhaps bleached, and the top row is perfectly straight. The bottom row is slightly askew but this detracts nothing from her prettiness.

"So Doreen, I'm going to do the Freud thing here," the counselor smiles to herself, "and ask you about your parents."

Doreen nods.

Lisa Griffin is wearing a colourful scarf. Her perfume is strong but not unpleasant. She has holes but no earrings.

"Tell me about your mother." It is clear to Doreen that Lisa Griffin finds herself amusing. Doreen is not really sure she gets the joke. As usual it feels as if there is something she's missing.

"What do you want to know?"

"Okay, let's start this way. What was your childhood like? For example, do you have any brothers or sisters?"

"Two brothers. One older, one younger."

"Tell me a bit about them. Did you get along? Did you enjoy growing up with brothers?"

"I wanted a sister but I got along with the boys well enough."

"Are they good men?"

"Very good men."

"Are you close?"

"Not as close as I'd like, I suppose."

Writing, as always, Lisa Griffin asks Doreen why she thinks that her and her siblings are not as close as she would like them to be.

Doreen wrings her hands together over and over again as she thinks about what to say. She feels sweaty and has an urge to open a window but there aren't any. The room is windowless.

"My older brother is too liberal with his kids and my younger brother is a homosexual. They are probably both going to Hell. Tom and I are hopefully going to Heaven."

"Why do you think that Doreen? That your brothers are going to Hell?"

Although Doreen is positive she has slipped and said too much, Tom would not want her talking about her brothers with anyone, the counselor appears unfazed.

"Tom says that when the Rapture comes both my brothers will be left behind."

The Counselor clears her throat and writes.

Doreen stares at the wall. Unblinking. Tom's words ring through her head like church bells. Discretion. Unwavering discretion.

"Can you tell me about the word liberal? What do you mean when you say your brother is too liberal with his children?"

"They don't go to church. They don't pray. They let the kids watch Teletubbies and Pokemon. They listen to the non-Christian radio. Rock and rap and the like."

Doreen remembers listening to the radio in the living room the day she cut her hair. She has worried every day since that God might be angry, that as punishment someone will jump out at her and shove her face into the concrete. After she had cleaned the hair from the sink she had been careful to re-adjust the stereo, spinning the dial in reverse and tuning it back into the Christian station that Tom insists upon.

"Tell me some more about this brother. What is his name?"

Doreen sighs heavily. She feels defensive.

"Jack. He has two kids. He has a wife. They don't believe in God. They will be left behind when the Rapture comes."

"Well, I'm not sure we can know that Doreen. Why are you so sure that's the truth?"

"Tom says."

"Okay. Well."

"We have Tom's family anyway. They are important. They are a priority. My brothers are not a priority. That's okay."

She has said too much again. She has never been good at speaking intelligently. She has a stupid mouth that doesn't know when to stop flapping. She wants away from the topic of her family.

"Can we go back and talk about the other brother for a minute."

Doreen wants more than anything not to but thanks to her stupid mouth the subject is in the room, unavoidable now.

"What is the other brother's name?"

According to Tom her brother's name is That Little Faggot. Tom calls him that as he assures Doreen that her younger sibling will rot in Hell. That he will, without a doubt, be left behind when the Rapture begins. He will suffer eternally for the unforgivable sin of loving who he does.

"Bruno."

"And Bruno is homosexual is that right?"

"Yes."

Doreen feels heat crawl up her neck, reach her face, and barrel toward her ears.

Little Queer. Flaming Fairy. Deviant. When he is really feeling passionate about the topic Tom puts the F word in front of one of these phrases.

"How do you feel about Bruno Doreen?"

"He is a sinner. He will be left behind."

"That's how Tom feels about your brother, I want to know how you feel about your brother."

Bruno as a young boy smiles at Doreen. Dark hair like hers, dark eyes like Jacob's. Scrawny, effeminate boy in a ripped t-shirt with one eye turning purple and both lips swelling into deformity. Yet still smiling. Still proud to be exactly who he is.

But I thought Tom, that God made no mistakes?

"Back when I knew him, he was the most wonderful person in the world."

The Counselor smiles. Doreen sees it from her peripherals.

"We hate the sin Doreen, but God tells us to love the sinner."

Something catches in Doreen's throat. An old raw ache.

"Why are we talking about my brothers?" Doreen squirms in her seat. She looks at the clock, willing the session to be over, willing the hour to just hurry up and pass.

"I'm just getting a glimpse into your past Doreen. Just common practice in this profession."

Silence. Doreen can feel the counselor's eyes on her. She stares down into her own lap.

"Shall we talk about your parents now?"

"Yes. Let's."

"Tell me about them. What was your childhood like?"

"Strict."

"Strict?"

"Lots of rules. Lots of punishment."

Silence again. It appears that she needs to say more to satisfy the counselor so she speaks again.

"When we were bad my mother put us in the closet. When my dad came home he would punish us. Usually with a belt."

"That must have been quite frightening for you."

"It was."

She sees her own children locked in places. Tied to things. Her heart thumps heavily. Something hurts.

"Was there affection in the home?"

"Affection is for infants."

The Counselor writes.

"How often would you say you were punished with a belt?"

"Often. My brothers had it worse. They were boys."

Doreen sees Jacob.

"You know Doreen, that that was not okay. Our parents usually only have the tools they are given by their own parents and can only do what they are capable of. Sometimes they don't know any better."

"He who spares his rod hates his son, but he who loves him takes care to chastise him," Doreen says. Out of habit. Because she has no idea what else to say.

"The Bible says that, you're right, but interestingly there are many Biblical scholars who argue that this passage, among others, is not to be taken literally. Sheppard's used the rod, or staff, to gently guide their sheep, not to strike or beat them."

Doreen reaches up and touches her Dumbo ears. Her mouth tastes salty and the sickening smell of worms comes out of nowhere and almost knocks her sideways. She hears a few hurried whispers, a string of quick unintelligible words that rape her ears and then scurry off into the corners of the room and disappear.

"We raised our children in a very God-centered household, but neither of them has ever been spanked."

Doreen stares and remains mute. She retrieves from her memory the satisfaction of stinging Faith's backside with her calloused hand. How good it feels for that split second when shock renders the child mute.

"And although your parents were only doing what they knew how, it is never okay to lock a child in a closet. You were hurt by that, and you will need to heal those wounds in order to become the best mother you can be."

Gracie against the utility shelf, Faith in the bathroom, all of them in the van, in the garage, time and time again.

Locks and darkness and terror.

"We can begin to work through these things Doreen. This is why it's important for me to know about your background."

Doreen wonders what Tom would think if he knew how very wrong he is about so many things.

Forgive me Lord. I seem to have fucked up again.

November, 2000

Martha is gone and the puppy has begun to chew things and everything outside is brown.

Gracie's bowel movements are becoming too large and human for Doreen to tolerate diapering her anymore and yet the child is so insolent. So reluctant to do anything structured or mandated. Doreen fears this one and the one who shares her bedroom. These girls will one day be large and have breasts and pubic hair. Doreen is very frightened to be sure.

She beat the dog when it chewed her leather boots. She has nothing nice of her own and she loved those boots. Tan leather broken in so nicely that wearing them was like wearing a pair of often-washed cotton socks. The dog got hold of them while Doreen was exercising in the basement and tore his needy fangs right through them. Ruined the only thing she truly loves to wear. With the boot that belonged once on her right foot, she beat the dog's body and head as it yelped and ran frantically through the living room searching for cover.

It cowered for the rest of the day, slinking out from behind the couch only when Tom came home.

"What's wrong with you Champ? Huh Buddy? What's the matter boy?" Tom petted the thing gently and kissed the side of its face. He looked at Doreen accusingly. She shrugged and said nothing.

Doreen had turned thirty-nine without celebration. She sat at the kitchen table and ate a small bowl of ice cream after the kids and Martha had gone to bed. Tom interrupted this lone birthday indulgence by instructing her to go upstairs, wash her vagina quickly, and lie down on her stomach. Her ice cream went unfinished, melting into thick sugary liquid.

Halloween had passed too and this was the first year that any of the children had made a fuss about not going Trick-or-Treating. Delilah had questioned both her parents about why they weren't allowed to take part in the simple traditions that the others at school were so excited about. Tom went into his speech about evil and witchcraft and Satan.

Doreen sat at the table listening to this tired explanation and watching her eldest daughter's eyes fill with water and her bottom lip tremble. But Delilah would not break. Not one tear escaped. Eden on the other hand, standing beside her, bawled as if in mourning. She did not whine, because she does not. Doreen is convinced that the child is too stupid to complain, to articulate with drawn out and high-pitched words her desires and discomforts. So instead she cries silently and shakes her head as if the act of willing away what she is hearing will bring more satisfactory results.

Once Delilah had relented to the fact that there would be no Trick-or-Treating and began to prepare instead for the church function they would attend on the thirty-first, she set her heart on being a black cat rather than a princess or a Barbie. This displeased Tom once more and prompted him to lecture his daughter for a good half hour about sacrificial animals.

Delilah went to the party dressed as a princess.

The Sunday after her haircut, at church, Doreen could only imagine what was being said behind her back by Tom's sisters. She caught them staring. Whispering. To her face they smiled. To her face they said nice things. But behind her back she knows. She knows it is altogether different when her back is turned. She imagines how sorry they feel for Tom having to be seen out in public with his wife and her ears. How pitiful they must find it that Gracie has inherited her mother's subpar DNA.

Doreen came around the corner and into the nursery and was sure she walked in on some conversation that needed to abruptly be brought to a finish because of her presence. It seemed the sisters were wiping away smiles and sobering themselves for her benefit, after a joke that had been shared just moments before.

"Doreen," The sister named Vicky had said, gathering one of the young nieces into her arms, "How has everything been?" The other sisters in attendance, the ones named Beth and Gwen, stared at her, waiting with held breath for an answer. Doreen wasn't sure what they were looking for. For her to say something stupid? For her to mention her hair? For some nugget of something they could laugh about together when she left the room?

"You're hair looks really cute like that. I think." The one named Vicky said. The ones named Beth and Gwen looked at her and nodded. They were taunting her. She was sure of it.

Doreen touched her ears, feeling them burn. She snapped at Delilah to hurry and gather Eden and Jacob and she pulled Gracie into her arms and tugged Faith's small hand. Faith whined and resisted until one of the sisters pulled her up and began tickling her, causing the child to break out in laughter.

"I've got her," the sister named Beth looked at Doreen with snide eyes.

Beth. Flawless, unwrinkled skin. Not one gray hair. Thin and well dressed. Mother of two over-achieving and gorgeous teenage daughters. Wife of Tony, financial advisor. Owner of a four bedroom home, a salt water pool, a cottage and a boat. Sister of Tom. Daughter of Martha and the late Lloyd Rutherford. Small-eared and God-fearing. Makes a mean cabbage roll.

Doreen wished a blemish on her. A boil or a mole. Something. But Beth remained perfect as she carried a contented Faith out to the van and buckled her into her car seat. Doreen quickly asked the Lord to forgive her for thinking such thoughts.

"If you need any help Doreen, anything at all, I'd be glad to stop by any night of the week and give you a hand," Beth offered as she slid the van door closed and pulled her sunglasses from her purse. "I can't imagine how hectic it is with five kids, I remember how it was with just two. I don't know how you do it, Hon."

There was some sort of amusement to her tone. Doreen envisioned bloodying her sister-in-law's lip, creating flaws on a face where none existed. The word "Hon" so condescending she wanted to somehow stuff it back into Beth's mouth and down her throat.

"What do you say Doreen?" Tom had joined them and was making his way toward the driver side door.

"Thank you Beth," Doreen choked out. The words tasted vile and bitter. She had the strong urge to spit.

Beth nodded as if she had done some favour to Doreen by offering her assistance and drawing attention to the fact that Doreen cannot handle things adequately on her own. Spiders of rage crept down Doreen's back, her ears burned. Humiliation.

Always humiliation.

Now the children are making their way through the candy they acquired at the church celebration. They are high from sugar and bouncing off walls and using voices much too loud for indoors. Tom has gone hunting for the weekend. Martha has promised to stop in. The dog is bounding around the room, jumping up on the children, joining them in their frenzy of sugar-induced energy.

Doreen hears the voice briefly. It is quite strong this time. The words are very pronounced. It tells her that she is capable of sparing her children great misery. It must be God. She's almost sure of it.

Delilah is wiggling her hips with a red sucker sticking out of her mouth. The other children are laughing and Eden is trying to mimic her sister's actions. They look happy.

She hears herself say it out loud, "They seem happy."

She waits for a response but there isn't one.

She pulls out her Bible and reads it.

> **Children, obey your parents in the Lord, for this is right. Honor your father and mother — the first commandment with a promise: so that it may be well with you and you may live long on the earth.**

That night, the Friday of Tom's three day hunting trip, goes fairly well. The children eat their candy and dance and play and when Doreen tires of the noise she sends them to the basement with a movie and a bowl of chips. Faith of course is a nuisance, coming upstairs every ten minutes while Doreen is trying to mop the kitchen floor. Wanting this or that. Whining. Oh the whining with that one. It grates on every nerve ending Doreen possesses, leaving each of them frayed and exposed.

Eventually Doreen calls Delilah up and asks her to please keep Faith quiet in the basement and not let her come back up. At one point she can here Delilah pleading with her sister, begging her to not go back upstairs and bother Mommy. Doreen is emptying garbage and half listening. The whining begins and escalates a bit and then she hears Delilah become agitated and harsh. She hears her own voice coming out of the throat of her eldest daughter. Delilah says through clenched teeth, "I mean it Faith *now*, or I'm going give you something to cry about."

At that the younger child concedes.

Martha arrives just after seven and sends Delilah up to have a shower, instructing Eden that she will be next. She sets the egg timer for five minutes and leaves it in the bathroom with each of them. Showers are to be finished when the gadget rings and vibrates. The girls seem to love this.

While the girls are showering Martha is taking laundry downstairs and sorting it, she is pulling blankets down on beds and fluffing pillows and laying stuffed animals in place so that when the children are ready they'll be waiting there for them. She is looking through story books and deciding which ones to read. She is immaculate this woman. It amazes Doreen the things that Tom's mother can accomplish in the span of ten minutes.

When Eden and Delilah are both showered and wearing flannel night-gowns Martha brushes out their hair while she runs the bathtub. "Put the other three in the tub," she tells Doreen, "While I read to the girls."

"Together?" Doreen asks. "With Jacob?"

"Yes Doreen, with Jacob." Martha's hands still themselves, resting in Eden's yellow hair and she looks at Doreen with intent. "Don't tell me you've been bathing him separately all this time."

Doreen looks down, once again feeling stupid, but also feeling a sickness worm its way through her at the thought of penises and vaginas float-ing around together in the warm bath water. She sees beautiful Jacob tempted to climb on top of one his sisters and hammer himself into her. She feels the nausea of this image run through her like anesthetic, burn-ing her veins as it creeps.

"Doreen?" Martha's voice. "Go turn off the bath water."

Doreen does. She undresses Gracie as Faith undresses herself and dumps a bucket of toys into the frothy water. The girls clamour into the tub. Jacob stands there staring like he has no idea what is going on. He has never bathed with his sisters before. Doreen just stares back at him, willing herself to start pulling his shirt up over his head.

"Doreen." Martha is now standing in the doorway. "Doreen, what in Heaven's name is wrong? Put Jacob in the tub with the girls and let's get on with this."

"I don't bathe them together."

"Why in the world not? They're babies."

"He's a boy."

"A *three year old* boy Doreen."

Martha begins undressing Jacob, talking to him in a voice that exudes enthusiasm about the adventure ahead. Jacob becomes excited. As Martha plunks him into the tub beside his sisters the girls squeal with pleasure. They call out their brother's name. They laugh. Their genitals disappear under a blanket of bath toys and soap film. They become, not boys and girls, but children. Generic and innocent. Sexless. With their hair wet and their mouths open with laughter they all look alike. There is no difference between them and Doreen cannot tell one from the other.

While they are in the bath Martha reads to Delilah and Eden.

When the bath is finished Martha tells Doreen to read to Jacob and Faith while she gets the baby off to bed. Faith whines that she wants Grandma to read the story and pushes her mother away. Jacob cuddles into Doreen's side, fuses himself with her body and looks up with deep eyes. He says, "That was fun Mommy. I like the bath." He smells like Baby Dove and fruit.

Finally Faith gives in and sits beside her mother to listen to *Love You Forever* and *In a People House*.

Gracie only cries for about three minutes and then settles.

Eventually everyone is sleeping and Martha takes the dog out back and lets him do his business and she cleans it up and throws it away in the garage. Doreen watches this woman, marveling at her. How does someone her age still have so much energy? So many wits about her? Her own mother has been seemingly going senile for over a decade, and wouldn't be able to handle more than an hour with the kids, after which she would have to lie down for an extended nap. Martha is a powerhouse. All five feet and ninety-five pounds of her.

When there is nothing left to do Martha gathers her coat and her purse and says to Doreen, "I put a casserole in the fridge for you to heat up for supper tomorrow."

"Okay. Thank you Martha. So much."

The old woman nods. Her face is like leather. Deep lines cut through it. She looks at Doreen purposefully.

"If I could give you one piece of advice Doreen, after raising seven of my own children, it would be that if there is any way you can make a job easier or quicker, you should. If bathing the kids together simplifies life, then bathe them together. They are just little."

Doreen nods. "Thank you."

"And enjoy them. They'll be grown in a blink."

Doreen becomes aware of her heart. The heaviness of it.

She remembers when Delilah was born.

There she was all pink and flailing and alive. Her face was squished and her nose was covered in white spots that looked like pimples. She had ten fingers and ten toes and peach fuzz hair and elbows and knees and nipples. She was perfect and complete.

Martha came to the hospital and held the infant to her chest. Delilah was one of many grandchildren before her. Martha had experienced this moment so many times before, holding a new grandbaby in her arms, feeling the warmth of the body against her chest, looking at the perfect newborn features. And yet her eyes lit up like she was seeing something miraculous. Something she had never seen before and would never see again. Her eyes had filled with tears that dripped without apology down her leathery face.

She had looked at Doreen and said, "Children must be beloved." Then to Delilah, "God bless you and keep you Delilah Jayne," and had kissed the baby on her head, love undeniably flowing from her and filling the small hospital room.

Eighteen months earlier when the baby had been born dead, Martha had held his body too, lifeless and blue, and to him she had said the same words. "God bless you and keep you little one. You are beloved."

Doreen awakens, for the second time in a month, not to darkness, but to light pouring in her bedroom window. Beside her there is nothing but blanket and empty space. There is a child standing at the door.

It begins to whine.

Faith.

Doreen sits bolt upright, throws her legs over the side of the bed and grabs her robe from the chair in the corner.

"Faith," she says, "Mommy must have slept in."

The child reaches out to her and her first reaction is to recoil. Faith had been beginning to cry and so the face is wet. The lips are moist. There is a smell like that of a duffel bag that has sat unopened for too long and has just been unzipped.

She reaches for Faith's hand. It's the best she can do.

The child seems pleased by this, albeit surprised. Immediately she stops making noise and wraps both her small hands around the one Doreen has offered her. She is warm.

"Let's go to the kitchen and get you some juice." Doreen speaks in a whisper and tip toes. Faith does the same, her mother's tiny shadow.

When they get to the bottom of the stairs and climb over the baby gate to land in the kitchen, the mutt barrels toward them panting like a maniac. Faith shouts with what can only be described as glee, "Champy!" delighted to see this thing as it snorts and drools and makes low moaning sounds.

"Shhhh!" Doreen snaps at Faith.

And to Champ, "Down Champ, go!" pointing a finger and stomping a foot.

Of course the animal is too stupid to shit where it is supposed to never mind obey a command and finger gesture. It just continues to do spastic things with its body and make walking through the room much more of a challenge than it should be.

Doreen says to her daughter, "Faith can you go open the sliding doors and let Champ outside for Mommy?"

Happily she does.

But instead of going off to do what it needs to do, it stands at the doors and presses its face against the glass defiling it with whatever is constantly moistening its nose.

Clearly it does not need to eliminate, which means that Doreen will sometime today come across a pile or two in the house and likely a fresh wet spot.

After a few minutes of listening to it whine Doreen instructs Faith to go ahead and let it back in. Faith and the animal chase and wrestle while Doreen puts the kettle on and pours juice into a sippy cup.

Shortly Grace Isabella begins to scream and the rest of them emerge too with tangled hair and thirsty mouths. Doreen sends them to the basement so that she can do her sit ups in the living room undisturbed. They take the dog with them.

And so begins another day.

Thank you Lord. For the many blessings.

After lunch Doreen takes the children into town to a park with a large piece of climbing equipment and several swing sets. She leaves the dog tied up in the yard despite the children's desperate pleas to bring him along.

It is mid November now and the air is chilly but not yet cold. The children play as if it is a warm spring day. For them there are no stipulations on joy. The sky is gray and the day itself has turned dreary and depressing, but the children run with mouths that open and close with laughter. Delilah keeps Gracie with her, holding her hand, lifting her up and down, sitting her on her lap to slide down the enclosed spiral slide. The baby squeals and laughs and claps her hands. Doreen sits and watches. She is able to breathe.

When she gets home no one will be there demanding anything of her. No one but that stupid animal, but all he will want is to come in and jump all over everybody for a few minutes and then to maybe be given something to eat. He will not care what time supper is on the table or if the children have dirt under their fingernails or if her vagina is clean.

She could stay here all afternoon. She could get back in the van and drive in the opposite direction of the house and just keep on driving. Set the children up in a new school in some other province, re-name them, put Faith in JK. Sleep soundly at night without anyone touching her.

She could get in the van without the children.

She could walk off right now, without anyone even turning to look, and start up the van and drive away. Someone would eventually realize that the kids had been left and they'd call the authorities and Delilah would make sure to tell them the right phone number and Tom would be called away from his hunting trip and life would change for him indefinitely. The mere idea of the look on Tom's face is so delicious that Doreen catches herself laughing out loud, like some loon on a park bench. Tom would likely lose control of his bowels the shock would be so great. Doreen can't wipe away the smirk that must seem very strange to anyone bothering to glance her way.

And then again, as she's picturing Tom's tormented face as he realizes his fate and his intestines betray him, she hears the whispers that have recently become part of her days.

She tries to focus in on what they are saying. The whispers are from several different sources all overlapping, talking overtop and around each other, cancelling out what the other is saying. They are quiet and chaotic. She can't understand any of them.

She tries to choose one strand, one hushed voice and tune into it. She can feel herself squinting as she tries to catch even one word of the nonsense in her head. But there is no sense to it.

It becomes louder as the seconds pass, more static-y. She becomes agitated, rubbing her face and shaking herself a bit, trying to shake loose the cause of whatever this is.

Hands on her knees. A voice, one she recognizes.

"I'm thirsty Mama." Dark brown eyes. The smell of gravel and cut grass.

Jacob.

The whispers die instantly.

Doreen reaches for the diaper bag where there are cups and bottles of water.

In an act of complete rebellion Doreen does not return to the house to heat up Martha's casserole. Instead she takes the children to McDonalds for Happy Meals and more climbing equipment. They eat and jump in a ball pit and drink Coke and tear open cheap toys and there is not an issue, not one crying session, not so much as a whine or a whimper from any of them.

By the time they get home they are all exhausted and Martha is waiting inside.

"I took them to McDonald's," Doreen tells her mother-in-law. She hangs her head in shame. "It wasn't in the budget."

Martha scoops Gracie up into her arms and asks her, "Did you have fun?"

Gracie nods and shoves her happy meal toy toward her Grandmother "I got this!" she says, her words perfectly formed, "See Gamma?"

"I see my love," Martha says. Then she looks at Doreen, "It's between you and me Doreen. Eat that casserole tomorrow."

Doreen nods.

She has spent more than a decade viewing this woman as the enemy, assuming that she could not be trusted, believing that she was as wicked as the daughters she had raised. She had never let herself think of Martha as an ally. As a resource. She feels confused now by her mother-in-law's behavior. She is sure there is a trick here somewhere.

Baths, stories, bed, dog outside. "I will pop by in the afternoon tomorrow and see how you are doing okay?"

"Sounds good."

Martha heads for the door.

"Martha?"

The old woman stops, turns around, waits.

"I just, um," Doreen is not sure how to articulate what she means to say.

"Just, again, thank you."

"Try to get some sleep Doreen."

As she opens the door to leave she lets cold November air into the house along with the smell of something burning in a nearby yard.

Doreen sits and has a tea and turns the radio on quietly and turns the dial and listens to people sing about things other than God.

She feels guilty but at the same time pleased with herself for her acts of independence. She felt this way once before. Proud of herself for shrugging off the rules and doing things her own way. Nothing good came of it. She can still feel the sting of her father's hand against her already swollen face. Can hear his words as sharply as if they had just been spoken, "You reap what you sew."

Still listening to demonic music she prays.

Forgive me father, I have been ungrateful and rebellious and I may have let you down. Please Lord, do not punish me. From now on, I will be a good girl. Thank you Lord. Amen.

With Tom still away on his hunting trip, Sunday during the day is peaceful. After church the children play outside and in the basement and in their bedrooms. Doreen feeds them breakfast and lunch and snacks and Martha stops by in the late afternoon to make sure everything is going well. She brings stickers for the children and a paper cup full of hot chocolate for Doreen. Doreen sits in the living room with her mother-in-law and they have a discussion about house training puppies, another topic Martha instinctively seems to have knowledge about.

When she leaves, the children wet their grandmother's face with enthusiastic kisses and Doreen has to stop herself from reaching out to wipe Martha's leathery face with her sleeve as the old woman is saying goodbye.

"Thanks for all your help this weekend," Doreen tells her. "I would have been lost without you."

"You just need to relax a little," Martha says, "you don't give yourself enough credit."

Doreen doesn't know what to say to that. She feels her ears crawl with heat and out of habit she reaches to pull her hair in front of them and is startled yet again by the fact that there is none. She touches the tips of her ears, pulls one gently and stares at the ground.

"Take care," Martha says, and leaves them with a gust of cool air and late afternoon sunshine.

At around five thirty Doreen heats up Martha's casserole which is made of noodles and tuna and some sort of sauce that the children all make a show of appreciation for. They eat their grandmother's food until their plates are clean. They smack their lips and rub their bellies. Lick forks and drain glasses of milk.

By herself Doreen begins to repeat the bath routine from the previous night and the night before that. While the three younger ones are splashing and laughing in the tub, Delilah and Eden get into their beds and read. They do not ask for anything, they do not need of her, they do not complain or demand to know when she will be tucking them in. They read and they are quiet. They are good girls.

Although Eden of course is not actually reading, but merely turning pages and looking at pictures. Words are lost on her. She can't even recognize single letters never mind string them together to create language. Thinking about this makes Doreen's skin rash with stress bumps, so she tries not to.

She tries to focus on the task at hand.

The bath itself is fine. The children play and Doreen washes Grace Isabella while Jacob and Faith use soap and facecloths to scrub themselves. She doesn't need to shampoo any of them as it was done the night before.

When the water is turning cool and the skin of her three youngest babies is beginning to tighten and prune, Doreen reaches into the tub and pulls the plug.

Placing the plug on edge of the bathtub she says, "Time to get out."

Jacob stands up and reaches his arms out to her and it is as she is extending a towel toward him that Faith's protest stings her ears and disorients her slightly. The child makes a sound so high pitched that, had it been any more so, it may have reached the point of being inaudible to the human ear.

Doreen drops the towel meant for Jacob and strikes her daughter in the side of the head, the blow instinctual, intended to stop the deafening noise.

There is a split second where Faith goes quiet. The room itself goes quiet. No water drips, no furnace hums, no human exhales. Even the walls seem to hold their breath, shocked by the hard thump to the head the toddler has just endured, and bracing for the result.

And then the silence breaks.

Faith screams.

Not as high pitched as the first time, but louder. So much louder.

The sound causes Jacob to recoil. He crouches back into the bath water and puts his hands over his ears. He tucks his head close to his knees.

The baby begins to cry too. Her arms shoot out toward her mother and her hands begin to open and close in a gesture of need. Through her sobs she utters, "Mama, out, out, Mama, out!" There are strings of mucus on the face. On the mouth. Doreen gags.

Faith continues to make noise. She is growling, her sounds wet and guttural and relentless. She is speaking while she screams, words come out of her distorted and raw. It is unclear what she is trying to communicate other than rage.

Jacob curls into himself while on either side of him a female child is making unbearable amounts of noise. Doreen grabs him and yanks him from the tub. She throws the towel around him and all the while she is saying, "Stop it Faith. Stop it now. What's the matter with you?" Her body tightens. Her head swims. Both girls are making noise. Unnecessary fucking noise.

Faith gets louder. Insistent and shrill.

The baby is getting more worked up as well. She stands, her hands continuing to open and close, open and close, her mouth doing the same, snot everywhere mixed with water that has now turned cold. Doreen grabs her and pulls her from the tub. She can't find a towel for Gracie. She looks and she reaches and she gropes blindly hoping to find something to wrap the child in as it continues to cry and leak.

There is no towel. The baby begins to shake. "Cold, Mama, cold!!" The skin rashes over with goose bumps.

Faith is still screaming. She has put the plug back in the tub. Through guttural gasps she is telling her mother that she is not getting out of the tub. She sits on the plug, an act of complete defiance, and Doreen, struck dumb by the enormous amount of noise in the small tiled room, can think of nothing but the need for silence.

She goes to pull Faith from the tub but the child resists. Doreen is telling her to shut up. To be quiet. To please just shut up. The child thrashes around and growls. She resists being pulled from the tub with unwarranted strength. She fights and she screams until Doreen's arms ache and her ears begin to throb.

In an act of desperation she grabs the child by the throat.

The noise becomes less.

She can feel the sounds. Her fingers vibrate with what is going on inside Faith's throat. She squeezes a bit tighter. The noise goes on. The throat pulses and squirms under her fingers. The noise is muffled but still there, still pummeling her eardrums.

She eases up. Loosens her grip. The child gasps. It then immediately winds up and lets go a sound that shakes the bathroom windows. Her eyes fix on Doreen, almost in challenge. Her lungs expel everything that exists within them. It is the loudest sound Doreen has ever heard.

She puts both hands around the child's neck and slams its head sideways into the water.

There is no noise.

There are bubbles and there is splashing, but the screaming has stopped.

The child kicks its legs. Its hands reach up and grip Doreen's arms. Doreen becomes aware of the fact that she is saying "SHUT up" over and over and over again out loud in the small ceramic room.

"Mommy let go!"

Shocked by this voice Doreen stops talking. Stops moving.

Jacob.

She turns around and sees him there. He is naked. His towel is on Gracie who is convulsing with cold and staring wide-eyed and silent.

"Stop Mommy! You're hurting Faith!"

Doreen's eyes widen. She becomes aware of her hands, of how tightly they are clenched and she loosens them. Pulls them from the toddler's neck.

Faith sits up. She spits water. She gasps. She takes huge lungfuls of air. She coughs. Doreen stares at her, lost for a moment, unsure of what just happened. Unaware of why her own clothes are soaked and droplets of water are running down her face.

Faith's face is deep red, almost purple.

Doreen stands up.

She backs away from the bathtub, from this scene in front of her.

Her head fills with voices. Whispers that confuse and irritate her. They come on like a swarm of insects nesting in her brain. Buzzing and flying and smacking themselves off the inside of her skull. She shakes her head back and forth violently. She puts her hands over her ears. She backs further and further away from the tub.

Then the voice.

Over top of all the whispers it begins to tell her things. It is clear and precise and she does not like what it is saying. She cannot listen. She smacks her hands over her ears. She does this three, four, five times. The voice continues.

She screams out loud, "STOP!"

Something snaps, dislodges. The voice recedes.

Once again she becomes aware of the sounds of the room. Her children's sobs, water dripping, her own laboured breathing.

All she wants is quiet.

———————————————

When Doreen, wet and exhausted, goes to tuck the older two girls into bed, the house is silent. Eden is asleep with a book across her chest and a stuffed cow tucked under her arm. Her blonde hair is stark against the deep pink of her pillow case. Her eyes are moving under her lids, not calmly back and forth, but up and down and sideways in rapid little jerks. Her fingers twitch.

Doreen puts the book away and turns out Eden's bedside lamp.

She goes to Delilah who has been watching her quietly.

Doreen says, "Go to sleep now Dee," and turns out the lamp next to her oldest daughter's bed.

As she is leaving Delilah speaks, "Mommy?"

"What?"

"When is Grandma coming back?"

———————————————

Doreen lies in the blackness of her bedroom and can still feel the flesh of her daughter's neck against her palms.

She needs help.

She needs to tell someone. A doctor, the counselor, Martha. Someone.

She wants the pills the Doctor offered. The ones Tom told him would defile the temple of Christ. Just some valium, something for the stress, something to quiet her mind and calm her nerves.

She can't go on like this. Something bad will happen.

Forgive me Lord. Forgive me and please send help.

She is still awake when she hears Tom come in. She looks at the clock. It is 12:03. She prays some more. Prays that tonight he will spare her.

After some time there are footsteps on the stairs. The door opens. Light from the hall comes in and gets shut out again. Doreen begins to breathe deeply, intentionally making the sounds of sleep.

His clothes come off one piece at a time. Shirt, belt, pants, boxers, one sock, the other. She hears it all blindly and continues to breathe and pray. She does not stir.

Not tonight God please.

The bed moves under his weight. There is a smell. Something musky and thick. Steel and sweat and animal flesh.

He pulls up her nightgown. His hands are cold and they wander up her legs and he flips her over from her side onto her back. His breaths become heavy. Without care he pulls her legs apart. She says his name. She says please.

He puts his mouth between her legs, something he never does. He takes greedy tastes of her, he pulls her apart roughly. Sticks fingers in so deep it makes her gasp.

"Tom..."

But she knows there is no use. He will take what he needs. A woman should not forsake her husband. A woman should never forsake God.

After a few minutes he comes up from between her legs and he fumbles toward her face looking for her mouth with his. Doreen is genuinely startled. She cannot remember the last time her husband has touched her mouth with his. She has all but forgotten what it feels like to be kissed.

She smells something that stirs a memory as his tongue opens her lips and pushes into her mouth. Her initial reaction is panic. There is a face, there is laughter. She pushes him away.

"Have you been drinking?" Tom never drinks but the distinct taste of alcohol is in his mouth, the smell of it coming out his pores.

"Shut up Doreen," he says, and covers her mouth again with his. His kissing is needy, his hands wander over her and he makes noises of pleasure, low moans in her ear, hot breath against her throat. His body writhes against hers, creating sensation. Causing the blood in her veins to quicken its pace.

The panic begins to shift into something willing, into something she barely recognizes anymore. She tries not to feel it. She tries to stiffen and withdraw. There is danger in pleasure. Vulnerability. Need and want only make one susceptible to a great many dark and terrible things .

She dampens against her will. Her body betrays her.

"Remember when we used to fuck Doreen?"

"Tom!" She pulls her mouth away. He comes back at her.

He says, "You used to like it. I know you did. Remember?"

"Please Tom, don't do this."

He pushes himself into her. His breath is soaked with booze, his hands are everywhere, squeezing her in places she can't remember him ever touching.

He pushes and pulls and pushes.

Her knees fall open. There is something in his need, something in the way he seems lost in her flesh that makes her body pliable and co-operative. The foreign smell of alcohol. The unfamiliar stubble that scratches her face as his mouth falls all over her. She feels her legs begin to tremble. Something inside her contracting. Waves preparing to break.

Then, in a swift urgent motion her husband pulls himself from her body and positions himself so that he is near the top of her, aiming himself at her face.

"No Tom!"

Every fragment of pleasure dies and he lets go of himself and pins her arms to the bed raising himself higher.

The smell of what comes out of him, the feel of it hot against her face, the stench of alcohol that has suddenly permeated the room – it pulls her into the darkness, shackles her, makes it difficult to breath.

A face flashes before her eyes, wild and laughing. She feels her flesh tear. Tastes blood.

Tom rolls off of her and begins to take deep heavy breaths that very quickly become loud snoring. Doreen lies with his fluids drying and crusting on her face and nightgown.

The voice comes out of nowhere.

It tells her to go clean herself. It says enough is enough.

All night she dreams of bonfires and beer kegs and sadistic laughter. All night her body is penetrated and torn and pissed on.

All night she tosses and turns and wakes up sweaty only to fall back to sleep and keep dreaming the same dream.

The next evening when she finally gets the children to bed and Gracie has quieted down after a good forty minutes of screaming and Doreen has explained away the marks on Faith's neck with lies, she sits next to her husband on the couch.

Tom is watching basketball. He does not look at her.

Doreen says her husband's name. He grunts and continues to stare ahead at the television screen. There is a bowl of chips on the coffee table in front of him, the strong smell of vinegar. Crumbs gather on his shirt, stick in the fabric along his chest and stomach.

"I need to talk to you about something."

He turns to look at her as if she has just said something absurd. And really she has. This is not how their marriage works. Tom talks and Doreen listens. It has always been that simple.

"What?"

"We need to talk."

"Fine," Tom says, his voice seething with defensiveness, "talk."

Doreen's heart is beating violently in her chest, her hands are clammy and her head has begun to fuzz over a bit again. The whispers are distant but threatening. She needs to get this out before they come closer and overwhelm her. And yet she is so nervous to communicate her needs to her husband that she considers just telling him to never mind, that she forgot what she wanted to say. She knows he wouldn't ask any questions. He'd simply turn his head back toward the television set as if she had never been there at all.

"What Doreen? Christ. I'm trying to watch the game."

Doreen takes a deep breath.

"I think I may need some help."

He looks at her again like she is speaking absurdities. He twists his face into an expression that tells her he's confused, or that her statement was asinine.

"What do you mean? My mother was here all bloody weekend was she not?"

"Not like that. I need help. Like, with my brain."

Tom scoffs. Lets out a gust of irritated air. Rolls his eyes.

"For the love of God, what are you on about now?"

"I've been hearing voices."

Tom becomes still and stares at her like she is something unpalatable that he is nonetheless going to attempt to digest.

He rubs his eyes. He shakes his head. Doreen sits silent and motionless waiting for a response.

Tom laughs.

"Voices?"

"Yes."

"Explain this to me."

"For the last little while I've been hearing voices. In my head."

Tom shakes his head again. He looks down at the floor. He chuckles.

"You're a piece of work Doreen." He laughs again. "Tell me, please, what is it that the voices are saying?"

"Some of them I can't understand. But…"

"What?" Her husband wears an amused grin. Her stomach starts to turn. It comes to her as a stark revelation. There will be no help.

She says a hurried prayer, *Please God.*

"One of the voices is very clear. It says things that scare me. I'm becoming afraid Tom. And I get so frustrated with the kids, so overwhelmed. Faith and Gracie are so difficult."

He cuts her off. "You've got to be kidding me here. What is this? We're not getting a nanny if that's what you're fishing for."

"No Tom. I need help. I need to talk to someone."

"You're talking to what's-her-name are you not? Smiley says she's fantastic. She will help you sort things out. God woman, nothing is ever good enough for you. My mother raised seven kids and never complained. Never needed to *talk* to anyone. I don't know what your problem is. Is there some reason, Doreen, that you can't do what millions of women around the world seem to be doing without all the drama?"

She feels herself deflating. Shrinking into the fabric of the couch.

"I was thinking maybe we could consider looking into whatever medicine the doctor was telling us about. Maybe I could…"

He cuts her off again.

He leans in so that his face is very close to hers. She can taste his breath. His eyes are viscous.

"Now you listen to me," he points a finger toward her, makes jabs with each word he speaks. "That is not happening. The body is a temple Doreen. If you pollute that temple you won't be coming with us. When the Rapture comes you'll be left behind with those deviant brothers of yours and you'll never get to hold Isaac again."

His words disable her. Isaac's name sucks the air from her lungs, slices her down the middle. She looks down into her hands but Tom puts a finger under her chin and cranks her head back up so that he can look back into her eyes. His are colourless and cruel.

"Is that what you want? Huh? You want me and the kids to be gone, you want me to have to explain to that baby where his mother is while you're back here suffering damnation with that faggot-ass little brother of yours and the rest of the low-lifes? Is that what you want Doreen? All because you're too selfish to just grow the hell up and be a mother?"

"I'm sorry Tom," she says. There is no point. There will be no help. Life will go on and on and on. The days will start and end and start again. She will wake and breathe and sleep and wake again. Over and over and over.

Tom stares at her. He keeps his finger under her chin, her face propped up so that she has no choice but to see his eyes and the hatred in them.

"God forgave you once Doreen," he says, "I think you better make damn sure he doesn't need to do it again."

He lets go of her face. Her head hangs. She is suddenly depleted. Empty.

After a minute of silence Tom says, "Now, go wash," and he points toward her crotch.

Doreen sits on the side of the cold bathtub and washes herself in one spot using soap and warm water. She remembers the beer on Tom's breath the night before. The contamination of the temple. The rules are malleable for Tom and yet so rigid for her. Tom is the head of the home as Christ is the head of the church. It is not for her to question.

Forgive me patient Lord for being such a terrible mother and wife. I will try to do better Lord. I promise.

"So. How have things been going?" Lisa Griffin's pen is poised.

"Fine, thank you."

"How have your stress levels been, with the kids and just generally running the household?"

"Good. Fine."

"Excellent. So you're feeling better then? More relaxed?"

"Yes. Everything is fine."

"That's wonderful Doreen. I'm so glad to hear it."

"Thank you."

December, 2000

November ends in grayness, bleeds into December colourless and damp. Wind bites at Doreen's gigantic ears whenever she leaves the house, which is as seldom as possible.

The dog shits, the baby shits, Doreen cleans up shit.

Tom comes at her almost every night. Stiff and careless. The smell of Ivory soap from between her legs. Her face pushed into the pillow.

She prays, *No babies*. She begs in silence. She hopes that her body has had enough. *Please God, no more.*

Parent-teacher interviews take place at the beginning of the month. Tom puts on a clean shirt and cologne. He puts product in his hair. He tucks away expressions like, 'for the love of Christ' and 'faggot-ass', reserving those for supper time and annoyances brought upon him by his wife. For the teachers he is shiny and God-fearing. For the other parents he is amusing and involved.

Delilah's teacher doesn't have much to say except to tell them how exceedingly well their oldest child is doing, how well mannered and

considerate she is, how her marks are the highest in the class, how she
excels in art and dominates in Phys Ed. Delilah is a dream she tells them,
every teachers dream student. They should be very proud.

Despite his desire to keep up appearances Tom can't seem to help but
be smug. Doreen says very little while he asks questions about what they
can do at home to make Delilah even more exceptional. The whispers
come and go as her husband and her daughter's teacher converse.
Every day the whispers seem to occupy more of her time than the day
before. During the interview they pester. They get loud only to quiet down
again. They disappear only to return. They pluck at the inside of her head,
create an itch she can't scratch.

Eden's teacher has allotted them some extra time. She has some important things to discuss with them and doesn't want to be rushed. Doreen
should feel anxious. She feels very little of anything.

"First of all let me just say," the teacher begins, "That Eden is a delightful
child to have in the classroom." She smiles brightly and waits to be validated for her positive assessment of their child. Doreen just stares numbly.
Tom thanks the teacher who is probably in her late twenties or early thir-
ties and quite heavy. She is wearing a sweater with Christmas trees on
it, and smells like she has been experimenting with her Grandmother's
perfume. She has a mole on her right cheek. Once Doreen spots it she
cannot look away from the mole. She stares at it, fixated.

"That said, I've noticed some things that have begun to concern me
slightly."

Tom demands to know what things without giving the woman an opportunity to explain.

"Eden doesn't really socialize here at school. She keeps to herself and
hasn't formed any friendships that I'm aware of."

Tom asks why this is a problem. He says Eden is one of five children, he says that with that many siblings perhaps she just doesn't need friends at school.

The mole is about the size of a kernel of un-popped corn and similar in shape.

"That alone wouldn't necessarily concern me," the teacher tells them, "but I have also noticed that she is very reluctant to make eye contact with anyone, even when I purposely try to engage her, she refuses to look directly at me."

It is the colour of feces.

Tom makes indignant grunting sounds.

"And have you noticed, at home, any flapping?"

"What do you mean by flapping?" Tom asks. He looks at Doreen, she can feel him looking. She is supposed to be getting worked up like he is. She is supposed to be worried and feeling defensive and asking sharp accusatory-toned questions of this chubby soft spoken woman who seems to be suggesting that something is wrong with their child. She has no energy for it. She knew this day would come. She has always known that something with Eden was not quite right. Probably one more reminder from God of how important it is to live by his rules.

She stares at the mole. There are a few very small hairs growing out of it. It moves up and down on the cheek while the teacher talks. When the mouth is still, the mole rests.

"By flapping I mean just that. Flapping of her arms and hands. When she gets excited or nervous or frustrated." The teacher demonstrates, flapping her chubby arms up and down like some sort of disabled bird.

Doreen can picture it in her head, the flapping. Eden does it all the time. It is something she has done since she was very small. In her head Doreen says, yes. Out loud she says nothing.

Tom is silent for a moment, perhaps thinking, trying to recall his daughter flapping her arms and hands in a way that would suggest abnormality. Then he says, "I've never noticed. I mean, I guess she could do that at home but it's not something I've ever made note of."

He turns his head toward his wife, "Doreen?"

Doreen nods.

"You have noticed some flapping then?" The teacher asks.

Doreen nods again.

The teacher continues to talk and Tom challenges her and questions everything she says and behaves as if he is being accused of something he is innocent of.

Doreen hears a lot of words.

She thinks that if she had a mole like that, right there on her cheek, she would like to have it removed. She's sure the procedure is a simple and inexpensive one. She thinks about how God makes no mistakes and she wonders what the purpose is then, of that shit coloured blemish on an otherwise unmarred face.

She hears more words being spoken by the teacher and by Tom.

She hears doctor and diagnosis and evaluation and Autism.

She hears the word Autism.

After that the whispers ambush her and she can hear no more.

She closes her eyes against it. Behind her closed eyes she can still see the mole.

When they leave the school the night is cold and the wind is whipping the bare tree branches into a frenzy. Doreen pulls her coat up around her face.

Tom is livid. He is talking and talking with his hands flying all around. He seems to be aiming his anger at her, something she is so accustomed to that it does not faze her. Of course this is her fault. She knew it would be.

As he talks the whispers soothe her. They create a static in her ears that blocks out all of Tom's angry words. They begin to feel like a lullaby, comforting and protective.

At night in bed after Tom has taken her savagely and is snoring beside her, the voice comes. It says again what it has said before. It tells Doreen to think of all of the suffering she might spare her daughter Eden.

Doreen does not fight the voice this time. She has no energy with which to do so. She thinks of a little blonde girl flapping her arms in desperate attempt to fly yet staying agonizingly in place despite her efforts. She thinks of Isaac's peaceful blue face.

She lets the voice say all that it needs to say. And then she sleeps.

December is a busy month, what with it being Jesus' birthday and all.

There are extra church obligations, the girls are part of a Christmas concert at school, and Doreen is expected to host several parties and dinners all while keeping the house immaculate and caring for five children, two of whom are demons and one of whom is half retarded.

Tom has been on a mission ever since the parent-teacher interview, obsessing about Eden's informal diagnosis and insisting on all kinds of intervention. The teacher had said that she wasn't willing to label Eden yet, and that they should all just keep an eye on things and communicate and wait and see if there were changes by the end of the school year. Although Doreen heard very little of this herself, Tom has reiterated it to her a thousand times and yet will not stop coming up with new plans of action. He speaks about the situation as if Autism can be evaded somehow. Nipped in the bud and corrected. Doreen says very little except for yes Tom and no Tom and sure okay Tom.

Tom tells her to make doctor's appointments. He tells her to call the children's centre and get Eden in for assessment. He wants the kids in swimming lessons now. He wants her doing at least thirty minutes of homework a night with Eden and reading educational books to her and taking her on play dates so that she can socialize and learn to make eye contact.

Yes Tom. No Tom. Okay Tom.

Eden's sixth birthday is on the eighteenth. Despite the already over the top busy-ness of the season Tom's entire family is invited over to celebrate. Despite Doreen's breakdowns, her recent trip to the emergency room, and the fact that she is regularly violent with the children, she is to go about planning a birthday celebration.

And she does. She bakes cake and buys decorations and sends out invitations and blows up balloons and scrubs the house all while cleaning up dog shit and trying not to smash Faith's head off the floor or lock Gracie in the cold cellar.

She is not to talk about the teacher's assessment of Eden to anyone other than Tom. It is not to be discussed. One more thing that is never to be spoken of.

Martha comes to the party and so do several of the sisters and some of their husbands, and a bunch of Tom's nieces and nephews. Doreen's brothers, of course, are not welcome.

Her mother and father are invited but they choose not to come. Too many small children in one room. Too much noise. Too much of an inconvenience.

Doreen's father still has trouble making eye contact with her. He manages to look briefly in her direction but his eyes refuse to rest on her, and instead take refuge on anything else in the room they can find. The wall, the floor, the empty space beside her head. Doreen knows he still sees her as she was that night. That even though decades have passed and she has devoted her life to Christ her father still sees her as she was a lifetime ago. Bruised and bleeding in a ripped Pink Floyd t-shirt, snot and tears pouring from her face, her body wracked with sobs. Soiled. Desecrated. Permanently diseased.

No matter how many years have passed and how immaculately she has tried to live them, she has never been able to recover herself in his eyes. No matter how pious a life she creates she will remain, to him, a whore. A rebellious teenage girl taught a lesson she asked for. A dirty used up and contaminated soul, unworthy of being looked at. When her parents decline the invite Doreen finds herself, more than anything, relieved.

At the party everyone sings and Eden blows out her candles and there is clapping and cake gets cut and eaten and presents are opened. Doreen floats through it all barely aware. At the end of the night when she is picking up the last of the torn paper and stuffing it into a garbage bag she has very little recollection of how it all got done. It just did. Like it always does.

Tom doesn't touch her that night.

He makes her turn on the light and stand in front of him facing the wall. He tells her to hike her nightgown up and pull her panties down to her ankles. While she stares at the wall Tom pleasures himself. Doreen listens to the *smack, smack, smack* of it with the taste of something vile climbing up her throat and spreading across her tongue. The taste is dirty and human. She feels her mouth excreting saliva, preparing itself for vomit.

When he's finished Tom says, "Dismissed," and Doreen pulls her clothes back on and curls up in bed beside him so that she can dream of being gang raped.

Thank you Lord for the beautiful life. Amen.

Doreen prays sometimes for cancer. She asks the Lord, *Father, if it has to happen to someone, I'll take it. Let it happen to me.* She thinks about how nice it would be to rest. To lie down in a hospital bed and have someone bring her meals and then take away the dishes and wash them while she watches game shows, or soap operas, or whatever it is people watch on TV other than sports and evangelism.

She thinks about morphine. Lots of it. A constant drip numbing any pain, distorting any thoughts, allowing calm. Creating a resignation that she can only imagine would be comforting. There has been very little comfort in her life. The only she can remember came at the hands of her younger brother who would come to her after she'd been hit with the belt and curl his delicate body around hers and sing songs he'd heard on the radio. She remembers comfort vaguely, but has had so little of it, that it is now nothing but a fuzzy half-memory she longs to grab hold of but never quite can.

Doreen thinks about having cancer and morphine and rest. She asks the Lord to inflict it upon her even though she knows Tom would disapprove. Another prayer she whispers into the darkness of empty rooms. She imagines fading away. Closing her eyes against all of the vileness of this world and sleeping. Never having to wake up again to the pain of being alive.

Please Lord, if you have to make someone sick, if someone needs to go, let it be me.

Christmas Eve constitutes a lot of church. The service is relentless, so drawn out and over the top that by the time it finishes Doreen is exhausted. She has had enough of the whole occasion and it hasn't even taken place yet.

Tom had insisted that Delilah forfeit the nursery and attend church with the adults and Eden begged to not be left behind, so the two oldest girls sat between their parents for what must have seemed to them like an infinite amount of time. Eden became fidgety first, picking at her nylons until Tom smacked her tiny hand away from them and gave her a stern look of warning. She tucked her hands under her legs and began to rock slightly, her bottom lip trembling and tears flooding her eyes. Delilah held out longer, but eventually she too began to wiggle in her spot and turn the pages of the bible and pick at her clothing and murmur under her breath until Tom gave her a slap too. A quick one on the thigh. Doreen looked at her daughter's faces, wracked with misery, and she felt very little other than the full body exhaustion that had overtaken her sometime during the first hour of the service. They were sad little creatures and it was Christmas Eve and her husband had smug eyes and a quick hand that seemed anxious, tonight, to sting flesh.

The voice came to her calmly and urged her to examine what was happening. It asked her about the way life should be lived. Then it was gone.

Now the service has ended and Doreen is standing in the reception area of the church with Tom and her two oldest daughters. She is smiling, she thinks. She is hugging all the members of the congregation who are making their way around the lobby. She is touching her ears as they burn. Tom's sisters are making a big fuss over the girls, and some of the nieces and nephews who have already been sprung from the nursery are running around. There is squealing and pulling and tripping. Children, wired with anticipation and adrenaline, encircle her. She continues to smile and hug and shake hands and say things in answer to questions she is asked. She continues to praise Jesus and the miracle of this, the night of his birth.

It is a performance. The voice comes to her to tell her this and once again vanishes. Life is a performance, it says and when it comes, when it says this, Doreen longs for it to stay. She feels reassurance in the words, in the pitch and the tone. She wants to somehow reach out for it but has no concept of how one goes about grabbing hold of a voice, of a feeling.

At some point Lisa Griffin appears amongst the crowd and makes her way toward Doreen. Doreen feels her ears turn scarlet at the sight of her, the heat almost painful.

"Doreen! Merry Christmas!" The counselor is bright, healthy. Her hair and skin and teeth shine. She smells like candle wax, like sensuality, like a life being lived. She hugs Doreen tightly to herself as she wishes her well and then pulls away to smile fiercely. Her energy makes Doreen feel even more exhausted. Even more inadequate.

Lisa introduces her husband, telling Doreen as well as Tom, who has come to stand beside his wife, that his name is Richard. Her daughters are around here somewhere she assures them, smiling at them as if this information should somehow make them happy. Doreen recognizes Richard. She is in fact sure that she had attended Sunday school with him at some point. Back before all the babies. When she and Tom used to stay after church to study and analyze the Bible with a group of peers and the good Reverend himself.

Doreen feels suddenly very vulnerable. Exposed. Secrets of hers, tales of her life, have been shared with this woman and now here she is, in front of Doreen, moving and breathing and dressed in fancy clothes and locking arms with this man who is her husband. Existing outside of the pale yellow room where they meet. Suddenly this woman is all too human and full of free-will and Doreen is sure that Lisa Griffin has shared her secrets. With her husband, with other members of the church. She starts to notice the looks on people's faces as they pass. They're looking at her strangely. They are smirking and giggling. She sees a man point and whisper to his wife who rolls her eyes as she scoffs.

Doreen wonders now why it was thought to be a good idea to have a member of the church provide therapy for her. She wonders, for the first time, why she agreed to it. Then she remembers her life and she shakes away that question. She was never given the option to agree with it or not. Of course. Her life is not comprised of options. She simply does what is required. She does what Tom and God and Reverend Smiley tell her she should do.

Now she is feeling immensely uncomfortable standing here with this woman who knows so much about her, and this woman's husband who Doreen is certain knows more than he should.

Tom is very stand-off-ish when Doreen introduces him to Lisa. Almost rude. So unlike Tom who puts so much emphasis on appearances. Doreen is surprised by his demeanor. He shakes Lisa's hand and states his own name coldly. He keeps his arm wrapped tightly around Doreen's waist, not in affection, but in an act of showing possession. Doreen is not foolish enough to mistake Tom's demonstration of ownership for something loving.

The husband initiates small talk. Weather and football. The husband is handsome. He has dark hair and green eyes and a friendly sort of face. A soothing way of speaking. Tom looks ugly and defensive standing next to him. Tom is ugly. Doreen has a flash of something she shouldn't. A memory of a face very much like Tom's that she does not allow herself.

Then she can't help but picture a hammer hitting Tom square in the face. Breaking his nose. She sees this hammer hit again and again his hideous face. Blood. Bone. A nameless clear fluid pouring from the cavity left in the middle of his ugliness.

The voice says nothing. Just laughs.

Doreen shakes away the thought, asks the Lord, silently, to forgive her depravity and her sin. She excuses herself to go get the rest of the children from the nursery.

When she returns with Jacob and Faith and Grace Isabella, Tom is still with Lisa Griffin and her husband. There are two women standing with them now. Delilah and Eden are standing next to Tom, fidgeting. One of these women has her arm around the waist of Lisa Griffin. The other is holding the hand of the husband Richard. When she gets closer Doreen realizes that they are not women at all, but girls. Tall, striking girls with breasts that stretch their sweaters underneath their open coats. They are blonde and smell, as their mother does, of something sensual and giving. Of something so very much alive. One has a perfect smile and the other has teeth with braces.

"Doreen," Lisa Griffin greets her again, "these are my daughters, Lauren and Rachel. Girls, this is my friend Doreen." The girls smile brilliantly and shake her hand, their own hands warm and pulsing. Their voices are sweet and soft when they speak her name, when they talk of Christmas and New Year's Eve.

The Children who have never been spanked, thinks Doreen.

She lets her eyes roam over them briefly once more. Long legs in black nylons, skinny waists, manes of pale hair. Their beauty makes her ache. It frightens her. They have vaginas between their legs, and anuses. Delicate, vulnerable holes. Doreen shudders.

She observes too the affection between these parents and their children. Arms around waists, hands in hands. The smiling and shrugging and nodding as if the four of them are part of some sorority. Some membership-only club that no one else is privy to. Somewhere impossibly deep within her, something aches. Some loss long buried dislodges itself from dormancy and rolls into the middle of her, expanding in her innards. She has the sudden urge to cry. For a small fragment of time she is aware of everything she's never had and never felt. For the smallest second she feels the pain of everything that is absent from her life as if it is alive and breathing in her guts.

But a second is all that she can bear. She pushes it down. Shoves it away. Averts her eyes from this foursome, so in love with each other, and back toward her children who are running around and making noise. Who Tom is introducing. Who the beautiful blonde girls are making a fuss over.

As the pain subsides, she begins to feel as if she is not really there. Even as she watches and listens and tries to focus on the task ahead, of getting everyone into the van and home, only part of her is present. There is a haze over what is happening. A numbness to her limbs. She goes through the motions, feeling half conscious. Half alive. Right now she is grateful for this feeling of only being half there. Anymore than that, any more lucidity would be too much to shoulder in this moment.

Tom and Doreen get the children out to the van in the frigid December air. Light snow is falling and this riles them even more. The children that is. Nothing excites Doreen except the idea of sleep, and Tom is simply agitated. He has been all night and the cause is unclear. He huffs and puffs and snaps and is somewhat rough with the children, tugging on them, pulling them along impatiently toward the vehicle. Doreen knows, however, that her children are used to being touched roughly. To being tugged and slapped and rag-dolled. That when they have grown to be bigger than her, they will not want to hold her hand or sling an affection-ate arm over her shoulder or around her waist. When they are grown they will not want her touch and it will be their choice and she will likely spend the last decades of her life with cold flesh. Without ever being touched aside from when Tom pumps in and out of her, grunting in the dark.

"Where are the keys?" Tom snaps at her.

Doreen, in a seemingly perpetual daze as of late, shakes her head, once again trying to clear it of fog. She tries to gather Tom's words and make sense of them.

"Doreen! The keys you moron!"

Now understanding, Doreen taps at the pockets of her coat. She opens her purse and dips her hand into it looking for metal, listening for the clanging of keys on a chain.

"Oh shoot!" she says, "I forgot the diaper bag. They're in the front pocket."

"For the love of Christ," Tom rolls his colourless eyes, "Go get it then. And hurry up."

"Can I come with you, Mommy?"

"Stay here Delilah," Tom snaps.

The girl hangs her small head.

Doreen walks at a quick pace back into the church and through the crowd of people which is gradually thinning out. She makes her way to the nursery where a few toddlers still remain. She asks one of the adolescent volunteers for the diaper bag and when she has it she quickly makes her way back out of the church into the relentless cold and back toward the van.

It couldn't have taken her very long. It couldn't have been more than four minutes.

As she approaches the van she senses panic. When she arrives at it she sees that Delilah has tears streaming silently down her face and Eden is openly bawling. Faith stands unfazed, a piece of red candy rolling around in her mouth, her nose snotty and bruised from the cold.

Doreen drops the diaper bag and her purse and kneels down in front of Delilah.

"Where is everyone?" she demands. "Where's Daddy?"

"Daddy can't find Jacob," Delilah says with a trembling lower lip. Guilt and fear distort her tiny features.

"What?"

Doreen doesn't wait for her daughter to repeat herself, her question a reaction not an inquiry. Instead she tells the girls to stay put and begins moving around cars through the parking lot.

She imagines cars on bodies. Bones shattering. A head rolling, independent. He's so small. No one would see him if they were backing up. Everyone is in a hurry. It's Christmas Eve. Oh God.

She begins to pray. *No God, not Jacob. Please, please, please, not Jacob. I'm so sorry. Whatever I've done this time Lord, I'm so so sorry.*

Why was he away from the van? Where in the Hell had Tom been while Jacob was wandering off? *He's such a sweet boy Lord. Such a good, good boy.*

She begins to call out his name. She begins to scream it.

"Jacob! Jacob, answer Mommy!" Raw emotion runs through her now. She has grown to depend on the haze that follows her through her days. She isn't used to this clarity and she doesn't like it. This authentic feeling of things. Of terror.

She darts around cars, she screams the name of her son, she smells him, damp dirt and weeds. She prays.

Then over her own voice she hears Tom's in the distance. He is yelling for Jacob. He is telling the boy that he better answer his father right now. He is saying that he is very angry.

"Jacob!" Doreen screams. She has to find him first. *Please God please!!*

She pictures Jacob as blue as Isaac. As still.

She becomes more frantic. She dodges cars and humans and forces her eyes to see through buildings and metal and she does not stop until she hears his little voice. Until his hand reaches up again and touches hers.

"Mommy?"

"Jacob!"

She bends down and pulls him into her, a hug so strong, so deep, it hurts them both.

"Daddy's mad." His eyes swell with tears.

Doreen scoops Jacob into her arms, his warm pink body, and tries to find her bearings so that she can return to the van. She calls out for Tom and as she does Jacob begins to sob into her neck. His small body rattles in her arms. Her stomach turns on itself. She and her small son both know that there will be a price for this. That with Tom there is a price for disobedience. A price for everything.

As it is with God.

All wrong doing is sin, and there is sin that does not lead to death.

A sense of dread coils around her and she finds herself wishing for that half-there sensation that has become who she is. This moment of clarity is unwelcome and she knows instantly and without doubt, that the night ahead will require a solid veil of indifference.

All the way home the baby screams in her car seat. She had been crying hysterically in Tom's arms when he had finally made it back to the van, angry and red. Doreen can picture Gracie's head being whipped around as Tom jerked in and out of parked cars and grew angrier in his search. The baby is covered in fluids, Doreen can hear them seeping out of her but refuses to look. She can smell them.

While Grace Isabella screams bloody murder and expels things from the holes in her face, Tom rants and raves about what just happened. He yells and slams his fist on things, the steering wheel, the driver's seat, the dashboard. This is Doreen's fault. He is, without a doubt, angry at her. If she had remembered the diaper bag, if she could get her shit together, if she wasn't such a dough-brain, if she wasn't such a useless thing.

Doreen rubs her temples. Her palms are sweaty for her son. Jacob sobs in the back strapped into his car seat, dimpled hands covering chubby wet cheeks. She can only bare a glimpse of him. If she looks too long she might be sick. Not from anything that's leaking out of his face but from the pain she already knows she will not be able to spare him. If she looks at his agonized little body she will throw up everything inside herself. She knows that his suffering has yet to begin.

She tries to calm Tom down. She says his name. She tells him it is her fault. She begs him to stop yelling.

"I told him to stand by the van! I told him not to friggin' move and as soon as I turned my back he took off!"

"He's only three, Tom."

"I don't give a rat's ass if he's only three! Thou shall obey thy mother and thy father! It's the first commandment Doreen! No son of mine is going to be rebellious. I told him to stay put and he didn't listen! "

Tom turns his head around as he's driving, looks into the back seat "Did you Jacob?"

Doreen hears Jacob's breath catch.

"That's right. Jacob didn't listen to Daddy, and you know what bad boys get don't you, Jacob?"

Bile rises in Doreen's throat. Chokes her. She wrings her sweaty hands, searches her brain for some way to stop this.

"You're gonna be taught a lesson tonight, boy!" Tom smiles as he says it. Looks smug and satisfied.

In the back seat Jacob gives into his tears and Delilah breaks into a sob. Something she never does.

Doreen sees that hammer again. This time it knocks Tom in the temple and sticks there. Blood pours from the gaping hole it creates and Tom goes cross-eyed, his mouth finally stilling itself.

"Stop your crying, Dee. Don't you dare start with me."

"Daddy, please don't hurt Jacob," Delilah pleads, "It was my fault, I should've been watching him better."

"Do you want it too, Dee? Do you want to know what it means to disobey your parents? I'll teach you a lesson too if you need it."

"Punish me instead of Jacob, Daddy. It's my fault. I'm a bad girl."

Get used to those words Delilah, Doreen thinks. Get used to being to blame.

"He's getting it no matter what, young lady!" Tom assures her. "You want it too?"

Delilah hangs her head, "No, sir." Her body shakes with sadness. With empathy and fear.

"That's better."

The hammer. The gratification of Tom's mouth finally, finally shutting the Hell up.

"You know, Lisa Griffin told me that some people claim that the Bible doesn't actually condone hitting your children. That they never spanked their kids. The rod is actually used to guide the sheep…"

Tom cuts her off.

"Lisa Griffin is a snooty cunt!" Froth flies from his mouth as he spits these words at her. Anger and rage mask his face so that he is no longer recognizable as a Christian, as a family man, as anyone she's ever known.

"Tom!"

"Is that right, Doreen? Is that right? Lisa Griffin doesn't spank her kids. Spare the rod, spoil the child Doreen, it means exactly what it says! Aren't you all high and mighty with your psycho-babble? Lisa God damn Griffin!"

"It's just that..."

"No! I find welts all over these kids constantly. What happened to Faith's neck while I was hunting, Doreen? Huh? Tell me that!"

He expels a gust of air. Stagnant and rotting. "Don't you dare sit here and act all holier than thou when I know what you do! You stupid ingrate."

They pull into the garage. Tom turns the car off. He grabs Doreen by the face. She tries to look down but he jerks her face toward him. "Look at me," he tells her.

The garage is bright with overhead light. Cries overlap each other in the back seat so that Doreen can no longer tell who is crying and who is silent, if anyone is silent by now. Her head hums with it. Her body irritated and raw.

Doreen looks at her husband because she doesn't have a choice.

"Don't you ever, ever tell me how to discipline these kids. Do you understand me?"

Doreen lets her eyes drop to the ground. The sound of her children's fear fills the van.

"I said look at me!" Tom jerks her face toward him again. Doreen forces her eyes to meet his. The hammer smashes him in the head over and over and over turning his face to pulp. She wants to spit. Right in his face. She says nothing.

"Do you understand me?"

Doreen nods.

"Sometimes, Doreen, I think you're still exactly what you've always been."

He lets go of her face.

God is nowhere. Again.

"Now get these kids into the house." Tom leaves the van, slams the door.

Doreen turns and looks into the back of the van. Gracie has cried herself to sleep. Faith is staring at her with wide eyes and red saliva caked around her mouth and down her chin in a crimson goatee. Delilah and Eden are sobbing and holding each other's hands. She looks at each of the girls but she can't bring herself to look at Jacob. She knows she won't be able to bear the weight of his anguish. The look on his face.

She doesn't look at Jacob. She can't.

Doreen is made to hand Tom the wooden spoon.

She is made to pull down Jacob's pants while he cries and begs her no, his small body shaking. Gracie has been put in her crib for the night but the other children are made to watch. They stand in a row, three nesting dolls, each one just a slight bit taller than the other. The oldest two cry. Faith rubs her eyes with sticky hands, and blinks.

Tom sits on the couch and puts Jacob across his knee. "Ten should teach you," he smiles. He is about to embark on something that will bring him much pleasure.

Doreen turns away from him. She leaves the room. Tom shouts for her to come back but she doesn't. She disobeys her husband. She walks through the living room, up three steps to the kitchen, and through it toward the stairs. When she reaches the bottom step the sounds begin. Wood meeting flesh. Agony. The girls flinching and whimpering with each blow, feeling their brother's pain.

Whack! Whack! Whack! Each strike louder than the one before. Each howl of Jacob's more intense, more raw.

Doreen covers her ears.

Upstairs she shuts the door behind her, lies on the bed, and puts a pillow over her ears.

The voice comes to her more coherent than it has ever been. Linear and clear. But she doesn't want to hear the things it is pointing out to her, the things it has come to remind her of. She doesn't want to remember what it is insisting that she needs to.

"Stop!" She yells out loud. The voice is silenced.

When Tom has finished with the children Doreen is ordered to put them to bed.

After she is finished she is ordered to wash.

She lies on her stomach, her face in the pillow.

She won't let herself remember.

Thank you God for this wonderful Christmas Eve and for the glory of your son. Merry Christmas Lord. Amen.

Christmas Day.

Tom rises before any of the children, and Doreen is to get up with him. He is jolly this morning. Energetic. Excited about celebrating. Whatever restlessness he'd been feeling the night before had been spent when he'd blackened Jacob's backside with a wooden spoon. He's clearly feeling much better now.

He sets the video camera up on the tri-pod and has Doreen make coffee. Then she is made to wake the children. Snotty and piss smelling. She begrudgingly rouses the children from slumber before they are inclined to get up.

Once they have had cereal in their Bunnykins China, a Christmas and Easter privilege, and after they have urinated and wiped the sleep from their eyes, the children are made to sit in front of the video camera and open their presents one by one, one at a time. Tom takes still photos while they do this. Jacob cannot sit. He squats instead, feet on the floor, bum hanging in mid air so that it doesn't touch anything. Doreen notices his face twist in pain a few times from moving a certain way, from rubbing up against something.

The morning goes relatively smoothly. Grace and Faith are both too enthralled with the wrapping paper and the new Barbies and the chocolate and candy from their stockings to cause much of a fuss about anything. Their usual obnoxiousness is dulled by the festivities and the novelty of the day.

When the presents have been opened, meaning when the children have finished opening, as Tom and Doreen have not exchanged gifts with each other since the year Eden was born, Doreen is to make a big breakfast of bacon and eggs and hash browns and toast and fresh fruit and juice and coffee for anyone who is so inclined to stop in for a visit. She is also to begin preparation for the supper meal. She also has to bake a birthday cake. For Jesus.

She is also to clean up dog shit and wipe asses and noses and hands. She is to keep the children in line. She is to clear the floor of wrapping paper and ribbons and scraps of tape and she is to vacuum before anyone gets there. She is to be dressed 'decently' instead of sitting around in her pajamas like a lazy cow. She is to do all of this with a smile on her face.

Yes Tom, no Tom, Merry Christmas Tom.

Thank you Lord for this glorious and blessed day.

All day members of Tom's family take turns stopping in. Some bring presents for the kids. Some bring food. Some take pictures of groups of cousins in front of the tree. The dog barks and chews things and jumps on everyone. Doreen's head aches. It pulses and throbs at the temples. She wishes more than anything that everyone would just go away. That this day would just hurry up and end.

The house is full of the aromas of cooking. Of cinnamon and sage and poultry seasoning. Of chocolate and coffee. Doreen's stomach begins to roil and contract from the combination of it all. The smells stick to her clothes and her hair. There is no escaping it, and her desire for the food she is slaving over becomes nil. No matter. As long as everyone else is satisfied.

Martha comes over toward lunch time and so does the sister called Suzie with her husband and her five kids. The oldest one is twelve, the youngest one is three. The house is full of children.

In the chaos Doreen finds herself hopeful that the voice in her head will appear. Although it scares her, she longs for it. She longs for that one thing that is truly hers in the midst of all this family in front of her that she has never felt at all like she belonged to. Like it belonged to her. The voice, whatever it is, God, her subconscious, her madness coming to life, whatever it is, it is hers and hers alone. No one else can tell her what it does or doesn't mean. No one can take it from her. She longs for the whispers too, which have become less frequent as the voice has become stronger. She longs for that sweet white noise that blocks out the reality she so often cannot find a way to tolerate.

The phone rings at around noon. Doreen is to wipe food from her hands and run them under water quickly before rushing to answer it because Tom is busy drinking coffee and showing his sister the new camera he bought for himself the week before.

The phone has rung about ten time before Doreen finally gets to it and she isn't sure there will be a response when she finally says, breathless and agitated, "Hello?" into the receiver.

"Hey Sis! Merry Christmas!"

The sound of his voice is beautiful. The sound of her flesh, her blood, her own heart pumping in her chest. The sound of familiarity and connectedness and roots.

"Oh Jack."

Tears well up in her eyes. She wants nothing more than to slide down the wall, phone in hand, and bawl.

"How's it going? Was Santa good to ya?"

Doreen laughs a bit.

Her instinct is to answer this question the way Tom and Reverend Smiley have pounded into her brain, into the brains of the congregation. *Jesus is the reason for the season.* But she stops herself.

"The kids got spoiled," she tells him.

"That's the way it should be."

His voice is like a childhood blanket. Something cozy she wants to wrap around herself, to crawl into. She suddenly misses him so much it runs through her like a fever. She tries to picture his face. His dark features, the gap between his two front teeth. His Sasquatch hairy arms. But his image is fuzzy. Blurred. It's been so long.

"What about you guys? Gosh, how are you all? How's Shelley? The kids must be getting so big." She can't picture at all what her niece and nephew must look like now. She can't even begin to piece their features together to make anything coherent.

Jack tells her that Shelley has gone back to work now that Sadie, their youngest, is in school full time. She's working in an office in town and quite enjoying it. They are going on a cruise in the new year. He's lost twenty-five pounds since last summer. He and Shelley go to the gym together. They spent the summer camping. His life sounds full. Balanced. Brimming with experiences and contentment and progress. A sharp contrast to her own life. One full of nothing.

"Who is it, Doreen?"

Doreen tells Jack to excuse her a minute, cups her hand over the phone and yells to Tom that it is her brother on the phone. That it is Jack. That it is her brother Jack calling to wish her and her family a Merry Christmas.

"Well hurry up!" he yells back. "We have company!"

Back on the phone Doreen tells Jack that she has to go. She is very busy. Cooking, entertaining.

"You know how it is," she tells him. Then she says, quietly, cupping the receiver with her hand, "Jack, it was so good to hear your voice."

"Everything okay, Sis?" She can tell by his tone that he knows it's not.

"Everything is fine. Of course. It's Christmas Day!" She injects some fake enthusiasm into her voice, hoping it will convince him.

"Well, listen," Jack says, "we should get together soon. I'd really love to see those rug rats of yours. We could have you guys over for supper. Shelley makes a mean lasagna, if you recall."

"I would love that, Jack. I would. Let's do that."

"For sure. Sometime in the New Year then?"

"Sounds great. I'll tell Tom. He'll be excited." Tom will tell her to forget about it. Tom will tell her the last thing their kids need is to be exposed to hedonism and disregard for the Lord's word. That the last thing their family needs is to break bread in a Godless home.

"Okay then. Well, see you in the new year then."

"Okay. The new year."

"Love you, Sis."

Doreen cannot remember when she last heard those words. Not from anyone. She wants to digest them slowly. She wants to keep them in a jar on her bedside table for those moments after Tom has spilled himself inside of her, so she can turn to them in those moments of vast emptiness and take little bites of them. Feel something other than grave sorrow and worthlessness.

"I love you too, Jack." It comes out as barely more than a whisper. Her eyes sting as if there are tears there, but there are none.

When Doreen returns to the kitchen Tom asks her what her brother wanted.

Martha says, "Tommy, it's Christmas day, what on earth do you think he wanted?"

Tom laughs and looks down like a shy little boy.

Martha comes into the kitchen to help Doreen do some chopping and washing. She asks Doreen how her brother is doing. How old his kids are now. She says it must have made Doreen really happy to hear from him and that she hopes his family is enjoying the season.

Doreen can't pin down in her mind whether hearing from her brother has made her happy or not. There is now something in her stomach that is heavy and hollow at the same time. There is an awareness of something missing. A limb. A digit. One of her senses. There is a sadness, an ache, that before the phone call had been subdued, but is now screaming inside her. Insisting on being felt.

Doreen says nothing. Just nods and smiles. As it is with her. Smile and nod. Agree. Keep going.

Martha continues to talk but after a minute or two Doreen stops hearing her. The white noise returns, relieves her, fills her up. Rises in her brain and seals it tight. Seals out thoughts and words and even voices for seconds at a time. She rides on a wave. Calm. Her body is still moving. Chopping, rinsing, seasoning, shuffling between sink and stove and refrigerator. But she is not conscious of any of it.

The noise in her head is akin to having an air conditioner on in a small bedroom. She hears nothing else, and is therefore not disturbed.

The unsettling part is when it leaves. When a sharp voice, a dropped lid, someone touching her arm snaps her abruptly out of that place and plunks her right back down in the middle of reality.

This time she hears Martha calling her name. *Doreen. Doreen.* It starts as faded and low. A whisper. Then, with each utterance it becomes a bit more focused. Louder. Closer.

Finally there is the sensation of being lightly shaken and the noise in her head evaporates. She is then standing in the kitchen looking at her mother-in-law. Martha looks worried. She says, "Doreen, are you okay? Have you eaten today?"

Doreen doesn't understand the question. She's been cleaning and cooking and wrapping and hosting and spreading her legs and incubating humans and pushing them out of her dilapidated body. She's been scouring and praying and smiling and nodding. And yet, has she been eating? That seems like such an odd question when there are so many other things to do. And she doesn't know. She cannot remember eating.

Tom is standing there. Near her now. He is glaring at her. She is an embarrassment. Again. Always. She remembers those eyes. The disgust in them. She remembers the look on his face. Him holding himself. Disgusted.

The smell of dead flesh now. Bird flesh.

Doreen's stomach clenches. It contracts. Bile rises up inside of her. Suddenly the smell of the spices, all of the different oils and garnishes and starches, come at her, burrow into her nostrils. Into her cells. She can feel the grease of the turkey settle into her organs.

She gags.

"Doreen?" Martha puts a hand on Doreen's shoulder. "What's the matter?"

Doreen holds her stomach and runs toward the bathroom. It's coming up. All of it.

It's as she is just about at the door of the main floor bathroom that she hears Martha's concerned voice say, "Could she be pregnant?"

Doreen reaches the toilet just in time. Fluids come out of her. Fucking fluids. Why is God's masterpiece so full of vileness? So God damn gross?

Retch and gag and heave and wipe and flush.

Please, God. No. NO!

If you give me another baby, I will kill us all.

The day passes in more work. In children eating and crying and needing while the dog barks and chews new things and ruins them. While Martha looks at Doreen with empathetic eyes. Behind them there is malice. There is resentment. Her concern is an act. She whispers to the sisters when they arrive. They talk about Doreen in the corners of her own home. Of Tom's home.

It is well after supper and only Martha and one of the sisters remain when the doorbell rings and no one is sure who could possibly be there now that every single member of Tom's family has stopped in to get a look at what a mess Doreen is. To judge her housekeeping and her cooking and her mothering. To question her about whether or not she's feeling okay. As if she is too stupid, too incompetent, to handle even the simple task of keeping herself alive.

"Well, go get it," Tom orders her, with a tired Gracie on his lap and his new camera in hand. He says this to her like she is retarded. His tone makes her aware of the dim expression on her own face. One of unmasked confusion.

Doreen is holding a plate. She slips it into the dishwasher. She dries her hands on a tea towel and goes to straighten her hair. There isn't much to straighten. She touches her jagged bangs. Her ears.

She moves through the house to the front door. Whispers go with her. They don't feel comforting to her suddenly. They are disjointed and irritating. She shakes her head. She pulls her shoulders up toward her ears in attempt to shrug them off. They persist.

When she pulls open the heavy door, the whispers go. She doesn't know where they go. She knows they are waiting for her somewhere.

"Heeyyyy!" Cold air blows in, evening air. Fresh and frigid.

She doesn't recognize him at first. It has been so long. Time has made them strangers. Unrecognizable to each other in a crowd. But here he is. Her baby brother. Skin and high cheek bones. Immaculate hair. The smell of cologne and winter.

Doreen drops into his arms. It is instinctual. Relief floods her body.

"Bruno."

He laughs, holds her tight. Says jovial things into her ear. Into her big, hot ears. His lips brush them and he does not seem repulsed. It had been Bruno who had held her in the aftermath. The only person that had still been able to bring himself to look at her face, to touch her.

After a time of being in his arms he says to her with a laugh, "Are you going to let me come in or what?" He pulls her away and looks at her face. He smiles. Perfect white teeth. Likely bleached. Smiling eyes. Moist, bright eyes.

It is only once they are inside the mudroom that Doreen realizes her brother has not come alone. There is someone with him. A man. Slight like Bruno, and not quite as good looking, but pleasant enough to the eyes. They are wearing matching coats, both of them with scarves and gloves. The stranger has earrings in both ears. He has a thin beard. His skin is bright and healthy. He smiles at Doreen.

"Sis, this is Christopher. Chris, my big sister."

The stranger reaches out his gloved hand. He takes hers and shakes it. Leather and cold. A gentleness to his touch.

Bruno turns and closes the door. Doreen is so foggy. So confused. By this day. By the smells and her tormented innards. By the static in her head.

She remembers, from her youth, feeling drunk. Being high. The feeling of not quite being present. Of not being able to grab hold of words and their meaning. Watching them float away, ignorant of what their purpose was. She used to love that feeling. In the present moment it is just disorienting. It makes her want, more than anything, a bit of clarity.

"Merry Christmas!" her brother is exuberant. How is it possible to be so happy? So alive? She can hear his pulse. The venous hum of blood rushing through his veins.

"It's so nice to meet you," says the stranger. This Christopher. He too glows with life and a joy she does not comprehend.

"Yes," she manages, "you too."

The Chris person is holding a bag of presents.

Doreen looks down at them. Ribbons festoon out the top of the bag. There are plastic candy canes full of Smarties sticking up, hooked to the edge of the shopping bag.

She looks back up at this Christopher.

It is the voice who tells her they are lovers. Finally it has come to her. She will not have to endure whatever lies ahead all by herself. Something uncomfortable is surrounding her and the voice brings respite. It brings back-up. It announces its presence with the simple statement that the two men in front of her are lovers.

Dread kicks her in the chest.

Tom.

"Well," Bruno says. His voice is shockingly masculine. One would expect with his appearance and his mannerisms, a tight, effeminate voice. One that ends each sentence with a question mark. But instead his voice is deep and gruff. That of a man. "Can we come in and see the kids?" He is looking at her much like Tom did when the doorbell rang. Like she is a simpleton. Like something with her is not quite what it should be. Only his look does not hold the contempt that Tom's did. That Tom's always does.

She swallows. She prays.

Please God...

But that's all she can come up with.

———————————

The kids don't know who Bruno is, and they are too exhausted to be excited now. The day has worn even them down. Instead of a wave of excitement, instead of a swarm of children jumping from their spots around the room and barreling toward their much missed uncle with his bag of gifts, there is a quiet awkwardness when Bruno and his lover enter the room. An uncomfortable stillness. The room itself seems to hold its breath.

"Hey kids," Bruno takes the bag of gifts from his lover's hands and holds it up in front of him. Makes a show of it. An offering. No one moves. They all just stare and blink. Doreen refuses to look at Tom. She can't. She can feel his disdain burrowing into her without needing to witness the look on his face. Her body becomes rigid.

"Delilah," she says. "Remember Uncle Bruno?"

Delilah nods even though she likely has no concrete recollection of the man in front of her.

"Hi, Uncle Bruno." She steps toward him. Such a good girl. So helpful. Delilah. *Thank you God, for that one.*

Delilah goes to Bruno and hugs him hard around the waist. He laughs. He puts the bag of presents down and stoops to look at her. He tells her she is beautiful. He says she looks like her mother. Doreen forgets who Delilah's mother is and wonders if it's true. Does Delilah look like this mother of hers who Doreen cannot recall?

Jacob gets up from the floor near his Grandmother's feet where he has been crouching, a toy car in each hand, and he too walks to greet his uncle. He stands in front of Bruno. He looks up, craning his neck just to make eye contact. "Uncle Bruno," he says, his "R" coming out more like a "W". "Did you bring presents?"

Bruno laughs. Tom snaps, "Jacob, mind your manners."

Bruno smiles down at the boy. "I might have, Jacob. Do you like presents?" The lover stands silently, smiling. Jacob nods his little head. Bags have settled under his eyes. There is a food stain around his mouth and, in a moment of being present, Doreen makes note of the fact that it is surprising Tom has not noticed this and demanded she rectify the situation. Tom hates the kids to be messy. What might people think, he says. We're not raising slobs, he says. Be a mother, Doreen. Stop being so useless.

There is then a flutter of activity as gifts are handed out and unwrapped, and Bruno introduces himself to Martha and to the remaining sister, and introduces, too, his friend Christopher. "And this is Christopher," he says, without mentioning how it is that the two of them have come to be together. The voice tells Doreen how much Tom will hate this. She already knows.

Doreen tries to remember how long it has been since she has bled. She can't. She tries to think. Tries to count. It's no use. It has been a while. She can't remember bleeding. Her stomach sinks. Her bones go cold.

The children have gotten a second wind and are loud again, and mobile. Both Bruno and Christopher are on the carpet with the children. Bruno on his knees, Christopher cross legged. They are opening boxes and cutting twist ties. They are showing the children how everything works. They are enthusiastic and very playful. They look at each other. A lot. With eyes that admire. With eyes that exude mutual adoration. Eyes that flicker and blink and stare into each other.

"Doreen!" Tom's patience with her has long worn away. She has been particularly difficult today. She turns her head to acknowledge that she has heard him speak her name, and that she is ready to listen further. "Get a bag for the wrapping paper. Now please."

Robotically, she does.

Tonight in bed will be trying. She can sense it.

Doreen gathers more ripped paper and ribbons and pieces of tape stuck to the carpet, and shovels it all into yet another garbage bag. She then sits down. She is in a chair holding the garbage bag between her knees and watching. Just watching and waiting for another cue from someone around her, so that she will know what to do next.

Tom's voice, "Jacob! Look at the mess you're making with those Smarties. I swear boy, that wooden spoon is getting closer and closer to your butt."

The voice begins speaking in her ear again. She is becoming more convinced that the voice is not just her sub-conscious or some manifestation of her insanity, but that it is in fact God. That she may have finally found connection with spirit.

She clears her throat. She shakes her head. She stands.

"Does anyone want coffee or tea?" She asks.

"He got ten whacks on the butt last night for not listening," Tom grins. He is boasting. Proud. Martha looks at Jacob. Sadness crawls over her expression. Doreen sees it. She can't help but see it. For once, Martha is not proud of her precious youngest son. Of precious fucking Tommy.

Bruno looks at her as if to say something. As if to tell her something he is feeling. Something he thinks. When they were younger they could do that. Look at each other and know what the other was thinking. Glance or cough or rub the corner of an eye and convey deeper meaning. A secret sibling code that kept them connected without the need for speech. In a home where free speech was forbidden, where one was not allowed to be or think or feel anything other than what they were told to, this was a useful skill. One of survival.

Now, Bruno is looking at her, he is trying to tell her something but she cannot understand, and the result is a grave sense of abandonment. She is a twin that has been ripped from the womb and separated from the only other heartbeat she has ever known. She is deaf and mute. She is nothing.

Kettle on, teabag in.

She waits for the kettle to boil, watches the people in the living room. Tries to stay alert and part of what is happening.

Tom's voice. "So, Bruno. Tell me. How is it that you and, sorry what was your name… Christian?"

"Christopher."

"Right. Right. Of course it wouldn't be Christian. How is it that you and Chris know each other?"

"Well," Bruno is still on the carpet with the kids. He is holding a plastic mini-van, "we met through a mutual friend actually."

"A mutual friend, huh?"

Doreen pours hot water into a mug.

"Yeah, a guy I work with, Glenn, who is friends with Chris's sister, introduced us."

"Hm." Tom is sitting absurdly upright. He is leaning forward. His voice is coming out rather forceful. He has set his camera on one of the end tables. "Why?"

"Excuse me?" Bruno is feeling unnerved. Doreen can tell by the tone of his voice, by the way he keeps looking down at what is in his hands.

"Well, it just seems strange. Some guy you work with introduces you to his female friend's brother? I mean, how did that come up? Do you guys both play hockey or something?"

Bruno laughs. "Hockey? No."

"Then what? I don't get it."

"I'm not really following you, Tom. What is there to 'get'?"

"Just why anyone would think to introduce the two of you."

Bruno picks up a hard plastic doll from the floor. He puts it into the fake minivan. It is the father in a set of family members he bought for the girls. For the dollhouse they already have. A black father. With a yellow shirt and blue pants. He is now sitting in the driver's seat of the plastic minivan.

"Well, Tom," Bruno chuckles. Cockiness edging its way back into his voice. The bravado that got him so many black eyes and fat lips in high school. "It's a crazy world. People just randomly decide to introduce people to each other all the time."

Tom laughs now too. But his is something sick. There is no humour in his laugh, but there is a degree of joy there. Something satisfied.

"Is that so?" He leans forward. "I'm wondering Bruno, are you familiar with this little book we like to read around here, it's called The Bible?"

"Tommy, I'm going to get going now." It's the sister. One of the oldest. Wrinkled and weathered and talking out of the blue. Doreen hadn't noticed her until just now. She forgot until she heard her speak, that she was in the room at all.

Tom keeps his eyes on Bruno as he says to the sister, "See ya at church," and then to Bruno, "You've heard of church haven't you Bruno?"

The sister comes into the kitchen where Doreen is standing at the counter with her tea. The tea has milk in it now. It is hot in her hands. She should move toward the living room. Her feet are dead things. Carcasses attached to the ends of her legs. Useless. Stationary.

The sister leans in, hugs Doreen. She smells of poultry seasoning and slight body odour. Savoury and sour all at once. "Thanks Hon," she says as she pulls out of the embrace, "The day was great."

Doreen just looks at her. She can feel her mouth hanging open a bit. Can feel the blankness in her own eyes. "Make sure you're taking care of yourself," the sister says. Doreen is tiring of this.

Martha gets up and sees Tom's sister to the door. Doreen turns her focus back to the living room. Back to the scene unfolding for which she is now the only audience member. The children are there, but they are as good as deaf-blinds at tuning out what is happening around them.

She has missed part of what was being said. Interrupted by the departure of the old, sour smelling sister and her insistence that Doreen is an invalid.

Bruno is for some reason describing their childhood. He is talking about church and belts and oppression. Christopher is silent. He is staring at the floor, still cross legged on it.

Tom leans in even closer now, he scoots down on the couch so that his body is right next to Bruno's although above his slightly, Bruno on the floor, Tom seated on the couch. He brings his face so close to Bruno's that her brother stops talking, mid sentence, clearly uncomfortable and waiting for some sort of physical confrontation. He is used to it. Primed and experienced. Instinctually knowing when he is about to be violated, having lived through it so many times. They are alike that way, Doreen and her brother. Accustomed to being violated. Taking it as part of life. Adjusting accordingly.

"I know what you two are." Spit flies out of Tom's mouth as he speaks. He rubs his hands together, making them into fists and then releasing them again. Bruno does not budge. He lifts his head back up to meet Tom's stare, to look him in the eye.

"And what are we, Tom? Please, enlighten me."

Tom stares a few seconds longer, hatred in his eyes. Then he pulls back.

Bruno continues to look Tom in the face. He is still holding a plastic minivan, now full of black people with plastic hair and primary coloured clothing.

"Listen, Bruno, there are certain things I don't want my family exposed to. If you catch my drift."

"You listen here, TOM," Bruno is the one to lean closer now. Doreen still stands like a mannequin in the kitchen. She is aware of her breathing. In. Out. In. Out. "This is my family too. That woman you order around all day, that's my sister. Do you catch my drift? These are my nieces and my nephew. Get it?"

Tom scoffs. "Here's something for you to 'get'. If a man lay with another man the way man lay with women, he has committed a detestable act."

It is Bruno who scoffs this time. "Thanks, Tom. You're so well read. Thank you for educating us."

Christopher stands. "This is enough. Let's go, Bruno. This is done."

"Oh is that how this works then," Tom asks, "Chris is the man of the family?" He looks at Bruno, "You must be so proud."

Bruno stands. Tom stands. Doreen watches. Steam from her tea rising and creating warmth.

"You like being a bully don't you, Tom? Spanking little boys and snapping orders at women. Yeah, YOU must be so proud of yourself. Such a big man."

Christopher reaches down for Bruno's arm and pulls on him. Doreen notices that Martha is in the room. How long? How much has she heard? How does she feel about her precious Tommy in this moment before them?

Bruno is in fight mode. Doreen can tell. Has seen it before. His eyes are wild. A vein throbs in his neck.

Tom gets right in his face with a finger, "You watch yourself. This is God's house, you understand? God lives here." Tom pulls at the cross around his neck. A delicate chain he wears without exception. He pulls it from under his sweater and undershirt where it has been hidden. He holds it up for Bruno to see. Chris is tugging at Bruno's arm with impatience, muttering about it being time to leave.

Holding the cross in Bruno's face Tom says, "You see this? Huh? You see that? This means something in this house. Don't you come back here until it means something to you too. You got that? Men with men committing indecent acts will receive the due penalty of their error."

"I think, Tommy that you are forgetting what I know about you and your inclination toward indecent acts. Everyone else might walk around acting like that shit never happened but I haven't forgotten. I fucking remember!"

"Bruno!" Doreen hears this escape her own throat. A voice she barely recognizes as her own and which shocks her with its sudden presence. "Stop!"

She is unleashed from her trance. She moves toward the living room quickly. The dog almost trips her. Jacob reaches up. She passes it all. She reaches the three men. "Bruno, just go," she says to her brother. His beautiful dark eyes take her in. Something in them is instantly injured. She has betrayed him.

"Just leave now, please." She looks to Christopher, "Please."

Her soul begins to crumble. The look on her brother's face is too much. But she knows that in this moment she has no choice. She has to save herself.

Tom looks smug as Bruno concedes. Her brother drops all defenses and begins to make his way to the mud room. He says no goodbyes to the children. Doreen follows him but he will not look at her. He will not speak. She says his name. She tries to touch his arm. He pulls away.

Why didn't he just shut up? Why did he have to bring up a past that she needed to stay buried? Why did she love him more than anything else this world had ever offered her? Bruno. Isaac. Jacob.

The door opens and the winter air comes barreling in. It is no longer refreshing, it is violent. Angry. She shivers.

Just as he is about to step out into the night, her brother turns around and grabs her. He pulls her tight to his chest, to his warm, girlish frame, and he squeezes her until she feels her ribs ache. Against his chest is a brief moment of darkness and quiet.

When he lets go, he leaves without words, closing out the winter with the slam of the door.

Staring at the blankness of the closed door, feeling the frozen air still wrapping itself around her, Doreen is sure that she has just now experienced the last moment of safety life will ever afford her.

She walks back to the living room. Martha is tidying up and Tom is sitting on the couch again, watching his mother. There is something on his face that goes beyond his usual smugness. He appears victorious.

On the floor the girls are playing with the dollhouse furniture that Bruno and Christopher brought as presents. Delilah has a couch and a chair set up, Eden has hold of the minivan. She reaches in and takes the Dad out of the driver's seat. "Time to go into the back now," she tells this plastic man, pushing him into the back of the van through the sliding doors.

"That's right," Tom tells her with a smirk, "put those niggers in the back where they belong."

Christmas was three days ago. Doreen has not bled. She has looked at the calendar but in doing so felt like she was looking at something foreign and inaccessible. She has tried to count days. She has tried to remember. She has prayed. *Please God, let me bleed. The abundance of your blessings has been plentiful, Lord. I am not worthy. Bestow your gifts on the infertile and the young. Please God, just let me bleed.*

The children wake and need. They cry and feed and leak. They emit odour. The girls especially. Vaginal smells.

Doreen listens to her body. She tries to feel her insides cramping . She squeezes her own breasts to see if they are tender. She prays.

No cramps. No tenderness.

The dog. Nothing is more satisfying than the feeling of her foot against its snout. The yelp it lets out when shoe meets face. She beats that thing in the days after Christmas. She beats it for no reason other than to feel the satisfaction of fist against bone. Punches it in its muzzle. Kicks its ribs. It yelps and scurries away from her. It cowers. In this experience something in her feels soothed.

She fiddles with the radio while Tom is absent. She hears all sorts of language and ideas. She turns the dial back long before she anticipates her husband's return.

She prays to bleed. She sticks fingers up inside herself even though God doesn't like that. Not for women.

It's not for pleasure, Lord, she tells the ceiling as she sits on the toilet seat jabbing at her insides, hoping that if something is growing up there she can dislodge it. If only she pokes hard enough. Prays well enough.

But she does not bleed.

She begins to pace the floor. Her head is a mess of voices and whispers and white noise. She finds herself rocking from time to time. Comes to, as if waking from a dead and dreamless sleep, in a corner of the room, knees to chest, rocking. Back and forth, back and forth.

No, no, no, says the voice that her throat creates. Please no.

No.

Doreen lies in bed, Tom snoring next to her, her inner thighs wet with his semen, and thinks of cancerous cells devouring not only her, but whatever lies within her as well. She envisions the disease as an entity. Something animate and ferocious. It barrels through her in this imagining, destroying everything in its path. It tears through her veins and her arteries. Ravishes her. It has worked itself into a cyclonic frenzy when it reaches her womb. It destroys not only life, but the potential for life as well. It obliterates her reproductive organs. Ovaries, fallopian tubes, uterine lining. Demolishes her innards. Then screams its way through the rest of her, leaving her hallow and lifeless. Leaving her at peace.

Tom's snoring has reached obnoxious volumes tonight. She turns to look at him, taking in his features in the dim room. His mouth hangs open, his Adam's apple rises and falls with his sounds.

She sees an aluminum baseball bat come down against his face. His nose shatters pleasingly. Perfect fragments of bone explode and fly in different directions around the room, along with a spatter of blood that feels warm as it sprays her face.

She reaches up. Wipes some from her cheek. Licks her fingers. Beside her Tom is a quiet gaping cavity. He is silent and faceless.

Doreen drifts into a sleep that is calm and without disruption. Dreamless.

It is Friday and Tom is late again for supper. The children are restless and hungry and begging for please, just some crackers to tide them over. Doreen refuses. She denies her children food.

She has not bled.

She has made soup with the leftover turkey. She has added potatoes and carrots, celery and onions and garlic. She has added oregano and thyme. The house smells of Christmas all over again. Her stomach twists and protests. She nibbles on soda crackers to stave off her nausea. She watches the clock and waits for Tom.

Gracie has worked herself into an agitated state, driven by hunger and fatigue, by the time Tom finally arrives home. She is sobbing at the bottom of the stairs, trying to climb them, while an irritated Delilah continuously pulls her back. The children barrel up the stairs when they hear the door.

"Daddy!" they jump and climb and shout. Tom ruffles their heads. He hugs and kisses and lifts. The mutt jumps and barks and tries to trip people in its stupidity. Tom ruffles its head too.

Eventually they sit and Doreen serves the soup along with a green salad with tomatoes and cucumber and two loaves of crusty bread.

"How was your day?" she asks Tom.

"Fine." He tells her.

"Good," she says.

He spoons soup into his mouth.

"I'm late," she tells him.

He doesn't need to ask her what she means. They've had this conversation six times before.

He smiles with an arrogance she can't quite make sense of. What does he have to be proud of himself for? His body's ability to make sperm? Ejaculating inside of his wife without regard for what she may or may not want? Big man. Bruno's words from Christmas Day. *Big man*.

"Late for what, Mama?" Delilah asks.

Tom smiles at her, laughs a bit.

"I think God wants you to have a new brother," Tom tells her.

Doreen feels herself becoming fuzzy. Detaching from the reality of this.

Delilah looks at her mother with eyes of concern. Wise beyond her seven years. Wise beyond her father's capacity for common sense. "Mommy, are you having another baby?"

Doreen doesn't know what to say. She shakes her head and stares down at her soup.

"Enough with the turkey already," Tom says, "If I come home to turkey tomorrow I'll be going right back out. I'll go get myself a burger or something. Christ, Doreen."

Doreen stops shaking her head. Stills herself.

"I'm almost forty years old, Tom."

"So?"

"For how long are we going to do this? I'm getting tired."

"For as long as He sees fit."

Doreen stares into her hands. She wants to cry but she has long ago forgotten how. There is no relief.

"Pick up your spoon Doreen, and eat something. You can starve yourself like a moron all you want, but you're not going to starve my son."

Doreen pictures the children, only twenty minutes earlier, pleading for food. Crying for just a few crackers or grapes.

She picks up her spoon.

"If God intends it, nothing can prevent it," Tom reminds her.

She puts her spoon into the turkey soup and proceeds to eat.

January, 2001

"My goodness it feels like it's been ages since our last meeting," Lisa Griffin says, removing the lid from the top of her pen and sticking it on the other end. She then takes the pen lid into her mouth and chews it momentarily while staring at Doreen.

Then, removing the pen from her mouth, she asks, "How have you been? How were your holidays?"

Doreen breaths an exhausted breath. There is no point to any of this. This is all so futile. Fake questions and guarded answers. How does anyone think that sitting in this windowless room exchanging lies and false courtesies with a stranger is possibly going to help her?

She is still going to go home and lock her children in cars. She will continue to choke their necks and slap their faces and pull tiny arms from sockets. She is still going to wander around half in and half out of reality praying for the end. Praying for the Rapture. Praying to just bleed and bleed and keep on bleeding until her organs fall out of her and make meaty splattering noises on the bathroom tile.

Out of nowhere the voice knocks her in the side of the head. It coaxes her to tell the truth.

She feels herself recoil from this idea. The truth. The truth is not something to be spoken of.

Tom says.

Again and again, Tom says. For years and years and years the truth is buried and forgotten, and never, ever spoken of.

Tom says.

But the voice is God. She has come to the definitive conclusion now that this is God speaking to her. And she must listen, always, to her Heavenly Father.

"Horrible."

Lisa stops all movement, even that of her perpetually restless pen. She stares a minute.

"I'm sorry to hear that, Doreen. What made your holidays horrible?"

"My life."

"Your life." The pen jumps back into action. "Can you explain?" Lisa asks as she writes.

"The kids and Tom and so much work. The dog. My goodness, that fucking dog." Doreen never swears out loud. Ever. She is unaware of Lisa Griffin's reaction to her profanity. She does not look at the counselor's face. She stares at the carpet. It is light brown, a colour one might describe as tan. There are flecks of darker brown within the base colour. It looks clean and freshly vacuumed.

"Did something happen to make your holidays horrible? I know it can be overwhelming. The holidays often are. For lots of people. And you with five kids and a new puppy. I mean, you have to expect to experience a certain level of stress."

"Stress." Doreen laughs the word, amused by the simplicity of it.

"Was there a particular incident that made things horrible, or was it just the overall strain of getting everything done?"

Why she is so concerned is beyond Doreen. What is it that she is looking to uncover? Something that will justify calling the Children's Aid? Having her committed? Putting her on heavy duty meds?

But as Doreen stops to think about this for the briefest of seconds, as she weighs all three of these possibilities in her mind as options, she realizes that each of them is viable. Appealing. Even a combination of all three does not strike her as entirely unpleasant.

Rest.

"I sometimes wish I had cancer," Doreen tells Lisa.

"I sometimes wish I had never met Tom at all and that I had stayed infertile."

"Stayed infertile?"

"I did this on purpose. I don't think God intended me to be a mother. I messed around with his plan. Tom said it would be okay. I sometimes wish I could just have cancer. Maybe of the brain. My memories would be gone and I could rest. Do you ever wish that you could just rest?"

Lisa Griffin, ever the professional, begins to deconstruct, sentence by sentence, everything that Doreen has just vomited up onto the nice tan carpet.

"What do you mean you went against God's plan?"

"I couldn't have babies. We tried and tried. There were just so many nights of Tom crawling on top of me. So much surrender. And no baby. For years. I was a disappointment. To Tom, to his family. To myself." Doreen shrugs, a gesture that suggests she has had no other choice but to accept her own shortcomings. "I couldn't get pregnant. Just one more thing I couldn't do. I can't make cabbage rolls either."

Doreen can see the pen, from her peripherals, moving frantically on the guarded pad of foolscap.

When the counselor finally stops writing she looks back up. Doreen looks up too. Looks her in the face. Lisa Griffin wears a frightened expression.

"Okay, so. I didn't realize you had suffered from infertility, Doreen. That is a difficult thing for many couples. But you did get pregnant. Right? And now you have five healthy children. So perhaps it was in God's plan."

"Then what about Isaac?"

"Isaac..." She lifts pages and scans them with eyeballs that twitter and twitch and Doreen imagines punching her in the face with a closed fist. How does she not know who Isaac is? How in the world does she have to look through her notes for this?

"My dead son."

Lisa stops flipping pages and looks at Doreen. Mouth closed. Eyes wide.

"God killed him. Because I was a whore."

Lisa stares. Says nothing.

"I didn't deserve babies. I wasn't supposed to have them."

"Oh Doreen, now, you can't possibly believe that these things are true."

"Why not?" Doreen asks.

"Doreen? Are you okay? "

Doreen has been staring at the carpet but she looks up again now, up into the face of Lisa Griffin.

"Oh no," Doreen tells her, "Don't worry about me. God is with me now. Everything will be fine."

Lisa Griffin wants to talk to Tom at the end of the session. Martha had stayed with the kids while Tom drove her in. She is not allowed to drive herself to counseling. She isn't sure if this is because they think she might run off, go somewhere else instead, or if Tom thinks that his mere presence in the same building will prevent her from saying anything to make him look bad. That by simply being in the waiting room he can stop her from opening her dumb stupid mouth in a way that might betray too much.

Doreen sits in a chair while the two of them move to a space as far across the room as they can be from her. They whisper. They look over at her and she curls herself into a ball on the waiting room chair. It is made out of some sort of polyester. Itchy fabric. Metal legs. Hard and uncomfortable.

The voice comes and soothes her. She can feel it petting her.

She doesn't need to care about much else.

Everything will be fine.

On the way home in the van Doreen is pretty sure that Tom is yelling at her. His hands are flailing about as they tend to do when he is angry, and his lips are flapping. Fat, wet lips continuously opening and closing and expelling breath. Polluting the air around them. Spit flies from his mouth, his face is the colour of a cooked beet.

She looks at him.

She sees him.

She sees all of this going on, the gestures, the saliva, the odd colour of the skin, but she hears nothing. White noise fills her to capacity. Hums almost violently in her head, rattles her brain. She doesn't mind. She'd rather not hear what Tom has to say anyway.

About half way home she stops even looking at him. She stares out the dashboard window into the January evening and lets her body vibrate with the noise in her head.

She thinks it might be time for another haircut. Girls are wearing it short these days. Like that character from that show. She thinks. But then again, she doesn't really watch television.

That night Doreen tosses and turns and sweats, falling into sleep only to be ripped back out of it by her dreams.

An infant screams. The goat-like cry of a newborn ricocheting off barren walls. She searches for the child with a sense of urgency she can't explain the reason for.

There is laughter in the corners of the room. She is petrified. Waiting for something to jump out at her, to take her. Afraid to move, terrified to stay still.

She is being chased. She is looking behind her. Boys are laughing. Her breasts are leaking milk. The baby continues to scream.

She bolts upright, makes a noise that comes from her guts painful and sharp.

"For Christ sake, Doreen," Tom slams himself back down and rips the blankets away from her in order to cover his own shoulder. "Go back to sleep."

Doreen lies staring at the ceiling, terror still gripping every molecule of her being. She is trembling, sweating. Her bladder aches and stretches. She does not want to get out of bed, but her body insists. Her kidneys demand.

She remembers being a child and building forts with her brothers out of blankets and couch cushions. Jack would turn out all the lights and point a flashlight around the room, riling her and Bruno with stories of men with hooks for hands and babysitters getting calls to tell them the children upstairs were dead. There was a joy to that terror. A satisfaction and a thrill. Afterwards her younger brother would go with her to the bathroom. He would hold her hand. He would stand against the wall and look away as she peed.

There is no one now to hold her hand. Her terror, like everything else, is an annoyance to Tom. There is no one to watch over her while she pees.

Terrified, she has no choice but to get up and go to the bathroom alone.

When she wipes, there is blood. The toilet paper is stained bright red. Instantly she is wracked with relief.

Thank you, Lord. Oh you are so gracious, God. Thank you. Thank you.

Eden and Delilah return to school, Doreen's period lasts five days and finishes with a day of spotting. She gives thanks each time she wipes blood from herself. She prays and thanks Him and means it. Oh how deeply she feels her gratitude. To the core of who she is. And with it, guilt. Deep down in the marrow of her bones, for so passionately wanting an empty womb. Ingrate. She knows. She is thankless and unworthy. So she prays about that too.

Forgive me, Lord for rejecting the gift of motherhood. Your gifts are my blessing Lord. I am a fool.

On a day when Doreen was feeling somewhat coherent and the white noise was at bay, the voice quiet, Tom had explained to her the consequences of her most recent visit to the counselor. He wanted her to stop all contact with Lisa Griffin immediately. "What the Hell are people going to think, Doreen? That woman goes to our church and you go in there acting like a complete loon. Seriously." Doreen apologized repeatedly for her behavior. For embarrassing Tom again. I'm sorry Tom. I understand Tom. Never again Tom.

Only because of Reverend Smiley was she allowed to see Lisa again at all. Reverend Smiley had advised Tom that it was in the best interest of the children, the best interest of the family, for Doreen to continue to see her counselor on a regular basis. He suggested making her visits more frequent even, but Tom had put his foot down on that. Doreen would see Lisa once a month now instead of every two weeks. And she would be very, very careful what she spoke of. "I swear to GOD Doreen, one more incident from you and I will go against Smiley on this one. I will yank you from that office so fast it'll make your crazy head spin, understand?" Doreen had nodded. She had apologized some more. She had gotten on her knees that night and let Tom take jabs at the back of her throat. His hands pulled her hair, he slammed her into himself. He was angry, and she took her punishment like the sinner she is. Repented on her rug burned knees until Tom was spent.

February, 2001

What follows Doreen out of January and into the breathtaking cold of February is a feeling very different than any she has been experiencing recently. It is an energy. A buzzing in her veins. Friction heating her up and causing her to move. She begins to need less sleep, begins to find it difficult to fall into. And that makes her happy. She has more time to clean and less time to deal with her subconscious trying to sort out her past and her present. She does her duty with Tom and then when he begins to snore she gets out of the matrimonial bed and goes to the kitchen and cleans cupboards and organizes drawers and moves things around in the fridge. She dusts and tidies and wipes and scrubs.

It is a sweet span of time where she is alone. No one clings to her. No one needs or cries or pries her legs apart.

Staining, slightly, these moments of solitude, is that dog that smells like the underside of testicles. Like something sweaty that should be housed inside the body but for some reason dangles outside of it, its loose skin creating stench.

But all it takes is a quick step toward the animal to make it cower. It has become too familiar with her shoes and her knuckles to waste time trying to get affection from Doreen. Realizing its mistake after barreling toward her excitedly, it retreats in short order. Every time. Good she thinks. Leave me the fuck alone.

And then she is free to just be.

Alone.

Untouched and unbothered.

She reads the Bible glutinously. Devours large portions of it at a time, running her fingers along the pages, under the words, ingesting each one studiously. Letting them fill her up.

She feels them the next day slithering up and down her veins. Words from the Bible.

Sin. Repent. Righteous. Punishment. Thou. Shall. Not.

Some nights, when she is absolutely sure that every other living soul under her roof is in deep slumber, she turns the radio on, the volume so low she has to lean in to hear it herself, and she listens. She adjusts.

It is on one of these nights of solitude in the earliest days of February, that she realizes for the first time that she can tune Him in. She can find Him when she needs Him. And she can hear His voice, His words, with acute clarity.

On these nights the world makes sense. She sees into a future without suffering. And she sees the alternative. She focuses and she tries to remember. Every word.

When she goes to bed she is satiated. As if she too has reached orgasm. As if she has climaxed and been brought to it again immediately afterwards.

And it is only then that she sleeps.

February is icy and gray. Getting the children bundled in hats and mitts and coats and boots is an exercise in frustration. Getting the girls to the bus, picking them up, carting the others to play group and library and in and out of stores, it is all so tedious. And so cold. The cold penetrates Doreen to the bone. Makes her ache. Her fingers are constantly red and half numb, as she cooks and cleans and wipes and slaps and turns the dial on the stereo. Her poor red fingertips. So worn, so stiff and weary.

Thank you Lord for my strong and steady hands. For the work that they do. You are a gracious and wonderful father. Amen.

When Doreen had broken the news to Tom that he did not have another son on the way just now, he was not pleased. He had scoffed at her as if in not getting pregnant with his child for the seventh time, she had committed a sin. Or at the very least, had failed once again. How many babies would it take? How many sons until Tom would feel Doreen had done her time? As many as God wills it, Tom would tell her. We will have babies until we no longer can. Until there is no life left to create. What else have you got to do anyway, he would ask her. What the hell else are you doing with your life?

But in her ears these days, God has begun to tell her differently. One night in front of the radio, in the wee hours of one of the first February mornings of the year, He had explained to Doreen what her children are destined for. What her sin has created. Unrighteousness, ungodliness. Generations of it.

And Tom, Tom may not think he's a sinner. He may think that his repentance has saved him, that the Rapture will be a glorious day for him, but Doreen knows differently now. Tom is a sinner to his core. Deep down in him those urges still exist. God tells her this. And God shows her this each time Tom mounts her and relieves himself without words or care. Each time he pushes into places she would rather he didn't touch. Each and every time her eyes beg no and he pushes her head into the pillow so he can finish instead of honoring her body, ignoring fully, her soul.

Tom is a sinner too.

There is no hope for any of them.

But reverend Smiley says be fruitful and multiply. Reverend Smiley says take pleasure in your wife. Fill her insides with your seed. Fill her with babies. And if those babies die just make more. And more and more.

Doreen thinks to go to the Reverend and tell him what God has been saying in her ears. She thinks to tell him that it is no longer her, but he, the Minister himself, who is confused. That some people just aren't supposed to have children because those children will never be anything but damned. And that when God proves his point by rendering a woman sterile and killing her babies, it is not necessarily a wise thing to continue to go against his wishes. That some children just should not be born, or even conceived, and that some people are not meant to be parents.

She thinks to tell him this. But she knows it would do no good. He wouldn't listen. He is so sure of his own beliefs. So arrogant in his version of the truth. And already he thinks she's crazy. He knows she slaps the children and ties them to things. Yet still he says, be fruitful and multiply. Yet still he says, spread your legs for your husband and take his fluids into you so that you might create more life.

––––––––––––––

The second week of February gives birth to another meeting with Eden's teacher. Tom is once again irritated. He has no tolerance for anything being said. Takes it personally. With a calm acceptance Doreen watches him huff and puff and rant. She wonders what the teacher thinks. But only briefly does she contemplate this. Then she begins to think of other things.

Eden is still not making friends. Her flapping continues, God forbid. She has begun to do repetitive and out of the ordinary things. It is all pointing to where the teacher thought originally.

"Autistic is just a politically correct way of saying she's retarded. I'm not buying into this. This is complete crap," Tom says in the van on the way home.

After listening to his tirade for what feels like days, Doreen finally looks at him. Flatly she says, "God makes no mistakes Tom." After she says this Tom looks over at her with an expression that can only be described as bewildered. She is to be quiet and agree. She is to hang her head and listen to Tom rage. She has broken protocol. His mouth hangs open with the shock of it.

Instead of looking down into her lap, as she would normally do, Doreen stares right back at her husband after she speaks this sentence of non-compliance. And then it happens.

She winks at him.

She doesn't even know what makes her do it. Perhaps just the newly acquired knowledge of how wrong Tom is about everything. For so long he has made her feel the idiot. But now she knows that Tom is nothing but a fool himself. So she winks and makes a small clacking sound with her mouth after having repeated her husband's own overused expression back to him. This makes him so palpably angry that all he can do is stare at her and turn a shade of blotchy pink that does nothing to make him look as if he should be taken seriously. Doreen turns away from him and looks out the window.

The teacher had explained to them how Eden spends centre time lining up different books on the floor. She opens them and lays them next to each other creating a train of five or six or seven books. She then begins to tell the story, as she sees it, using this combination of books opened up beside each other. When she gets to the last book she reads the page, then goes back to the first book and begins to turn all the pages, telling more of the story. A hybrid of many stories mashed together. Never actually reading, but just using the pictures as a guide to make up her own tale. She would likely do this for hours if she were allowed, the teacher had told them.

"Well," Tom had scoffed, "I think that sounds highly intelligent if you ask me. It takes brains to be able to do something like that. And creativity. I mean, come on, what other six year old would come up with such an interesting way to tell a story?" He had crossed his arms over his chest looking arrogant and satisfied. He had laughed. He said, "Maybe she'll be a writer when she grows up. Eh, Doreen?"

Doreen had nodded.

At home now, Tom paces the floor as he had done after the first meeting with the teacher. He begins again with his list of instructions on how to fix this. He curses the teacher. He calls her fat. He calls her a left-wing idiot.

"Call right now and get something going, Doreen. Swimming lessons and tutoring. And I want you working with her, DAILY. This needs to be rectified. No one is telling me my kid's a retard."

Doreen goes to a drawer in the kitchen and pulls out the phone book. She begins flipping pages looking for tutors, looking for facilities in town that offer swimming. Tom continues to talk and talk and talk.

When he finally stills his mouth Doreen says to him, "Damaged goods Tom."

"Pardon?"

"Do you know what happens in the wild when a baby is born damaged? The mother takes it out to the woods and leaves it there."

Tom is still for a moment. Doreen has a finger pressed against the name of a tutoring agency in town on the newspaper-y pages of the phone book.

"What did you just say?"

"There's a place on Charing Cross that offers tutoring to primary students. Does that work for you?"

"What is wrong with you? Seriously Doreen you better watch your mouth."

"First Isaac and now this. I mean, seriously, Tom. We went against His will. And we both know the price of that." Once again, Doreen is looking right into her husband's eyes, unblinking. "Me more than you I suppose."

Tom glares at her. She moves toward the phone. Tom goes to move toward her but then stops himself.

"Make that phone call right now," he tells her. One of the younger girls is winding up in the basement, a noise from its throat escalating toward a cry. Doreen can hardly tell the difference between those two anymore. They are the same noises, the same smells, the exact same emissions. Tom shouts down at Delilah.

Doreen makes the call. She books Eden in for weekly tutoring. One more thing on a list of things. On an already long and exhaustive list of things.

Tom stares at her the entire time she is on the phone. He hates her. It pours out of him, this hatred. Unabashed contempt.

As soon as she hangs up the phone he grabs her arm. He pulls her, shouting down at Delilah again to calm the agitated sibling. He tugs Doreen without care, without mercy, just as Tom does everything. He pulls her up the stairs by her elbow and into their bedroom. He shuts the door. He pushes her down onto her knees and she is sure her mouth will be full of him before she can utter a word of protest.

But no. He grabs hold of both her hands and slaps them into one another, pulling hard on her fingers to make them stand in prayer position. He turns her on her knees toward the bed and pushes her body forward into it.

Doreen is on her knees like a little girl, bent over her bed, with her face buried into the crook of her arms.

She remembers being little and bruised. Praying on her knees for the beating sounds and her brother's anguished groans to stop emanating from the room across the hall. Praying with all her might, *Please God, make Daddy stop. I will always be a good girl, God. I promise. Please, please, please*. The desperate, hurried prayers of childhood.

Tom gets down beside her in the same position. "Repeat after me Doreen."

Doreen says nothing. Just waits. Waits, as always, to be told what to say.

"Forgive me father for I have sinned…"

Tom prays and Doreen repeats. They do this for what feels like an hour. Her body is cramped and her knees are sore but still Tom talks into his hands and waits for her echo.

When it is finished and she stands, Tom takes his wife's face in one of his hands. He looks in her eyes. He says, "Now go be a mother until it's time to be a wife," and he releases her face with a shove.

Doreen walks, zombie-like, down the stairs to her children.

She wakes up to a bright white bedroom. Snow. Outside the ground is covered and the sky is full. Everything is white-gray and blinding.

She listens to the local radio station to hear that school is cancelled. She hears some songs while she is waiting. Tom is still home and going in and out of cupboards. "Turn the station back," he tells her as soon as the cancellations have been announced. Doreen grins at him obediently and turns the dial back to the gospel of Christ. Even though she knows now that these people are wrong too. These singers. These disc jockeys preaching between songs. Claiming to know. Claiming to see.

She knows.

She sees.

God's word is not on this channel but on one further down the dial. Where He talks and makes clear His intentions.

When only weeks ago she was wracked with it, Doreen has all but stopped feeling guilt now for not wanting another baby. God tells her that these ones were never meant to be at all. She knows now. The trouble will be in convincing Tom.

Gracie is rubbing herself on Doreen, drinking a bottle. Doreen rubs the child's back in a moment of calm. The snow. God has given her respite. A day off. The child smells like milk and something left over from the bath. There is a powder smell to her. She does not sicken Doreen presently. She is warm and quiet and clean.

"Have a nice day," Doreen tells Tom. He stops moving around and looks at her funny. "In a hurry to get rid of me?" he says. She has committed a wrong doing by wishing her husband a good day. She should just shut her dumb mouth for once and for all. But she doesn't dwell on it today. She continues to rub her daughter's small back. Flannel and warmth.

"Can you put the kettle on for me?"

Tom looks at her like he has never seen her before. Like she is a leper.

"Are your legs broken?"

"I have the baby."

Tom scoffs. "She's not a baby Doreen. We don't have a baby." Accusatory glare, pissed off tone.

"So you can't put the kettle on? You're standing right there."

"I'm leaving for work," he tells her and picks up his own coffee before exiting the kitchen.

Doreen looks down at the baby. She *is* a baby. Small and helpless. Needy and demanding. A baby still. Doreen tries to picture her growing into something as capable as Delilah, but in this moment she cannot.

"Silly Daddy won't make mommy a cup of tea," she says into the child's hair.

Gracie loosens her lips from the bottle, holding the nipple with only her teeth and says, "Silly Daddy." She giggles, frothy milk bubbling up and surrounding her mouth and teeth. Doreen gags a little as she pulls the child from her lap and walks to the adjoining kitchen to turn the burner on for tea.

———————————

Snow day. The kids eat bowls of oatmeal with heaps of brown sugar. They drink chocolate milk. They pull snow pants and boots and hats and mitts and scarves onto their eager bodies. Outside they go, taking precious Champy with them. The animal is so excited it pisses itself within seconds of hitting the outside world, blemishing the pureness of the snow with trails and drops of yellow.

Doreen does some sit-ups and pushups while the children play outside. She can see them from the sliding glass doors. Their footprints vandalize the snow's canvas, desecrating it completely.

She drinks another tea and sits on the couch, the children still in her view, with the Bible in her lap. She reads, sips tea, and takes glances up at her offspring so full of life in the yard. They laugh with wide open mouths, sticking out their tongues to catch what's falling from the sky. They roll snow into balls and push them through the yard making them bigger and bigger as they go. They lie on the ground and stretch out their arms and legs, moving them away and toward their bodies again and again, creating angels. Five little angel outlines in the snow.

Doreen looks back into her Bible. She reads.

> *Be merciful, just as your Father is merciful. Stop judging and you will not be judged. Stop condemning and you will not be condemned. Forgive and you will be forgiven. Give and gifts will be given to you; a good measure, packed together, shaken down, and overflowing, will be poured into your lap. For the measure with which you measure will in return be measured out to you.*

She looks back up. The dog chases the children in turn, Jacob now, around the yard. Jacob looks back over his shoulder at the dog as he tries to escape him. His face is red with cold and bright with laughter. The dog rushes past him and begins chasing Eden who also looks back with a red face and a delighted mouth. Jacob falls into the snow, lies back in it, takes a handful and puts it to his mouth. Tastes. Smiles.

They have each passed through her vile insides, her used up and despoiled vaginal wall. Her crude lips spreading around their small heads. Her sin seeping into their pores as they entered the world. Created, at the basest level, by Tom's deviant seed.

Poor Creatures. Not a chance. Not a prayer.

The children fly and fall around the yard. Arms and legs outstretched. Tongues out. Eyes wide. There is no crying, no needing. There is nothing but bliss. A yard full of freshly fallen snow and a sky that keeps giving and the exhilaration of abandon that only childhood allows. They are pure joy. All five of them. They are breath and energy and happiness personified. Small bodies pummeling, with excitement, the ground, the air, the sky.

Doreen finds herself snapping out of watching them, realizing her tea has gone cold. Realizing she had lost herself, momentarily, in their delight. She finds herself in a living room she doesn't recognize as her own, her mind filling up with doubt. She finds herself turning off the radio. Turning off the word of God for now. Putting down her Bible. Pulling on a coat and going out into the cold February morning, to the surprise and elation of the children. She finds herself attacked and accosted with their hands and their arms, their mouths and the sounds of their joy. Screeches and screams and full bellied laughs.

She tilts her head toward the sky and opens he mouth wide to the heavens; lets cold snowflakes land and melt on her outstretched tongue.

Tom telephones at four to say that he will be away for the night. The snow is too heavy. Roads are blocked, he is out of town, he will have to book a hotel and stay overnight.

"You're on your own tonight," he tells her. She can't help but wonder what he thinks she is, on every other night of their lives, if not on her own.

She feeds the children at five o'clock. They do not have to await their father's arrival. They come to the table hungry but not famished. Not cranky and miserable from pangs of deprivation. They eat grilled cheese sandwiches and thinly chopped vegetables with dip. Delilah asks for a plate of pickles and Doreen instructs her on how to get them from the fridge and bring them to be served. Delilah brings a plate to the table piled with dill pickles and all but Faith slurp and crunch the tangy goodness until the plate is empty of anything but droplets of greenish juice.

"Pickles are yucky," Faith says.

"Pickles are good," Doreen counters, picking up a thick dill and crunching down on it. There is sensation in her mouth. A burning as she salivates. Taste buds screaming. Pleasure.

She thinks about Isaac suddenly. Does a quick calculation in her head. How old? He would be eight and a half. Eight years. Time has certainly gone by. Given things and taken things away. Slowed and sped up, but passed all the same. And in doing so has turned strings of her hair gray, and wrinkled the delicate skin around her eyes. She looks down at her hands and is reminded of her own mother. The harsh knuckles. The protruding bones and veins. Calluses. She remembers those hands. Coming at her. Pulling, pushing, tugging. Locking closet doors. And here she is with the same hands. With the exact same hands that are all too capable of those very same things.

Later she bathes the children without incident. She reads to them. Gracie barely whimpers when her mother lays her in her crib. She nurses the rubber nipple of her bottle, suckling noises filling up the room, and although she makes a slight protest as Doreen shuts the door, that is all. No ruckus. No temper tantrum. Just submission and quiet.

By the time Doreen makes it to Eden and Delilah's room, the younger of the two is already asleep. Doreen removes the book from Eden's chest, noticing that there are two more beside her. She thinks of the teacher's description of her daughter and touches the child's blonde hair. She knows it's her fault. God has tried and tried to show her. To stop the madness of Tom and Doreen's incessant need to create humans.

But right now her daughter looks so innocent. Eden is the prettiest one by far. Blonde hair and tiny features. Perfect ears that sit snug against her head. It's what's inside her head that is ugly. Delilah, blessed with abundant intelligence, and poor, pretty Eden all screwed up inside. Her brain wired wrong. Because of Doreen. Because of Tom. Because of teenage rebellion and a night so long ago.

For a moment longer Doreen touches her daughter. Lingers there, fingertips tracing the features. She rarely touches her children in softness. Only to sting. Only to hurt. The sensation of this now, this gentle contact, is alien but pleasant. The skin is warm and there is a pulse underneath it. There is breath. The smell of sugar and lavender. Masking now what lies beneath. The smell of body. The smell of sin.

Doreen pulls the blanket up to Eden's small neck, watches the throat pulse. Tucks the blanket around the child. Turns out the bedside lamp.

Delilah has been watching her mother and as Doreen turns to look at her, it is as if the child is holding her breath. Waiting for something that might go wrong. Doreen sits on her bedside too. Looks at her face. It is not an unfortunate face by any means. Delilah is strong featured. Black eyes. Doreen sees her brother in those eyes. Evidence that she once belonged somewhere. Somewhere other than curled compliantly in Tom's shadow. In Delilah's eyes there is proof that Doreen came from somewhere. That she is responsible, in part, for creating something that didn't die. That isn't obviously defective. Delilah is proof that something went right somewhere along the way. Even if it was never meant to be.

Delilah stares at her mother pensively. God knows the child has good reason to be apprehensive. Doreen thinks to touch her. To run her fingers along her forehead and her eyes lids. To feel the twitches under the skin. The warmth of the flesh. But she doesn't. Not while the child is awake and watching. Not with Delilah. It has been too long. So long that the very sensation might startle them both.

She takes in the cheekbones, the reasonably sized ears, ripe lips, and tea coloured hair.

"Did you have a fun day today?"

"Yes. We should get hot chocolate at groceries."

"Sure."

Doreen turns out the light. Delilah sets her own book on her bedside table.

Doreen says goodnight and walks toward the door.

"Mommy," Delilah says, and Doreen turns back toward her, waiting for more words.

The child seems uncertain of what she means to say. She stammers a bit. Says, "um".

"What is it, Dee?"

"I hope it's a snow day again tomorrow."

Doreen nods silently and closes the door, hearing Eden's breath, in, out, as she does.

———————————

The following day, life resumes.

The dog whines and chews things and trips them all as he jerks around underfoot. The roads clear, school begins again with the nine o'clock bell, stranded husbands make their way home. Doreen must cart human beings from place to place and get them to and from at specific times. She must clothe them in layers that feel extravagant even though she knows they are necessary. She must share space with a man. Cook, clean and give her body over.

The following day and the one after that and the one after that. A never ending parade of obligation. This, then this, then this. Over and over again. That's the trouble with snow days, they always end, putting the rest of the days of the year into sharp, disheartening perspective.

Tom comes home earlier than normal and on a mission to find something she has done wrong in his absence. He inspects the house as if for pests, squinting into the corners of cupboards like he might find droppings or some other evidence of his wife's inadequacies. He seems disappointed when there is nothing to complain about and so he goes into a barrage of questioning about what Doreen has done to help with Eden's 'situation' over the last twenty-four hours.

To herself Doreen thinks, 'Why Tom, of course in between cooking and cleaning and wiping asses I've been very busy researching a cure for Autism.'

Out loud Doreen lies to placate her husband. Gives details of activities that simply did not take place. She barely feels guilty for the lies. Barely flinches in their aftermath.

Tom, clearly dissatisfied with his attempt at bullying his wife, picks on the children after that. Slaps Jacob hard on the butt for spilling his juice and even strikes out at Gracie for whining. A quick stinging slap to the child's outer thigh. Doreen just watches. She feels nothing about it. Not gratified as she once might have, and not angry or protective either. She just watches. Her husband smacks her daughter. The child cries. Doreen watches.

At some point in the early evening, without provocation or justification, Doreen makes her way out of the room.

"Where are you going?" Tom asks, seemingly confused. His wife has made a move to leave a room without announcement. Without permission. She did not wait to be dismissed.

"Upstairs to read the Bible."

After a brief moment where it appears that wheels have begun to grind behind the bones of her husband's skull, he smirks at her with his eyes and says, "Yeah. That's probably a good idea. Do more of that, will ya?" And now it is he, and not she, who has decided how she will spend her time. He is once again in control which is where Tom needs to be.

Doreen looks at him and turns her face into something sweet. The way to do this comes back to her from adolescence, something so practiced that it has remained perfected just under her skin. Just waiting for the opportunity to once again become a useful skill. She smiles, all syrupy, and then while holding eye contact, she curtsies. It comes out of her much like the wink in the van on the way home the other night. It comes out of a dusty place, a place where a window has just recently been opened, where the sunlight has begun to once again illuminate all the dirty parts.

To Tom it's like a slap in the face. She can almost see her handprint swelling on his cheek. But before he has an opportunity to say anything about it, the voice comes and tells her to walk away from the imbecile before her. And Doreen does just that. She turns on her heels and leaves the room, white noise impregnating her brain as she does.

In the wee hours of the morning Doreen, alone in the living room, reads her Bible. Curled on the couch with a tea and a blanket she reads. The dog is asleep at her feet. It snores.

If there is a young woman, a virgin already engaged to be married, and a man meets her in the town and lies with her, you shall bring both of them to the gate of that town and stone them to death, the young woman because she did not cry for help in the town and the man because he violated his neighbor's wife. So you shall purge the evil from your midst.

She turns on the radio. She adjusts the dial. She lets the words spill out of the speakers in whispers as she continues to read. She listens to all that God has to say with great care. With a meticulous ear. Details. She pays close attention to them all.

It has been an awakening.

Guilt subsides. Resignation sets in.

She reads until the sun begins to crawl up over the horizon. Until it brightens the backyard, turning it pink and then white.

She reads and listens until she hears Gracie begin to whine, and she goes to her daughter with a head full of clarity.

She knows.

––––––––––––––––––––––

"How have you been since we saw each other last? You know, I was a bit worried when we parted ways last time."

"I've been fine. Good."

"Good. That's great to hear." Predictably Lisa Griffin lifts some pages of her paper pad and chews her pen lid. "I was concerned last time Doreen, when you were speaking about wishing you had cancer. Do you remember us discussing that?"

"Yes. Why wouldn't I remember?" Doreen is very tired of being conde-scended to.

"I guess there's no reason that you wouldn't, it's just that, you seemed a bit agitated the last time we met. Like you might be suffering from a bit of anxiety or depression. I just want to make sure that you're okay."

"I'm fine."

"And have these thoughts, about wanting cancer, have those thoughts sorted themselves out?"

Doreen breathes a snort through her nose. "Sorted themselves out?"

"Are you still having those kinds of thoughts Doreen?"

"Sometimes." Tom is in the waiting room. Doreen expects to hear him on the other side of the door. The rustling of a coat, a sharp intake of breath, as she once again says the wrong thing. But she only hears the hum of the heat as it kicks on, creating a sort of white noise that makes her feel more secure. Protected from Tom's prying ears.

Lisa Griffin writes.

"Okay. How often would you say you have these thoughts?"

Doreen sighs. The question is a lot of work. "I don't know," she says.

"In a week say, how many days might you think about having a terminal illness?"

"I don't know," Doreen repeats. "Maybe three. Four maybe. It depends. I had such a nice day with the kids on Tuesday. It was a snow day. The kids made angels in the yard and I thought about how they really are angels. Like their brother. Y'know?"

Doreen leans in and whispers, "And Tom couldn't come home. It's so peaceful then. Like a little piece of Heaven. That's what that snow day was!" Doreen claps her hands together and sits back in her chair abruptly. This concept has just come to her. It was. It was like Heaven. If only Isaac had been there. Never-ending whiteness and no Tom. It was a day of Heaven on Earth.

"It just dawned on me that it was an image sent from God. He was showing me Heaven. The kids would all be there. And Isaac too."

Lisa writes. Feverishly.

"What do you write down?" Doreen asks her.

Lisa Griffin pauses as if the question has confused her. She looks down into her lap at the pad of foolscap. "Well, I just write down key points of the things you tell me. Things I would like to remember so that I can continue to help you."

"Who sees it?" Doreen asks.

"Just me Doreen. Our sessions are completely confidential. Anything you tell me in here is one hundred percent between you and I."

"What if I told you I hurt the children? What if I told you I tied Gracie up in the garage?"

Lisa stops all movement. Stares.

"Have you hurt the children Doreen?"

"I was just wondering if you would have to tell anyone."

"Well, I have to be honest with you, yes. In that circumstance, if I believed your children were in harm's way, I would be obligated to contact the Children's Aid."

"So you're lying then. Nothing is really just between you and I. Nothing is sacred except what happens between me and God."

"Doreen. Have you hurt your children? Did you tie Gracie up, Doreen?"

"Of course not." Doreen looks down at her hands. Wrings them.

"Because if that were the case, Doreen, you would be in need of a more aggressive form of therapy and perhaps some other kinds of help. The Children's Aid is there to help you."

"Oh that's a load of crap," Doreen surprises herself. Voicing opinions is something she has very little practice with anymore. "They're idiots and you know it. They take kids out of good homes and leave them in the bad ones. Give little girls back to their molesters. Place kids in foster homes where they end up beaten to death. It's a joke. Smart woman like you. You know it's a joke. I know you do."

Lisa pauses yet again. Then says, "Doreen, has anyone ever spoken to you about post partum depression?"

Maybe. Maybe she has heard that phrase before. Maybe when she banged her head. She isn't sure. No one has ever really seemed too concerned. Everyone has seemed to simply want her to suck it up and keep spitting out babies.

"I took fertility drugs to get pregnant with Isaac. Then after that it was like every time Tom looked at me I got pregnant." Doreen laughs a bit. It's a sad laugh. One that says, I have no other choice but to laugh or I'm afraid of what might happen.

"He wants more you know. Tom."

"More babies? Oh, Doreen that is not a good idea. Please listen to me when I say this, it is not a good idea for you to have more babies."

"Be fruitful and multiply,"

 Lisa Griffin leans forward, "Doreen, you have to take care of yourself and these children that are already here. You *have* been fruitful and you *have* multiplied. Are you on any birth control?"

Doreen looks at her, perplexed. "Birth control?"

"Are you on the pill or do you use condoms? The rhythm method? You know you can pretty successfully avoid pregnancy by being aware of your cycles."

"Tom would never allow it."

"Doreen. It's YOUR body. I understand Tom is your husband but ultimately you need to decide what is best for you. I believe that if you were to get pregnant again there would be consequences. For you, and for your family. I need you to take this into serious consideration, Doreen. If you take nothing else away from our time together please listen to this one piece of advice. No. More. Babies."

That this God-fearing woman has said this would have been much more shocking to Doreen a few weeks earlier. Before God began explaining things to her. Now she understands.

Doreen leans in again, close to Lisa Griffin, very close this time, their noses almost touching.

"I don't want Tom to hear this," she says, "But does He talk to you too?"

The day after this particular appointment, Martha is at the house again. It is a Wednesday. She shows up early in the morning and Doreen is still awake from the night before. Tom hadn't even touched her that night. He had been livid on the way home in the car. He and Lisa had chatted again, in a far away corner of the waiting room, in patronizing whispers. Doreen knows they think she is too stupid to understand that they are talking about her. She is insulted by this, but God soothes her, pets her head, fills her brain with waves of comforting noise. The sound of the ocean, of water breaking and rushing the shore. Of water receding and pounding against the surf once again.

She had comprehended none of what Tom was on about.

Martha arrives, uses her own key to enter and startles when she sees that Doreen is sitting on the couch. The old woman jumps and throws a hand over her heart, which Doreen guesses by this gesture had skipped a beat and is now pounding wildly in the old woman's chest, trying to regain its equilibrium.

How frail. The human heart. Doreen thinks about this as she watches her mother-in-law taking intentionally deep huffs of air in what appears to be an attempt to settle herself, to bring her ancient heart rate back to normal.

"My goodness, Doreen. You scared the living daylights out of me."

"I'm sorry," Doreen tells her.

How frail a thing the human heart. How easily it startles. How quickly it scares.

Doreen once heard about a boy who was hit with a baseball at the precise moment that his heart was between beats. The organ stopped instantly and he died right there. A boy of fifteen or sixteen years old. In the prime of youth. One minute strong and virile. The next minute dead. Just like that. Because of the vulnerability of this particular muscle.

Amazing, she thinks, that any of us survive our lives for very long at all. That hearts keep beating despite the terrors of living. That so many hearts go on and on and on beating no matter what type of commotion they may endure.

After a few more seconds of trying to breathe normally, Martha asks, "Why are you up? Is Gracie still struggling with that molar?"

"I couldn't sleep. I was reading the Bible." Doreen lifts the Bible from her lap, holds it up in presentation. *Look, I'm a good girl.*

Martha smiles at her but Doreen can't read it. The smile, the expression. It seems to be a reach, something the old woman has to force. She says, "It's important you're getting enough sleep."

"Yes," Doreen nods. "Would you like a tea, Martha? Let me put the kettle on for you."

"I'm fine. I had a cup before I left the house. I'm going to help you out today and we'll see how that goes."

Doreen goes backward in her head. What has she done wrong recently? She can't remember. She hasn't locked them anywhere. There have been no bruises. No ropes. But for some reason her mother-in-law has been sent again to keep tabs on her. To explain how mothering works. Doreen, the idiot. The bad mother. But it's not her fault. And yet it is. She never should have let Tom talk her into fertility drugs. She should've listened to her nightmares.

"Did I do something wrong?" Doreen asks.

"Of course not, Doreen. I just think you're under a bit of stress. It's fine. This is what family is for."

"You never needed help with your kids, did you? Tom says you never needed help."

"Well, that's not true. Tommy doesn't always remember everything accurately."

It's then that a look passes between them. A quick flash of mutual knowledge that dies out instantly. Martha looks away. Doreen wants the old woman to hold her stare. She is curious as to just how aware this woman is of her precious Tommy's faulty memory.

"Mm. Hm." Doreen nods.

"He was the youngest so by the time we had him I had done it all six times already. And by the time he has any recollection, there were no more babies in my house."

"Right. True."

"My mother helped me all the time. Lloyd's mother helped. And by the time I had the younger ones, the older girls were like second mothers. Just like our Delilah." Martha smiles the girl's name out of her lips. Her love of Delilah palpable and solid. Undeniable. She shakes her head, "My goodness that girl makes me proud."

"She is a gem."

"So bright. That girl has a bright future."

Doing what, Doreen wonders. Catering to her husband? Pushing babies out of a body that cannot remember pleasure and so it has learned to expect and endure pain? Wishing for things that will never be? Raised as a good Christian girl at the hands of Tom and Smiley, what future is there for Delilah other than one of compliance and relinquishment? Except of course for one of revolt and consequence.

"Sure does."

Doreen rises. Rests her Bible on the coffee table. Goes to the kitchen to make tea.

When soon the baby begins to fuss, it is Martha who goes to her. Doreen can feel the bags under her own eyes and yet the urge to sleep is non-existent. She wants to keep reading the Bible and listening to God's voice on the radio. But now with Martha here her days will not be her own. And perhaps not even her nights, depending on what the plan is. On what has been discussed behind her back by Tom and his mother and their Minister and her therapist. A whole team of people deciding the fate of a grown woman, without so much as conferring with her about any of it.

Doreen feels irritation begin to creep through her veins. She feels freedom, any sort of freedom, being ripped from her grasp. She paces a bit and prays.

Thank you God, for family. For those who wish to help me Lord. What would I do without your gifts. I am humbled and gracious Lord. Amen.

Doreen bleeds again and February finishes with slippery highways and mountainous snow banks and a cold that is painful and relentless.

Martha stays overnight some nights and some nights she sleeps at home. Doreen haunts the downstairs when everyone else is asleep. She roams freely around the kitchen and the living room even on the nights that Martha stays. Like everyone else, the old woman sleeps through.

The radio speaks to her, and her Bible pushes certain passages off its pages directly into her retinas, burning words into the delicate fibers of her eyeballs. Branding them there, as well as in her brain tissue. She recites. She memorizes. Sometimes she can feel the energy of the words pulsing within her, gushes of adrenaline as their meaning sinks deep into the cones and rods and membranes that make up who she is. Penetrates every opening she possesses. As the words and their importance finally, authentically, become part of her from the inside out.

March, 2001

Most days Martha is there at least for a short period of time. Sometimes she just drops off food and 'checks in'. Other times she stays and helps Doreen with the bath and bedtime routine that she, herself has established. All while Tom sits with his rank feet propped up on the coffee table and shouts at the basketball game.

Doreen spends endless hours, even while the children are awake, reading the Bible.

She bites her nails down to the quick so that they begin to crack and bleed. She used to do this when she was small. When she was confined and needed desperately to move. When there was nowhere to go and nothing much her body was capable of doing in such a small, dark space, she would gnaw away at her fingernails. It was motion. It was something to do with her energy. She would chew and chew, swallowing the fragments of her nail that she was able to preserve, feeling them cut the back of her throat as they went down.

Her mother would scold her afterwards.

"You are so homely already young lady! Look at what a mess you are making of an already messy body. Dirty body! You've made yourself bleed you vile creature! You disgusting, homely girl."

All of this in a thick accent. All of this with a raised hand and a face discoloured with rage, disfigured with repulsion.

Doreen would hide her hands behind her back. She would keep them
buried in pockets. Would curl the fingers up and under, tucking them into
her palms. Hiding herself. Always, in some way, hiding bits and pieces of
herself. A self created by God.

As she has begun to do now. Slipping her hands behind her when Tom or
Martha look her way.

"What happened to your fingers Mommy?" Eden asks her one night while
she is reading the child a story in bed.

"Shhh, Pumpkin. Don't say that out loud okay?" Her mother-in-law is in
the next room.

"Why?"

"Eden, I am your mother. What does God tell you about your parents?"

"Honour and obey."

"That's right. Now do as you're told."

Doreen does not want Martha to hear Eden asking about her mutilated
fingers, although she is sure the old lady has already seen but has chosen
not to say anything. It's interesting about Martha, sometimes she speaks
up and other times she does not. She tells Doreen that what happens
within a family is meant to stay there, and especially what happens
between a husband and a wife. Then why is everyone always so involved
in what is happening with Doreen? Why are so many other people con-
sulted about how she is to be conducting her life? Nothing, for her, seems
to be private or sacred. Unless of course, Tom decides it to be so.

Conveniently Martha bites her tongue and turns away when anything involves her one and only son. When he uses words like fag or nigger, when he beats Jacob with a wooden spoon until the boy's skin is blistered and broken. When he, in front of his mother, tells his wife to go take a bath and make sure she washes up good. Martha turns away then. Averts her eyes. Finds something else to busy her hands.

"My mother was a good wife," Tom has told her on so many occasions she could recite what comes next. "She kept a clean house and ran a tight ship with us kids. But when my dad stepped in, she knew her place. She knew when to let him do what the man of the house is supposed to do."

Doreen would smile. Yes Tom.

She had often wondered just how much deference it would take on her part to please her husband. How much more a body and soul could concede. Tom spoke as if she were still the rebellious teenage girl he met at a party in grade nine. A girl who said the "F" word out loud in every other sentence and wore her hair long and her shirt cropped above her navel. Tom spoke as if that girl were right below the surface of this skin Doreen had been wearing ever since. This compliant and sacrificial skin that he has violated over and over again without ever being gratified.

That's just the question though isn't it, Doreen thinks one night in March. Will Tom ever, ever be gratified? Of course, a long time ago, Doreen knew the answer to that question.

Yes Tom. No Tom. Three bags full Tom.

Fuck you Tom. She doesn't say it out loud, but she thinks it. On this night in very early March she thinks it. And she remembers the middle finger that used to feel so intoxicating when it was hoisted in the air and shoved toward just the right person. Fuck you Tom. And the horse you rode in on.

Doreen is unaware of how the idea came to her. Maybe it was God who told her to do it, but if she is honest with herself she can admit that in the last week or so it has become somewhat difficult to keep straight everything that God wants her to know or do. He talks to her incessantly these days, it seems. As the air outside goes from frigid to something only slightly more tolerable, God becomes unremitting in his lessons and commands. He tells her to go to the radio. He tells her to turn on the television, and there too, she has begun to hear him.

The first time this happened the children had been in the basement watching a video, and Doreen in the kitchen slicing things for Tom's supper. She had been wiping down the counter tops with disinfectant spray. She had been sweeping up carrot and potato peels. God demanded that she stop her work, lay down her broom, leave everything and go to the basement with her children, and listen. She had obeyed even though she knew she didn't have the time. She had descended the stairs, hearing the grating voices of Bob the Tomato and Larry the Cucumber growing louder with each step she took.

"You shouldn't sit so close Mom," Delilah had told her, "it will ruin your eyes. You'll have to get glasses."

"Shh," Doreen was firm with the child but not harsh. A quick finger to her own lip to show her daughter that Mother needed her to hush her mouth.

Cross legged on the floor she had strained toward the television, brought her ear as close to it as she could without touching it to the screen. She had listened. And of course, the Lord had not let her down, as it was between them these days. There he was. Full of wisdom. Full of grace and prophecy. Until the show concluded Doreen had sat like this on the floor. Like a kindergartner at story time. Spellbound.

But with so much to take in and remember, Doreen is aware that she is beginning to lose pieces of what may be vital. Things are recently, just slightly, becoming slippery.

So when she finds herself on her brother's doorstep in one of the days that begin March, she has no idea why she is there or how the idea to get there had ever entered her head.

It feels like early evening when she arrives. She stands shivering on the porch for what seems like a long period of time, waiting for the door to open to her. She knocks for a second time and pushes on the doorbell. She should have worn gloves. She should have called first, maybe. They may not be home. They may be eating supper. She definitely should have worn gloves. But how could she have imagined it would take anybody this long to open a door?

Thank you Lord for guiding me here. Thank you for the beautiful March air. Please Lord, let somebody answer the door.

Finally she hears the thumping of steps from inside, getting louder as if they are coming toward her, and then movement on the door handle, and finally the door opens away from her. A young and aesthetically pleasing child stands there. It has dark hair and dark eyes and a slight caterpillar of hair on the upper lip. She thinks it's a boy.

"Oh," Doreen says, feeling shaken by the appearance of someone other than Jack.

"Hi."

"Oh. It's Mason. Is it?"

The child looks calm and yet unsure. He is clearly not feeling threatened but has surely had many lectures on the dangers of giving out his name to strangers.

"Do you remember me, Mason? It's Doreen."

"Hi Aunt Doreen. Do you want to come inside?"

"Please."

The child opens the door wider and Doreen steps into the front foyer, a cubicle of space filled with warmth and smells. Garlic, starch, dirty boots, animal.

"Do you have a cat?"

"Two," the male child tells her, "Gretzky and Muffin. Gretzky is mine. He's black and white and has one little patch of orange, and Muffin is Sadie's and he is all orange with white whiskers. My sister's cat is mean."

"Oh."

The child yells then, startling Doreen, making her jump. "Dad!"

"Do you have a cat?"

"Oh no. Tom doesn't like cats. We have a dog."

"I like dogs. What's your dog's name?"

Doreen thinks for a minute. The question confuses her. She looks at the child who looks back at her obviously anticipating an answer. The lips are shiny, the cheeks are pink as if the face has been outside until just recently.

"Cupcake." That's right. She is sure that's right.

"Oh," the child says. "Did one of your little girls name it?"

"Whoa!"

Again Doreen startles. This deep voice has come out of nowhere and is gruff and loud. She has to shake her head to clear it. What on earth is the dog's name?

Before she can speak she is wrapped up in arms. Big ones. She smells musk and cooking oil and something else. Maybe sex.

Her brother squeezes her until her ribs begin to protest. He pulls her away and looks at her, then pulls her in again, crushes her against his chest, rocks her back and forth in abrupt jerking movements.

Finally, he pulls her away from him for what she thinks is for good.

"I can't believe you're here! Your hair. It's so short. I've never seen you with short hair."

Ears burn. Cheeks flush. Touch ears. Touch hair. Look down.

"What are you doing here?"

She doesn't know. She doesn't even remember driving herself here. She doesn't know if she did.

"Is my van here?"

"What? I don't know. Did you drive it here?"

"I don't know."

Jack goes to the door and looks out the small window in the top of it.

"Well, there's a van in the driveway."

He turns to look at her. "Are you okay?"

"I don't know."

There is a twister of noise in Doreen's head for a period of time as her brother leads her through his house. She sees things as she passes them, hooks with coats, a mirror, photographs in frames. Jack's mouth is moving but she does not hear. His eyes are wet and the expression on his face seems to betray stress. Doreen is almost dizzy with the noise in her head. Drunk.

It becomes something so aggressive that it annihilates anything else that might be heard. Her head is full and boiling. She finds herself sitting at a table, a woman leaning down in front of her face, touching her arms, moving her mouth flaps, expelling hot breath that reeks of spice.

Doreen shakes her head in an attempt to dislodge the chaos. It does no good.

She shakes it again, violently this time, hurting her own neck with the motion. Still the riot of noise rendering her deaf. Still the dizziness.

The woman shoos the children away. Waves her arm at them. A boy and a girl. Doreen tries to open her mouth to speak. To say, no, leave the children here, I want to know them, but nothing comes out. Her mouth remains slack.

Commotion. Confusion. Head so loud it becomes painful. Eardrums burning. Brain screaming and rattling.

She shakes and shakes and shakes her head while faces flash in front of her then jerk out of view again.

When she can no longer stand it, when she wants desperately to be coherent so that she might talk to her brother and his wife and their children after such a gaping time away from them, and when nothing else is helping, she reels backward with her head, craning her neck toward the sky and then propels herself forward.

Her head meets the wood of the table with a thud so intense she feels her brain shake inside her skull.

Blackness.

And quiet.

She floats on something warm and fluid. There is nothing but darkness and the voice of God. *Rest child,* it tells her, *you need your rest.*

She opens her eyes. Her head is pounding. Her vision is blurry. She hears voices now. She sees the fuzzy outlines of people she half recognizes. She feels them touching her. Her forehead, her arms. As images begin to crystallize, to sharpen and clear, she realizes her grave error and she wants nothing more than to fall back into that black silence she has just been roused from.

She trusted Jack.

Three faces now.

Jack.

His wife.

Tom.

There is a goose egg on her forehead that becomes larger and larger during the more than thirty minutes it takes to get home from her brother's house. She touches it and rubs it and pulls down the sun visor to look. It is bluish and quite alarming. Her already hideous face has somehow become even more so. Even more repugnant and unacceptable. She can only imagine what a kick Tom's sisters will get out of this. Martha is at the house and can make a full report. How much fun they will all have with the description of Doreen's malformed face, a product of her own doing. What kind of a loon knocks her own head off a table?

Tom is shaking his head. His breaths are coming laboured and loud from his nose. He has not spoken and this is frightening to Doreen. There is never a time when Tom is quiet. And for of all the times she has wished that he would just shut his mouth, that she could hammer him into silence, now that his silence is upon her, it is more unnerving than anything he has ever had to say.

"I'm sorry Tom. I didn't mean to leave them alone."

And the silence breaks.

"What do you mean you didn't mean to leave them alone? What is wrong with you? What in God's name is going on in your brain? Nothing, that's what! You left five kids alone in a house at suppertime! I should have you fucking committed!"

Doreen feels much more comfortable now that he has begun to demean and insult. Now that anger is spewing out of him in place of hot gusty breaths. There is a return to normal. This she can navigate through like she has a thousand times before. Repentance. Apology. Remorse. It's how she has always managed to survive.

"I'm so sorry. I didn't realize..."

"What do you MEAN, Doreen? What the Hell do you mean when you keep telling me that you didn't MEAN to do it? That you didn't REALIZE? How do you accidentally leave a house full of children alone?"

"I don't know."

"You don't KNOW? For the love of Christ, Doreen this is IT! I don't even know what else to say to you right now. What in the Hell did I pro-create with? I should've known. I should've God damn well known!"

Doreen is small in the seat beside her husband. Insignificant. She curls herself inward, puts her nose to her knees. There is nothing good about her. No matter how hard she tries, she will never be anything but a burden and an inconvenience. She will always be useless.

The eerie silence so foreign to her that had filled the van moments earlier, fills it once again. It suffocates her. The voice is nowhere.

She is nowhere.

"I'm so sorry, Martha."

Even Martha cannot look at her. Doreen hangs her head. She does not hear the children or sense them anywhere.

"Where are they?" she asks. First to Martha who does not answer but looks instead to her son. "Where are the kids?" She directs her question to Tom now.

"Well, they're not alone in the basement anymore. No thanks to you."

Doreen feels a sense of panic. Where are her kids? She can't feel them here. But then, her instincts have always been prone to periods of dullness. When Delilah was an infant Doreen had dropped her off her chest. Had fallen asleep on the couch with the baby on her and had gone into such a deep sleep that she had rolled over and sent Delilah's newborn body crashing to the hardwood floor. The sound of it sickening. Her stomach had heaved as her eyes opened to the baby's screams.

The sisters had said that they slept with their babies. That they did not fear rolling over on them because it would never happen. Because they were so tuned into their babies, to the breath and the presence. Because mother and infant were as close to being one as it was possible for two humans to be. One from inside the other, sucking life from the nipple, stuck chest to chest for most hours of the day. And Doreen had managed to drop hers. To fall asleep and completely out of tune with the one human being who she was supposed to instinctively be connected to. She is sure that had she tried to sleep with her babies she would have rolled over and suffocated them, not even waking until they were cold and rigid. Why was Tom surprised now? How is it that Tom, or anyone, can still find astonishment in her deficiencies?

"Did someone take the kids?"

"I don't even want to look at your face."

Martha excuses herself and leaves the room. A matter between husband and wife. None of her business.

"Where are the children?" Doreen has no idea what time it is. How long she has been gone. If the children are perhaps in the basement eating chips and watching religious cartoons and she is just incapable of hearing them, or if they are tucked up into their beds long asleep and she simply feels no connection to them because she is a mother who never should have been one.

"Get out of my face Doreen." Tom comes close and puts a pointed finger against her nose. "You go upstairs now, and do not come out of that room unless I tell you you can. Do you understand me? You will NOT disrespect me like this ever again, you can be sure of that."

He pulls on her arm now, takes her body and pushes it toward the stairs, "Go."

So she does.

She climbs the stairs and goes into her bedroom, the bedroom she shares with her husband. The bedroom where she is tormented and penetrated against her will both while she is awake and when she closes her eyes to sleep.

She sits on the bed with her knees drawn up and tries to think about what she has done. She feels nothing. She knows nothing. Nothing other than the fact that her own flesh and blood had betrayed her. Called her husband to tattle tale on her. He was supposed to be on her side. He was supposed to be refuge. How could he? *How could you, Jack?*

The betrayal sits inside her and becomes painful. It sets into her bones, into her marrow. There is nowhere to go. No respite from anything, for her.

God pets her.

Says, I told you so.

Doreen is nothing to anybody.

The room around her becomes too much. It overwhelms. There is too much space in which to realize all that has just happened. There is too much allowance for her to move and make decisions and reach out with limbs that seem to instinctively move her in the wrong direction.

She climbs off the bed and walks across the floor to the closet. She opens the doors, steps inside and sits. Clothes hang down in her face. Shoes dig into her bottom and the underside of her thighs. These sensations are familiar. Comfortable.

She closes the door.

Blackness.

She can hear her mother outside clanging dishes and cursing under her breath. She can smell paprika and Lysol. She curls up into nothing.

As she has done so many times before, she waits. Blind and helpless. She begins to rock and hum the old songs of childhood. The ones Bruno would sing into her swollen back. She hums and hums and hums. Waiting.

Martha moves in the next day. She brings suitcases instead of the usual overnight bag. She puts toiletries in the medicine cabinet in the upstairs bathroom. Her slippers appear beside the couch. It is as if she is there to stay.

No one says much to Doreen about any of it. Reverend Smiley comes to the house and talks to her. He talks about the gift of motherhood, about how to be a devoted wife, about God's high expectations of women and their innate ability to live up to that potential. It just takes a bit of effort, he tells her. Some strength. The wherewithal to put others before oneself and to be humble and gracious. God is counting on her to raise these children, Smiley assures her.

"He wanted you to have these babies, Doreen, or else he would not have let it happen under any circumstances. God wanted you to have these beautiful, miraculous beings come from your body. And I think, Doreen, that God has not finished with you yet."

There are more babies to come, he tells her. Which is one more reason why she needs to pull herself together, find her strength, and soldier through.

"God does not give us anything that we cannot handle. He only gives us the challenges he is sure we can meet. You are a child of the Lord, Doreen. Don't ever, ever forget that."

He tells her it is time to pray and so they do. They bow their heads and ask the Lord to forgive Doreen her trespasses, to provide her with strength, and to be with her in her hours of need. They pray until Doreen turns numb. She stops hearing what they are even praying for. By the time the session finishes, she finds herself, once again, fuzzy-headed and clueless, but she thanks the Minister nonetheless.

"Thank you so much." She hugs the tall, clean shaven man, having to reach up and stand on her toes to get her arms around his neck. Something in her stirs as she pulls away from him. His skin smells of cologne, his breath is minty. He reeks of cleanliness, emitting it. She feels heat in her belly and downward. Her thighs and knees get rubbery. This is a feeling of long ago. A feeling that creates danger. She quickly retreats from the hug.

Stepping back so that their bodies are nowhere near each other, Doreen says, "God bless you and keep you," and the Minister repeats the same words back to her, bowing his head toward her slightly as he speaks.

After that, he and Tom spend a great deal of time talking in the front room. Doreen helps Martha get lunch ready. She is an assistant now, an apprentice in her own home once again. For how long, she wonders. For how long now that she has transgressed so severely? She had put the children in danger simply by going about her day without considering them. And so is the burden of motherhood. In her presence or in her absence, these five lives are dependent upon her, and something as simple as getting in a van and driving off can be the difference between their survival and their demise. What a heavy load. What a gigantic and overbearing weight to carry. For all the hours of every day and every night. Eternally.

And now, she is a woman gaining on middle age, who will live with her husband's mother letting her help out in the kitchen when she has behaved herself. She wonders if she will ever again be allowed to live as an adult. But then she questions whether or not she ever actually has been allowed that privilege.

She thinks about those women who choose not to have children. Who earn degrees and travel. She thinks about being able to get in the car at will and drive to visit someone and not have it be a crime and a failure. She imagines coffee dates with girlfriends. Business suits. A cell phone. Flights from here to there. Oh the freedom of flight. Those women who don't have husbands to answer to. Who have lovers that make them feel good. That touch their bodies because they want them to. That kiss them long and deep, and look into their eyes, and do no control where they can go or how they wear their hair.

She itches with these thoughts. Thoughts of freedom.

But this has always been her problem, hasn't it. This longing for wide open spaces. This need for independence. A craving so relentless that it still nags at her and tugs her arm until she desires for nothing more than to inject herself with it. The sweet thrill of autonomy.

That night she dreams of flying. She dreams that she has wings, white and magnificent, that push out of the flesh on her back and spread large across the sky. Effortlessly she gains height and is looking down on the world she leaves behind. She can see her house below. Her yard. That ridiculous animal is barking at her even as she gets farther and farther from it. The children wave their chubby hands with enthusiasm, simple smiles on all their faces. Tom is nowhere.

When she reaches the clouds there is no noise. There is only stark whiteness and never ending space. No fences, no gates, no closets. No doors.

In the clouds she meets with lovers who come at her softly. Their mouths give instead of taking. There is pleasure.

When her dreams rouse her from sleep she does not startle and bolt upright, but instead writhes and groans herself awake. She opens her eyes and Tom is staring at her.

"What the Hell are you doing?" he asks, his eyes squinting with confusion and disdain.

"Dreaming," she tells her husband. "I was dreaming."

"Go back to sleep." He pulls the blankets from her to give them to himself and he rolls over in disgust. "Freak."

Between her legs is a thick moisture.

This time, it is not blood.

———————————

Due to Smiley's suggestions, Doreen is to go to see Lisa Griffin an extra time this month. As soon as possible. She is to go more often than Tom wants. Once a week if it is at all feasible. She is not to tell Lisa about leaving the children alone. This is said to her very clearly, repeatedly, and by several different sources, one of course, being Tom.

She is to tell Lisa that she has been feeling stressed again and over-whelmed, but only slightly, and that she would like some coping strat-egies for handling life stressors while parenting five very young children.

She does this. She manages somehow to keep all of it straight in her head and reiterates to Lisa exactly what has been recited to her.

One of Lisa's suggestions almost knocks her off her chair. She feels as if her prayers have been answered. Not the fake prayers that she is forced to say with Reverend Smiley and Tom and sometimes Martha now, but her real prayers. The ones she says quietly in dark rooms. The ones she whispers in the living room in the middle of the night when no one else is around. Her real prayers. The prayers that happen between her and God.

"I think it would be a really good idea for you to think about getting a part time job or taking a class or something. Something that is just for you, that you can do all by yourself, without Tom or Martha or the kids. Something to recharge your battery so to speak. What do you think about that?"

The thought alone makes her delirious. The idea of doing something completely for herself. Something that would not, in any way, involve anyone other than her. It is intoxicating. But terrifying too.

No kids. No Martha. No dog.

No Tom.

And there it is. As soon as this little nugget of possibility is given to her, it is snatched right back away as she utters Tom's name in her head.

"I really can't see Tom allowing it."

Lisa sighs. She writes. She looks back up at Doreen and bites her pen.

"Why is that?"

"Why wouldn't Tom allow it? Because Tom doesn't allow anything."

"Doreen, you have to be able to do some things, sometimes, that are just for you. It's okay and of course respectful to consult your husband about things, but he's your husband. Not your father. You are a grown woman, capable of making some decisions on your own. This is something that I believe will benefit you greatly."

Doreen just stares at her. She's right. Doreen knows it. God whispers something to her.

"He's just such a bully," Doreen says it before she can catch herself. "I don't even know how I would broach the subject. He'll have a fit."

"Perhaps we should have a group session. Maybe bring our Reverend here too. I think Reverend Smiley is really going to bat for you, Doreen. He wants to see your family thrive. If I talk to him and he talks to Tom, we might be able to work something out."

Doreen is elated and petrified all at once. She can feel her hand on the doorknob. The wind in her crimped hair. She longs to burst through the door into the open air, while also feeling an overwhelming urge to retreat back into that closet in the bedroom. To sit for hours, with clothes in her face, where it has always been safe and predictable. It is the unknown that she craves and fears. That she needs but that has always had a tendency to destroy her from the inside out.

"Is that something you'd be interested in arranging?"

Doreen nods. "You can try I guess."

"Great. I will try to set that up for next week. Now. Is there anything you can think of that you'd be interested in doing?"

It has been so long since she has thought about anything she might like to do as even a remote possibility. She has no idea what she likes, what she is interested in, or even what the world has to offer at this point. She's been locked away for decades. She feels as if she might step out there and see people in flying cars who eat pills instead of food, using technology she's never heard of.

"I have no idea. I don't remember what it's like."

"What what's like?"

"Living."

Tom is pissy on the way home in the van but says very little. More unnerving silence. So alien. Doreen looks over at him. His mouth is too big. The lips. The gums. He has too much gums. Too much wet when he talks. His face disgusts her. She imagines something sharp sticking into the neck, penetrating it in one quick jab and causing the head to fall sideways, the eyes to widen. She pictures the wet mouth drooling something that starts out clear and turns red and clotted. She gags a little. Gets a quick sensation of bile at the back of her throat. Tangy and sharp.

Lisa has given her a task. She is to go home and write a list of things she used to do for fun. A list of things that interest her. Things she might like to do during her 'me time' as Lisa has referred to it.

As of right now, Doreen's mind is blank. But she can feel the pad and paper in her hand. She can imagine ideas popping into her head and the sweet sensation of her hand creating cursive letters on the page. She pictures herself doing Lisa's job. Something important and prestigious. She pictures herself needing to write things down. Needing to remember facts so that she might later consult them. It is a decadent idea. One that excites.

But for now, she will need to come up with something more simple. A part time job. A course, a hobby. She used to take pictures. She used to like clothes. She used to write poetry. She used to hide her ugly face behind make up, her ears behind hair. She used to care what she wore. She used to go to the mall with her friends and smoke cigarettes in the food court, bags of clothes at her feet. She worked at McDonald's from the minute she turned fourteen. Back when she had plans. When she wanted to show the world that she needed no one.

Back then she had no intention of letting someone else take care of her. She was going to live on her own in an apartment. Have some house plants and a cat. Put art on the walls. Listen to music from speakers she would buy herself. She was going to move to Toronto, and walk down Younge Street in the middle of the night, and go to dance clubs where men and women morphed into one another and could not be told apart. She was going to move out West, and climb mountains, and go to night clubs, and take pills that dissolved under her tongue.

She was not going to live in another house like her Father's, where rules were made for her and breaking them meant repercussions. She had had no plans of being tied to anything.

But God had changed those plans in one fell swoop. She remembers the thrusting now. The relentless thrusting. The faces are blurred, but the laughter is still so sharp in her memory that she looks over at Tom to be sure it isn't him having a deep sadistic chuckle about something she has missed.

Tom's face is still.

Thank you Heavenly Father for Tom and how he cares for me. He really is a devoted husband Lord, for putting up with me. Thank you. Amen.

Her days become a routine that make her feel violent with the need for flight.

When she gets out of bed Martha is already in the kitchen. When she goes to sleep her husband is in bed beside her. Throughout her days children cling to her body and soil it. When she walks there are things in the way. Toys, other people's possessions, animals. She wants to kick and slap at things but she is not allowed. She is under constant surveillance.

Her nights in front of the radio take on an even greater degree of importance. She gets herself through her days by thinking about the nights and a time when there will be quiet and room and self.

She often becomes antsy just waiting for Tom to begin snoring. She sometimes wishes for a drug. Something potent and tasteless that could be slipped into his food that would cause him to collapse as soon as the meal was finished. A little bit for the old lady too, to prevent her from noticing her son's unusually early bedtimes, and to keep her from spending too much time cleaning and tending to the children. Even them, even the kids. A tiny bit. Half a spoonful. Something to sedate them to a heavier degree than what is natural. To keep Grace Isabella from crying out, Faith from climbing out of bed and demanding another drink, another hug, some specific stuffed animal that is always tucked somewhere obscure.

She pictures all of them drugged and lifeless. Limp bodies resting without the chance of wakefulness. The quiet. The still. The sweet liberation of knowing that no matter how loud she turned up the radio no one would hear and interrupt her in her pursuit of solitude.

She read Flowers in the Attic as a teenager. The mother used arsenic to slowly kill her children, succeeding with one of them. Doreen's only intention would be to keep them sleeping. Just to keep all of them asleep. A little deeper. A little bit longer than usual. That's all.

However, there is no sleeping powder in her cupboards, and the body is the temple of Christ, and so Doreen is forced to wait until the natural rhythms of sleep overtake each and every one of the seven other people who occupy her house and dictate her life. Only then is she able to retreat to her sacred spot on the couch. Radio, Bible, tea, God. And only when the sun begins to creep up over the horizon turning the sky bright behind the curtain of the sliding glass doors, does she sneak back upstairs and tuck herself into bed beside Tom so that if he wakes he will never know she's been gone.

Thank you Lord, for our nights together. I cherish your guidance Lord. You humble and better me. Amen.

Doreen is allowed to walk Delilah and Eden to the bus while Martha stands at the door and watches until the bus has driven off and the children are within a safe distance of their mother's care. Only then does the old woman turn away and go back into the house to tend to the other three.

As everything is under control once she gets back inside, she feels the true depth of her uselessness. What's worse, she cannot decide. Having overwhelming amounts of responsibility cloaking her, weighing on her with every exhaustive step she takes throughout the day, or being fit for nothing and hence as unneeded as shoes on a cripple?

She pulls a pad of paper from one of the drawers in the kitchen and thinks of Lisa Griffin. She poises the pen then pulls it up and chews the lid which she has secured to the opposite end.

After a minute she writes the words, *Things I used to like to do.*

She thinks.

The house breathes around her.

It tells her things. It reminds her of who she used to be and shame burns through her, reddening parts of her body and face. She used to like things in all their vileness. She used to embrace the dark, the pleasurable. She thinks of the list she could write and Tom's shocked face if he were to stumble upon it. She grins a bit at the thought of this. Tom liked it all too. Perhaps even more so.

She sees him as he once was. Young. Eyes still holding colour, hair vibrant. Body hard and lean and tight-skinned. Everything about Tom now is muted and loose. Ill-fitting.

His face, then, lit up by a bonfire. The smell of Jovan Musk. V-neck t-shirt. Tight jeans. Too much gums when he laughed. The idea of his laughter turns the memory sour. Too much gums. Too much wet. Something unspeakable behind the blue of the eyes.

She chews the pen lid, shivers away the image of her husband in his youth. By the time she had met up with him again he was already pale and softening. He was already turning into the Tom she dreams of seeing bloodied and split open.

She taps the pen on the paper. Martha and the children make familiar noises upstairs. Doreen can't think of anything suitable to write, and realizes that even in this lone pursuit she is not free. She must censor herself. She must be very careful what she chooses to disclose. Nothing is authentic. She will fill the page with lies and end up doing something that is of no interest to her anyway.

She writes down ten generic things that seem appropriate. Ten things that will make everyone else smile with hope for her. Good girl, Doreen. Way to go.

But it doesn't matter to her greatly anyway. As long as she is permitted to leave the house. She would spend the time shoveling shit if that was the only activity she was allowed to be dismissed to do. She would lie in the woods and let ants chew at her flesh, if it meant ten minutes away from the confines of the house and the endless sets of eyes that watch her in constant anticipation of her incompetence.

What she writes on this list is irrelevant.

The only meaning is in the time. In the escape.

Martha and the kids enter the kitchen and Doreen gets up and puts the pad of paper away in the drawer, first tearing off her list. She folds it and puts it in her pocket. The children clamour around her. The dog is there. It snorts and is like Tom, too much wet. Nose, mouth, eyeballs.

"There is a family swim in town at ten," Martha informs her. "Get your bathing suit and a towel, I won't be able to handle all three by myself."

And so her day has once again been decided. She does as she is told.

Thank you Lord for all the help. For sending my children's grandmother to help me raise them. Since I am so inadequate on my own. Thank you Father for the beautiful blessings of family. Amen.

April, 2001

Doreen gets a job working at a sprout farm. In all of her life, Doreen has never taken any sort of interest in sprouts, nor has she had any desire to work with plants or crops of any kind. And yet, this is where she has ended up. Surrounded by organic greens and young farmhands. The smell of manure accosting her nostrils with such a vengeance that on her first day of work she bites holes into her bottom lip and tongue, filling her mouth with the coppery tang of blood.

It had been a struggle, as she knew it would be, getting to this point. Tom was violently against it and took much convincing to see the benefits of his wife having time to herself. The meeting between the four of them tried everyone's last nerve as Tom protested and attempted several times to put his foot down. They had concluded the meeting still undecided on the topic, Lisa Griffin completely frustrated and Reverend Smiley looking a bit disappointed in Tom. Smiley had looked at her husband with irritation in his eyes, and a 'tsk' playing on his lips that Doreen could tell was just dying to be born.

It wasn't until Martha had sat with her baby boy and gently reminded him of how much knowledge Smiley possesses, and that some things just need to be turned over to God, put in His hands even when it doesn't feel like the right thing, that Tom had finally relented.

Doreen was in the bathroom, running the water for her vaginal washing and Tom had opened the door abruptly, startling her out of the conversation she had been having, out loud, with God.

"Fine," he had said to her, his face in a pissed off grimace.

"Fine?"

"You can go do something like this woman's libber quack Doctor wants you to. But if you're leaving the house for no God damn good reason, you might as well be bringing in some money. Get a job."

Doreen had stared at him, the noise of the bath water in one ear and something glorious feeding into the other.

"I can?"

"I said you can, didn't I? Get a resume together."

And he was gone.

And now here she is, working at a sprout farm just down the road from home. She figures they think they can keep tabs on her this way. Drop her off and pick her up. Drive by if they want. Bring her things unexpectedly. It's not as much freedom as a job in the city would have been. Doreen would rather be at the mall or at a bank or taking a course in photography at night with pretentious, artsy adults. But the sprout farm is something.

She works two days a week. Two. Which is more than she had hoped for. Mondays and Wednesdays for four hours each day. Martha takes care of everything like she is so accustomed to doing at this point anyway. Tom's meals are on the table and his children are clean and well mannered regardless of his wife's whereabouts. And there will be money. Spending money maybe. Doreen isn't sure yet if she will get to keep her cheques.

She's not sure what she would do with them anyway, but the idea is interesting. The idea of having a little bit of cash that she doesn't have to ask permission to have.

After only a couple hours of training she is put to work. It is menial and repetitive but she doesn't mind it. There are no children anywhere. Only adults. Some of them barely adults mind you, but none of them that shit in their own pants or cry out loud or leak stuff from their faces.

People talk about adult things. Things she feels strange about. She remains quiet. She has nothing to add. She doesn't know about music or movies or trends in fashion. She knows nothing about celebrities or reality television or award shows or brand names.

Profanity flows as if it were a necessary part of speech. She listens and works and remains quiet. She speaks minimally and only if someone speaks to her first. Answers questions. Avoids eye contact. She wishes more than she has since that fateful day with the scissors, that she had enough hair to pull in front of her ears. She is grateful that her bangs are long enough now to hang in her eyes a bit. To blanket her and hide some of those features that no one wants to see.

God comes to her in fragments. Whispers quickly in her ear and leaves. There is so much going on around her that there isn't much time for anything in depth with God while she is working. He checks in and then retreats. Even He has decided to give her some space. Just a little bit of time with no one needing anything. Not even for her to listen.

Her hands begin to move methodically and without the need of her brain's direction. She is trance-like at times. Time passes quickly. Mid-shift she gets a fifteen minute break where she has no idea what to do. She stands outside the greenhouse in the April air. She stares. She is still and silent and staring.

A racket from behind her and then a female voice saying, "What are you looking at? You look like a mannequin standing so freakin' still like that." The girl laughs. Doreen feels nothing but thinks perhaps she should be embarrassed by her own awkwardness. Still, even with the thought, she remains emotionless.

"Oh," she says to the girl, "nothing really. Just looking."

The girl puts a cigarette to her mouth and with it there, moving up and down as she speaks, she says, "You freaked me out a bit. You look kinda spooky. No offense." She pulls a lighter from her pocket, lights her cigarette, inhales, taking the cigarette from her lips with one hand and slipping the lighter back into her pocket with the other. She exhales.

"I'm Miranda." She holds out her hand to Doreen.

Taking it Doreen says nothing. Just stares.

The girl shakes her hand and then lets it go. "Gotta name or what?"

"Doreen."

"That's an old lady name if you don't mind me sayin'. How old are ya?"

Doreen thinks. Blinks her eyes. Stares at the girl, this 'Miranda'.

"Hello?" the girl waves her hand in front of Doreen's face with the hand that holds the cigarette. The smell stirs memory. It is familiar and woven into a zillion recollections, into countless goods and bads from a past that often doesn't feel like it belongs to her. Doreen pulls away, steps back a bit.

"Thirty…"

The girl waits.

"Thirty four?"

"Really? Shit, you don't look that old. I would've guessed you at like twenty-eight or twenty nine."

Is she thirty-four? Maybe she's not that old. Maybe she is only in her twenties. But that can't be right. She didn't have Delilah in her early twenties. No. There were no babies then.

"So, are you married?"

Doreen has no trouble coming up with this answer. "Yes."

"I was married," the girl tells her, dragging on her cigarette before beginning to speak again, "but it sucked." She laughs, blue smoke pouring out of her lips and nostrils as she does. "Got a baby girl out of it though. Chloe. You got any kids?"

"Seven," Doreen tells her.

"Holy shit! What? Seven kids! Are you crazy?"

"I guess."

The girl laughs. "Wow lady. You look good for spitting out seven kids. Where did they come from?" The girl looks Doreen up and down, smoking and laughing to herself, shaking her head.

"From God."

The girl chuckles. "Yeah."

She taps her cigarette, ash falling beside her feet.

"You're like a MILF."

"A what?"

"You know, a mom I'd like to fuck? American Pie?"

Doreen feels disoriented.

"Never seen it?"

Doreen shakes her head.

"It's pretty fuckin' funny. Wanna drag of this before I put it out?"

Without speaking Doreen reaches out and takes the last of the cigarette and puts it to her lips. It is hot and she can taste the grease of the girl's lip gloss on the filter. It burns her mouth and throat as she pulls on it. Mixed with the spring air it reminds her of a thousand different things, none of which she can name.

"Nice to meet you Doreen," this Miranda girl says, and she turns around and walks back inside, leaving Doreen to stand by herself and finish her glossy, used-up cigarette.

"So," Lisa Griffin looks excited. "How is everything going? How is the job?" She puts emphasis on the word job. Doreen sees it come out of her mouth in italics.

"It's really good," Doreen tells her honestly. "I really like going."

"Tell me what it is again."

"Sprout farm. I take care of plants."

"Excellent." Lisa writes.

Doreen nods. Looks down at the floor. A smile plays on her lips. She doesn't know why. She isn't even sure if she feels happy, but that smile tugs the corners of her mouth up nonetheless.

"Do you find that it's helping you be calmer at home?"

Doreen thinks about this.

"I think I'm feeling less stressed. I really haven't even thought about doing anything bad in a while."

Lisa stops. Looks up. "Anything bad?"

"No, I just mean. Well. Martha is there any way now. She is pretty much living with us now so she does most of the work, really."

"Let's go back for a minute Doreen. When you say you haven't thought about doing bad things, what did you mean?"

"I forget."

"You forget?"

She really does. Maybe she meant that there had been no violence involving the children lately. Things are different recently. She really doesn't have to deal with the children like she used to.

"I didn't mean it."

"What did you mean?"

"Just what I said. That's all."

"Doreen."

"I really like the job. The people there are so interesting. There is a girl named Miranda and she is raising a little girl all by herself. Without her husband. I mean he takes her daughter half the time, but they don't live together. She lives on her own. In her own apartment. She talks to me all the time and she thinks I look like I'm in my twenties. Can you believe that?"

"That's good. You're making friends. Do you find you have more patience after you have had some time away?"

"I really do. She is planning on going back to school in September. Raising a child alone and then going to school. To be a child and youth worker. Do you know what that is?"

"Yes, I do. Are we talking about your new friend from work?"

"Miranda."

"So you two have hit it off?"

"Well, I don't know. She talks to me. She talks a lot and tells me things and it's all so very interesting to me. The idea of living such a life."

"Explain that to me Doreen. What is interesting to you about the way she lives her life?"

"Just doing what she wants."

Doreen leans in, she looks back over one shoulder and then the other. She looks toward the door. She leans further in, puts her face next to Lisa's.

"She doesn't even believe in God."

She snaps back up in her chair. Claps her hands together once. Stares at Lisa with wide expectant eyes.

"Some people don't. I just hope this person doesn't influence you in negative ways. You must keep your faith strong through all of this. You and I both know, Doreen that Jesus is rest for the weary."

"I don't even know what that means," Doreen laughs and shakes her head, "I sometimes have no idea what you are all on about all the time."

———————————

Doreen's weeks take on a very structured way of playing out. Martha establishes pristine habits and routines that carry them through their days. Mondays she works and Eden goes to tutoring. Tuesday is swimming lessons. Wednesday, work again. Thursday they go into town for groceries while the girls are at school, and they attend playgroup in the afternoon. Fridays they go to prayer group, Martha, herself, and Tom while the children are minded in the nursery. Saturday is for catching up on chores and doing a free activity with the kids, like the park, or family swim, or the library, or a walk and some treats afterwards. Sunday they have church and often times some sort of family gathering back at the house. Lunch or supper or finger food in the afternoon. Lots of coffee and cookies and prying eyeballs. Questions and insinuations.

The sisters all want to know the details of Doreen's insanity. They all want to know how her cute little job is going and if she's going to give herself another cute little hair cut. No one asks about Eden because no one knows that her brain is damaged. No one is allowed to know such a thing. Doreen is not even sure if Martha is aware of the reason for Eden's tutoring and extra cirriculars. She assumes she likely is aware, that Tom would keep nothing of their family personal from his mother.

Doreen serves bowls of soup and crusty buns and platters of cut up vegetables and fruit. She serves Martha's cabbage rolls. Martha's casseroles. Martha's apple and pumpkin and pecan pies. Martha's homemade puddings. Martha's perfectly brewed coffee.

God's voice and white noise keep her company throughout her days but particularly on Sundays when Tom's family takes turns coming at her like a pack of something that thrives on flesh. Picking. Tearing in. The voice soothes. It tells her to be patient and wait for their departure.

Doreen is not responsible for much at the moment. Martha allows her to help out but otherwise runs the house single handedly. If only she could somehow take over the bedroom duties. But of course, that is impossible. Didn't God allow concubines? Second wives? Daughters to rape their fathers in order to impregnate themselves and carry on the family name? Surely there is some way that someone else could take over the heavy work in the bedroom. There must be some clause somewhere in the Bible that would make that okay.

Rise, help, work, eat, exercise, shop, drive, read, spread, tea, God.

Vince is Miranda's friend who also works at the sprout farm. On account of Miranda talking so much, Doreen learns a lot about Vince before she has ever spoken to him. Apparently he got Miranda the job on the farm after she left her husband only a few months earlier. Which still astounds Doreen. Just packing up and leaving. Just deciding, *this isn't good enough* and actually going beyond the fantasy of escape and doing it. Leaving. When Miranda talks about it, Doreen gets the same feeling in her stomach she used to get at the moment she was strapped into a carnival ride. A gut full of something fluttery and irritating, yet undeniably addictive. A feeling that frightens her, yet makes her want to stalk it.

Vince smokes cigarettes and he smokes marijuana. Weed, as the two of them refer to it. He is thirty one years old and wears nothing but t-shirts under flannel button-ups. The shirts usually have random logos or slogans on them. Things about hot dog stands or laundry detergent. He has dark eyes and a dark beard and wears tuques and baseball hats and jeans with rips in them. He wears big work boots that he keeps unlaced.

"He thinks he's Kurt Cobain," Miranda tells Doreen one day while the three of them are working side by side. Miranda laughs toward Vince as she says this. Doreen, of course, like with everything always, doesn't get it.

"Y'know, Nirvana?"

"Like the Rapture?"

"What the fuck are you talking about?" Miranda laughs, "Lady, you've lived one sheltered life." She shakes her head, looking down into mounds of wheat grass.

"You've never heard of Nirvana?" Vince asks her. He is much more gentle than Miranda. Much softer.

Doreen shakes her head, she thinks to explain her theory of Nirvana but knows they will only think she is weirder for it. "No."

"Really?" Vince in clearly surprised. "Smells like teen Spirit?"

The scent of armpits and gym socks comes into her passageways.

"Kurt Cobain? Pioneer of grunge? Got all fucked up on heroin and shot himself?" Miranda reaches up and tugs a strand of hair behind her ear, tucks it there.

Doreen feels like she has come from somewhere far away. Like these are natives trying to explain their customs to her, a foreigner. None of it makes much sense. She isn't even sure what exactly the topic is. She's sure they're not talking about food but other than that she has no bearings. She is once again lost.

"Well actually," Vince says, "It's debatable as to whether or not Cobain can actually be given as much credit for starting grunge as people tend to give him. There was an album called Deep Six that in some circles is considered to be what started the entire genre."

"Oh, here we go." Miranda rolls her eyes. Laughs.

There is so much strangeness in this world and Doreen has been locked out of it for too long to even fathom understanding any of it.

"I still think Courtney had something to do with it." Vince directs this statement at Miranda but then turns to Doreen and says, "His wife."

"Oh come on! Give up on that one, will ya? The guy was a junkie."

"So?"

"So. He overdosed and killed himself. His serotonin was all fucked up."

"Eww. Serotonin. Big words. You're so hot when you're trying to be smart."

"Fuck you Vincent." Miranda throws a handful of sprouts past Doreen and at Vince. It hits him in the chest.

Vince's face is playful. Light. He smiles and he has just the right amount of gums. Doreen can imagine his mouth on hers. Her thighs grow warm. Ashamed, she shakes the image away.

One of the lead hands walks down their aisle and yells, "Break time fuckers! Fifteen minutes! Smoke 'em if you got 'em!"

"Coming out?" Vince is pulling a cigarette pack from his red flannel pocket.

"Um, no," Doreen tells him, "I'm staying in."

"And doing what?" Miranda asks, her face screwed up into amused confusion.

"Praying."

They look at each other, Vince and Miranda, each of their faces blemished by the same expression.

"Are you for real?" Miranda says.

"Let's go Randy." Vince pulls Miranda away.

As soon as they are gone Doreen drops to her knees. She doesn't care who sees. She needs to pray. With a famished vengeance she needs to pray.

Lead me not into temptation and deliver me from evil. Forgive me my trespasses as I forgive those who trespass against me...

That night is tutoring for Eden. Doreen is still not allowed to do anything completely by herself with the kids, so Martha stays with the other four while Tom and Doreen take their dysfunctional child into town for six o'clock.

Doreen looks at Tom as he drives. Pale and non-descript. Doreen is tired of looking at Tom. So bored of it. She turns and looks out the window. Her husband doesn't say much. He is still silently fuming over her having a job. It pisses him off and she is well aware that he allowed it only due to influence. Doreen is sure it has emasculated him to some degree. He has been coming at her hard and with a point to prove.

They drive. They park. They get Eden out of the car and take her into the building. Doreen sits in one of the waiting room chairs and stares. Tom does all the chatting. Grills the receptionist, the owner, the very young tutor about what exactly the session will include, how his daughter will be evaluated, and what they can do at home to 'speed things up' as he puts it.

Doreen's mind wanders back to the sprout farm. To the smell of earth and grass. To Miranda. To Vince. Smokey and with fresh air clinging to them. Coming in from outside with faces slightly chilled. Vince, with such nice straight teeth. Moisture on his mouth that does not repulse her. That she thinks about touching.

Tom sits down beside her at some point and starts yammering about Eden and schoolwork and that teacher who he is sure is making this all up because she doesn't go to church. Persecuting them as believers have always been persecuted.

In the middle of one of Tom's run on sentences Doreen cuts him off. "What will happen with my cheques?"

Tom stares at her with annoyance. "I'm sorry, did you not hear me talking just now? Did the middle of my sentence interrupt the beginning of yours?"

"Will I get to spend the money? Will I have a bank account?"

"The money will go into my account. It's about time you started pitching in. What the Hell would you need money for?"

Doreen shrugs.

She looks away then, out the windows of the tutoring place. Lip smackers. That's what she wants to buy with her money. The Dr. Pepper one. She had stolen so many of them from the Eaton's Centre as a teen. The smell of it euphoric. Sweet and greasy.

She pictures Miranda slipping into designer looking running shoes before she leaves for the afternoon. The blonde streaks in her hair. The black makeup that rims her eyes and darkens her lashes. The magazines she pulls from her purse. The tattoo on her wrist. A small black heart.

Doreen sighs heavily.

Tom is once again blabbering beside her. She thinks about splashing something toxic in his face and watching his skin burn and peel. Watching his features disappear completely under a bubbling layer of poison.

Please shut up.

For a minute she thinks she may have said it out loud. But she did not.

She goes back to staring out the window, enjoying the rest that being a mental invalid seems to have afforded her. She thinks about music she knows nothing about. Names like Cobain. Words like Milf. She thinks about the big wide world. Sky and mountains and oceans and fields. Wings. Propelling her through the clouds. Flight.

The next day begins like a thousand other days before it. And ends that way too. Doreen rises with the sun, having spent a longer time than is usual these days actually sleeping. She had retired early as God had not been particularly talkative the night before. She guesses she was in bed by about one thirty.

She looks at Tom and gags.

She goes downstairs and does sit ups and pushups.

She thanks God.

Thank you Father, for this blessed day.

The dog goes outside, the children and the old lady rise. Tom's ugly face emerges, eats, spews words, leaves. She takes Delilah and Eden to the bus while Martha watches.

They all eat and change and brush and wash.

They go into town. They go to playgroup. They eat lunch. Grace Isabella naps and Jacob drifts while Faith demands attention and compliance from her elders. Give her her way and everything runs smoothly. Do not tell the child no or ask her stop or start or clean or help.

The baby wakes. The girls show back up on the bus. Martha cooks.

More eating.

Swimming lessons in town.

Children in baths. Stories. Sex with Tom. Couch. Radio. Tea. Sleep.

Thank you Lord, for another wonderful day. So fulfilling, Lord. What would I do if I were not doing your work by caring for this brood? Amen, Lord. Amen.

The following day is Wednesday. A work day. Doreen helps with the morning routine and then Martha drives her to the sprout farm and drops her off. She finds herself anxious all morning, in anticipation of getting out of the house. She combs her hair so that it looks somewhat decent. She stands in the mirror and tugs one of Tom's tuques over her head. Miranda had worn a tuque one day and Doreen had liked the way it looked. It was boyish, yet feminine. Cute. But then again Miranda is a young blonde with turquoise eyes and a pretty mouth. She is not an old raped hag like Doreen.

Doreen takes the tuque off and leaves it behind. Just before she leaves she wipes some Vaseline along her lips. She thinks of Lisa Griffin.

When finally Martha drops her off Doreen feels like she's about to walk through the door of her own birthday party. Anticipation. Just the idea of all the conversation she will hear around her; the information about the world that will confuse and excite her. The air of downtrodden light-heartedness as they all moan about the oppression of their job, yet make the best of it through banter and vulgarity. The idea alone has her restless and impatient.

She spends four hours listening to it. The profanity. The talk of popular culture which she knows absolutely nothing about. She absorbs it all. Lets it sink into her pores. Lets it dance in her molecules.

God is not around. He does not come to her. He does not invade this space. The white noise is at bay. It is unnecessary. She is glad for the calm of her brain today, for the absence of voice and noise. She finds herself actually wanting to be lucid, wanting to be clear-headed and aware. To maybe even be part of what is going on, even if that only means she stands and robotically does her job while taking in everything that is being and said and done around her.

She stands outside with Miranda and Vince on break while they smoke. She is offered drags but refuses them. Smoking the end of Miranda's cigarette the first day they met was a lot less enjoyable than she had remembered. It had left her mouth coated and her breath thick and rancid.

She tries not to look Vince in the eye. Doing so makes her entire core feel strange and electric. She knows this is the Devil trying to tempt her as he has tempted her before. As Eve was tempted by the apple. As Joseph was tempted by his neighbour's wife. The Lord is testing her, she knows it, and she refuses to fail. Not again.

> **Blessed is the man who endures temptation; for when he has been approved, he will receive the crown of life which the Lord has promised to those who love Him.**

She enjoys the company of these two young people who seem to so easily, for some reason, have adopted her into their fold. She wants to be out there with them, breathing in their second hand smoke and ingesting their second hand conversation. Listening. Watching the exchanges she remains on the fringes of. She feels something positive in their presence. Some kind of inclusion. Like an anomaly to be sure, but somehow like less of an idiot.

As Vince tosses his cigarette into the grass he says to her, "I like your hair today, Rutherford."

Doreen touches her ears, feeling them ignite. Her entire face bursts into fire and heat. She doesn't know what to say.

Miranda pulls open the door to the greenhouse and as Doreen is stepping through she says to her, "Your hair does look cute today," and smiles with what appears to be genuine good will.

Doreen smiles back at her, touching her ears, feeling them burn.

"Thank you."

When she gets home she is energetic. She is quick in the kitchen, helping Martha beyond what she has managed up until this point. She talks a bit to the old lady and is more enthusiastic than usual with the children, sitting at the table with Eden for over thirty minutes helping her with a booklet made up of crossword puzzles and word searches.

Tom gets home and is wearing his pretty fake smile and good manners, reserved for when his mother is around, which is all the time now, a perk Doreen has discovered, in having Martha taking up residence with them. Tom is on much better behavior most of the time. He slips back of course, accidently shows his true self when he can't seem to contain it anymore. But for the most part Tom is a much more pleasant human being in the presence of the woman who birthed him. Doreen thinks it interesting that a man could have such respect and adoration for his mother, but see all other women, particularly his wife, as beneath him. But then again, she deserves it doesn't she? Has she not earned every ounce of condescension her husband bestows upon her?

One night Martha had even gotten away with the unfathomable crime of feeding the children a bowl of grapes before supper when Tom had been late. He had said nothing about it. Just apologized for making everyone wait.

This was not her husband. This was some version of her husband that used to present itself much more often, but has rarely bothered in decades. The version that used to reach out and hold her hand when they were driving. That pretended to be tender with his mouth and with his fingers. This is a mostly dormant edition of Tom that has now been forced to the surface by his mother's image of who he is and his unwillingness to crush that.

The women clean up the kitchen and bathe the children while Tom sits on the couch watching sports and petting his pungent dog.

Doreen retires to her bedroom immediately after the last of the children, Jacob tonight, has been tucked in and kissed goodnight, and she reads the Bible.

She finds that she enjoys being in bed without Tom. The soft glow of her bedside table, the quiet. The down comforter pulled up to her chest. No one else breathing in the room, just her own lungs filling with, and then expelling air soundlessly.

She reads and reads trying to memorize. God whispers to her softly, nothing that seems of grave importance tonight, just his voice in her ear as a consistent reminder of his presence. *I am here,* he tells her.

The door pops open at around ten o'clock. Doreen doesn't bother looking up. She can smell Tom's feet as he enters the room. Can hear the overabundance of saliva as it moves around in his mouth, as he breathes and moves and vibrates. Worms. The taste of worms and something fecal. Her own mouth waters instinctively, preparing to regurgitate.

As he takes things off his body and moves and sits and pulls blankets and lies on his back beside her, Doreen keeps her eyes on the words.

"Turn out your light."

"I'm reading."

"You're done reading. Turn out the light."

Doreen puts the Bible on the bedside table, turns out the light.

"Are you clean?"

She doesn't feel like going through the motions so she lies, "Yes."

He pulls her toward him, pulls her legs apart, climbs on top.

Without kissing or touching his wife he masturbates inside her. Pumps in and out with his head turned to the side and his eyes closed. Doreen stares at the ceiling until it's over. He doesn't seem to take any notice of her unwashed insides. For all the fuss he makes about her soaping up, he seems to have no real distaste for her un-cleansed body.

On the days she works she is more tired than usual. Tonight sleep takes her before she even hears Tom begin to snore.

Blackness. Quiet. Peace.

Thursday. Grocery day. Doreen and Martha put the three youngest children into the van after Delilah and Eden have been safely put on the bus and driven away.

Doreen is allowed to drive, an adult privilege she is sure is only afforded her because the old woman gets anxious behind the wheel of the van. She imagines it being discussed that she might very well be capable of going into one of her 'spells', a term she actually heard Tom use one night on the phone to God knows which sister, and drive the children right off into a ditch. But with Martha there by her side she is allowed to drive into town for everything that needs to be done there. On days when Doreen works, Martha crams all three babies into the back of her four-door to avoid having to maneuver the giant vehicle that is their mini-van.

They get two carts, one for the children and one for the groceries. They stop at the deli first where the children are given free slices of bologna that pacify them for about two and a half minutes. Grace Isabella sits in the front of the cart with her legs hanging down and her rubber boots banging into Martha's thighs as the old lady walks. Doreen notices this. Pictures those bird-ish legs of Martha's buckling from the jabs. Pictures the loose skin around the knee caps, bone protruding through folded flesh.

Faith is in the back of the cart sitting down, taking tiny bites of the processed meat with only her front teeth. Nibbling, like a rodent, at the greasy nitrates. Jacob, for now, stands on the back of the cart holding on with one hand and feeding bologna into his mouth with the other. He is wearing a Blue Jays ball cap instead of a winter hat now. He has no mittens.

Doreen takes care of the food cart as abandoning it would not create the same consequences as abandoning a cart full of children might. They can allow her an attempt at being responsible for the food.

They get their lunch meat and their bread and bagels and then head into the produce section. The children are greasy, their fingers slick with the oils that come from bologna, whatever those oils may be caused by. A wave of something sour rises and falls in Doreen's guts.

Gracie is fine, Jacob is fine, Faith has already begun to cause problems. She is done her meat, she wants out of the cart, she is arguing with her grandmother who is trying to explain patiently to the child why she must stay in the cart. When explanations fail Martha pushes the cart to the bakery and gets free cookies for each of them. Their mouths go quiet and busy for a few more minutes.

Canned goods, meat, dog food, toilet paper, cereal, gallons of milk, dozens of eggs, litres of juice.

Faith eventually stands up in the cart and demands to be released until her grandmother gives in. Jacob is tired and wants to sit down. Gracie kicks her boots against the metal of the cart when she sees her sister set free and running without restraint down the aisles. Martha calls to Faith but the child just laughs, mocking the adults she seems to have no fear of. Gracie is eventually set loose too, to stop the racket of the banging and the whining that is obviously building toward a full fledged tantrum.

Jacob sits quietly in the cart. Doreen looks down at him and he looks up at her with dark eyes. He looks into her. "Hi Mommy," he says. Warmth moves through her.

What would Isaac have been like? Even tempered like his brother? Sweet? Would they have holed up together under bed sheet forts and built airplanes and light sabers out of Lego? Would he too have reached for her with warm dry fingers that always managed to bring her back from the depths of her own mind?

Doreen smiles at her son.

She lets Martha deal with reigning in the girls. Both are in need of a smack, a quick hard one to the bottom or outer thigh. A sting to the cheek. But not in public Tom has always warned her. Too many people have strayed from the teachings of the Bible and NOW Tom had emphasized this word during one of his rants, parents aren't allowed to discipline their children. "You can't even look at them the wrong way these days. Next thing you know the cops are at your door and your kids are being hauled out and put in paddy wagons. I've seen this happen on the news. They can charge you for spanking your own kids. It's blasphemy really. Isn't it, Mom?"

Doreen is most often discouraged from watching the news.

Don't spank the kids in public. Other people don't like it. Discipline must take place within the four walls of the home. So many acts that must be carried out in private only.

What's it like, she wonders, to get groceries for one? To come, unencumbered to the grocery store and shop at leisure. Skip the processed meat and the juice boxes and the diaper and wipe aisle. What's it like for Miranda with just her and one little girl. How much easier?

Vince's eyes. Dark and deep. The image digs into her. Penetrates places she can't name.

By the time they reach the checkout Martha appears to be frazzled. She becomes stern with the girls which only makes them laugh at her and rile each other further by tearing away and yelling out. They create a scene. People stare and shake their heads. Jacob asks to get out of the cart and he begins helping unload the groceries onto the conveyer belt. An old man in line beside them ruffles the toddler's hair and says, "That's a good lad. Helping Mom, are ya?" Jacob says, "Yep," and keeps working.

It takes a ridiculous amount of time to gather the girls and get everyone to the van and get all the groceries in and buckle children into car seats and begin the drive home.

"It'd be so much easier if one of us could get the groceries while one stayed home with the kids," Doreen has both hands on the steering wheel. She turns a corner slowly.

"Well, we can't do it that way now, can we?" There is irritation in the old lady's voice. This trip has rattled her.

"You must be tired," Doreen says, turning her head to look at her mother-in-law. "You must be tired of all this caring for everyone else. So many years of it, Martha. I'm so sorry."

She feels as if she might cry.

"Don't be silly. This is my work."

There is silence for a few minutes.

"I'm going to get better."

"Don't worry about me, Doreen. What else would I be doing?"

And that's just it, isn't it? There is nothing else for some people, so long impressed upon that they are only here to serve. There becomes nothing else. No other image, no other dream. Just the acceptance of what is. To the point that it is not just understood, but embraced. Until it is a lifeline. Something that defines and gives purpose. Martha wouldn't know what else to do. Like some sort of mule, she has grown to depend on being worked to death.

"I'm going to get better. Things are going to be okay." For a minute, as she pulls into her driveway and then into the garage and looks upon her handsome home and while all three kids are chatting happily in the back of the van, she believes it. For a split second she can see something other than what she has known thus far. There is a moment of untainted faith.

Thank you, Lord. Amen.

Martha makes a hot lunch for everyone. Homemade soup and warm bread with butter and a salad made up of iceberg lettuce and cucumbers that the children smother with ranch dressing and devour. They drink milk out of cups with spouts. They eat small red boxes of raisins at the conclusion of the meal.

Martha takes the baby upstairs but first hoists her onto her old, assuredly fragile hip and leans her toward her mother.

"Give Mommy a kiss," Martha instructs the child, "it's naptime."

Both Doreen and the child stand looking dumb and baffled.

Martha leans the child closer to Doreen. The lips are wet. The nose is moist around the nostrils.

The child purses her lips into a tiny rosebud and leans toward her mother, reaches for her with the mouth. Doreen gives the baby her cheek. Afterwards she wipes away what's been left behind.

Doreen takes Jacob and Faith down into the family room. She is alone with her children, a rarity these days. She puts a movie on for Jacob who hunkers down quite readily under a brown fuzzy blanket that smells like cookies and powder. He pulls the blanket up around himself, scrunches his shoulders under it. He curls his body into something small and inconspicuous.

Faith, at first sits beside her brother and watches the beginning of the movie. Doreen watches her to make sure her eyelids don't droop. Doreen is sitting on the floor. She picks at one of her nails momentarily and then stops herself. They have started to grow back again. She needs not add an extra ounce of repulsiveness to who she is. Bloody raw fingernails. Tom has mentioned them often enough. She tucks her hands underneath herself. Sits on them to stop the chewing that seems to come as an instinctual compulsion at times. She sits so that she won't absent-mindedly begin gnawing at herself again.

The room is still but for the images on the screen of cartoon animals talking and climbing trees and singing songs.

She listens for messages from God. None so far.

The stillness, of course, is fleeting. Soon enough Faith gets restless and sitting on the couch compliantly is no longer a viable option for her. She jumps down from the couch. She demands a game of Barbie and Kelly. She gets out a fake toilet and a box of doll clothes and a miniature hair brush.

"Play," she shoves a dark-haired doll at her mother.

Doreen takes the doll. She turns it so that its face is toward her and she pulls back the matted dark hair so to examine the perfect plastic features. The ears are precisely aligned with the head.

"Do you have another brush, Faithy?"

Rummaging through a box of small trinkets Faith produces to her mother a small purple hairbrush. In her hands is one exactly the same only pink. The two sit side by side, mother and daughter, brushing acrylic hair. Faith's doll is blonde. She has earrings where Doreen's brunette doll has only holes.

Faith steals glances at her mother, Doreen can see the child looking over at her cautiously yet with a hint of something excited in her expression.

"Your girl is named Honey," Faith continues brushing the blonde hair as she speaks. "Mine is called Tasha."

Doreen nods. Brushes.

"This one looks like me and that one looks like you."

"You think so?"

"Yep. Brown hair, blonde hair." The child points as she speaks.

"You have red in your hair though. Yours isn't really blonde."

"Can you braid Tasha's hair?"

Doreen puts her own doll on the floor and takes the blonde one and divides its hair into three sections. Faith digs around while she talks about getting a 'pony' to hold the braid in place. Her speech is fast but clear. She pronounces most words with a perfection very unexpected for a child of her age. While other mothers cooed and directed cute, mangled words at their infants Doreen spoke clearly to hers. Treated them like tiny adults instead of like something one needed to be gentle with.

She finishes the braid and hands the doll back to her daughter.

Faith looks at the doll. She puts her down and with the small pink brush moves toward her mother. Doreen isn't sure what the child intends to do or how to react to it. She remains still.

Faith crawls up on the couch and straddles her mother from behind, wraps her legs around Doreen's back as she remains sitting on the floor, leaning against the couch. Faith begins to run the brush through the bits of Doreen's hair that have grown back. The child drags the plastic bristles through her mother's ragged black hair. The strokes she uses are gentle and yet determined. The child means to make something of the strands that months ago were butchered and are only now resembling something slightly feminine.

Faith's tiny fingers run along behind the brush. They scratch at the scalp. Not tearing or hurting but scouring nerve endings that cannot remember being touched. Doreen's flesh turns to bumps all the way down her neck and back. The sensation is undeniable. She gives into it. Lets herself go weak, feels her lids droop.

Faith stops for a minute to fetch something else from a container somewhere nearby. Doreen's neck sways with relaxation. She wants nothing more than for the child's hands to return to her and stroke her flesh into slumber. She wants to sleep. She wants not to dream. Not of anything.

Faith says, "I'm going to put barrettes in. It will make your hair pretty again."

The hands begin working again. The tiny fingers. The plastic brush.

Doreen cannot remember pleasure. She cannot remember the last time she was touched in a way that made her want only to be touched more. She recalls so easily the prying open and the forcing into and the greedy painful sucking.

Closing her eyes to the pleasure she tries to find it somewhere else in her memory.

She remembers being ten years old. Sitting on her bed. Shirt lifted. One of the neighbour girls, slightly older than her, writing words on her back. Her job was to guess the word and then they would switch places and Doreen would use her fingertip to trace her name and the names of boys in her class onto the girl's aroused back. Doreen recalls the sensation. The flesh of her back jumping to life, rising in stimulation. The raw seductive power of the feeling of those fingers gently touching her bare skin.

And then her mother coming in. Gasping at the sight before her. Screaming. Yelling. Sending the neighbour girl home. The confusion as her mother tore her from the bed, and dragged her to the closet calling her names and assuring her of the Lord's disapproval. Always a consequence for pleasure.

Faith pushes barrettes closed in her mother's scarce strands. She clips things in and then removes them and begins again. She breathes the heavy breath of concentration in her mothers' ear. She speaks quietly and constantly to herself, commentating all that she is doing. Doreen falls into something trance like.

She listens for God. Her head is quiet. Her mind now still.

Tirelessly the child brushes and clips and rakes fingers along and through.

For a moment Doreen is calm. For a minute there is only pleasure, and she forgets to fear it.

Footsteps on the stairs and Faith speaking loudly now, "Grandma! Do you like Mommy's hair? I put barrettes in it, see?"

"Very nice. Doreen did you put any laundry in today?"

It is all she can do to speak, her body is so completely begging to give in to rest. "No. Not yet."

Martha walks past them then and into the laundry room where she creates laundry noises. The lifting of the washer's lid, the unscrewing of detergent caps. The moving around of clothes and bottles and knobs. Water beginning to run. Pipes screeching. The shuffling of feet on concrete floors.

Faith moves around to the front of her mother now, to face her.

"You look very pretty, Mommy."

A feeling Doreen has never managed to feel for anyone female, swells up in her and begins knocking at her throat. She swallows hard. Something burns behind her eyes.

She pulls the child on to her lap. Wraps her arms around her. She has always been unsure about exactly what love is. The concept has been blurry and hard to get a hold of. Love has always seemed to come with such a price. It has been harsh and punishing. Doreen has always felt much safer keeping a reasonable distance from it.

But something stirs in her now. A feeling. A memory. Bruno's face and spindly arms wrapped around her tightly. His hands in her hair.

"Do you really think I look pretty, Faithy?"

"Beautiful." Faith touches the front of Doreen's hair, pushes her mother's bangs back. The sensation of the warm fingertips against her forehead intoxicates her further. The little girl smiles.

"Do you love Mommy?"

The child's face screws into something confused.

"I love God."

Like a robot or a well-trained slave the child answers in the way she has been taught. She regurgitates the words breathed into her constantly since the day of her birth. The children have been taught the importance of loving God. Of knowing God's love above and before all others. It dawns on Doreen that in all the religion, in all the scripture and the prayers, they have overlooked themselves. They have forgotten to take joy in one another. It slaps her in the face like something wet and pungent. Overshadowed constantly by God, they have seemingly placed no importance on loving each other.

"Mommy loves you just like God loves you." She has no real idea if this is true or not, but she feels compelled to say it. She wants the child drawn further to her. Doreen touches the girl's nose. It is small, warm, dry.

"You do? Just like God?"

"I do, Honey."

"I love you like God too."

Small arms go so easily around her. Without anger or resentment. Without any memory, it seems, of all the times the hands have stung flesh and pulled arms and held down. The child's small arms go around her mother's neck without any demand for apology. There is no notion of blame. No need for the past. There is only this moment, and the only mother Faith knows is the one whose warm lap she is sitting in.

Doreen smells her daughter. Inhales the hair. Nothing dirty. Nothing damp and fishy. Only shampoo and something else sweet and pleasant. Something nameless but distinct.

Instinctively she begins to rock. The child's body in hers. The rocking motion lulling them both.

Naptime ends and Gracie awakens and cries and fusses and needs to be cleaned which Martha deals with single handedly. One load of laundry is done and folded and another is in the dryer. The sound of metal buttons battering the sides of the dryer's drum travels up the stairs to the women who are now preparing a plate of cheese and crackers and fruit for when Delilah and Eden return from school.

Jacob has a pile of Lego on the living room floor and a large plastic dump truck. He is humming songs from the movie he watched earlier as he loads Lego pieces into the truck, drives it along the carpet, and dumps the pieces at a different location. Gracie is strapped into her highchair with grated cheese on her tray. She picks up strands of cheese and grapes cut into quarters. She talks to herself as she puts food into her mouth. Faith sits on the couch with a book.

Doreen looks at the old lady and wonders if she is ever moving out. If she will ever go away again.

"I'd like to try it on my own again at some point."

"What's that?"

"Mothering."

"We'll see."

Doreen slices a grape in half and then in half again.

Burdens are given and then taken away. Everything happens against her will. She is tired of not having a choice.

"I'm an adult," she tells her mother-in-law.

"You just need some guidance for now. Keep reading your Bible. Keep praying Doreen. Stick with God and we will see."

Doreen sighs.

A few minutes pass without conversation between the women. Only the sounds of knives slicing and clothes drying and babies chatting to themselves.

Doreen meets the girls at the bus while Martha stands at the door and watches. What does she think will happen? That Doreen will push one of the girls in front of the bus as it prepares to drive away? That she will run away when the children begin to descend the stairs of the vehicle, and harm will come to them in her sudden absence. The prying eyes have begun to wear on her. The constant supervision. She can manage meeting her daughters at the end of the driveway. Someone brain damaged could handle that task.

The day turns to evening and into night with all the usual rituals. Snack and homework and Tom's return. Supper and baths and sex and bed.

Doreen spends a few hours awake in the living room. She reads the Bible, heeding her mother- in-law's words of counsel. Stick with God, read your Bible. Maybe one day we can let you take care of the children all by yourself like a big, big girl.

God has been quiet. He says very little to her tonight. His voice is in nearly inaudible whispers and cuts out intermittedly so that she catches only fragments of what he is saying. She is left to piece together what she thinks has been said and insert her own words where His are missing. What results, is a pile of sentences that mean very little to her. Eventually she just turns the dial to another station and listens to the lyrics of some hedonistic songs.

She wishes there were something to clean. Some chore with which to busy her hands. But the house is immaculate. Martha's domestic prowess is evident in every room of the house, in every gleaming door knob and dustless shelf.

Reluctantly she crawls into bed with her husband much before the sun rises. There is nothing to listen to and nothing to clean. So she sleeps.

Friday.

Again Tom goes to work and the girls go to school and Doreen spends the day with Martha and Jacob and Faith and Grace Isabella.

Her mind wonders to other things. To the world outside of the four walls she feels so constrained within. She thinks about fields and cloudless skies. Sand dunes. Oceans.

The weather is warm and the sun has come out and situated itself high in the spring sky in a way that exerts its intention to stay. On Doreen's suggestion they take the youngest three to the park. They pack Teddy Grahams and juice boxes and bananas. They bring thermoses of tea for themselves. Jacob totes along a pail and shovel and some small metal cars. The girls each have a doll tucked up under one arm.

The sun shines down on Doreen's face. She imagines it highlighting the years that have passed. The lines in her flesh. The spots on her skin. The time. All the time that has come and gone, mapped on the contours of her face.

Sitting at the park in the air she is okay. The afternoon passes in pleasantness.

At home she becomes antsy. She begins to chew her fingers. She paces. The repetition gets to her. The same things over and over again. They have just finished cleaning up a meal when it is time to begin preparing the next. The babies have just been put to nap when they awaken. The sun has just set when it again decides to rise.

The weekend passes this way. With everything ending only to begin again.

Church on Sunday. A family gathering. Preparing and feeding and cleaning.

She goes to bed on Sunday night with the satisfaction of knowing that the next day is work. The next day is something different.

Thank you, God for my job. For allowing me to work. I know you are testing me but I will do you proud, Lord. Amen.

"So how serious are you about this whole God thing?"

Doreen and Miranda are working side by side. Their gloved hands moving by rote, pulling and transferring and pulling again. This question seems to have come from nowhere, a sentence spoken perhaps, to interrupt the silence that had settled down in the middle of them.

"I'm not really sure what you mean."

"Randy." Vince pipes up from the other side of Doreen. He seems to be warning Miranda of something. Attempting to hush her with his tone.

"No. I just mean, like, do you follow the Ten Commandments to a tee? All the time I mean?"

"I try to." She does try to, although she is prone to failure.

"Did you grow up religious or just become religious?"

"Y'know, two things you should never discuss with friends, politics and religion." Vince's eyelids are heavy, half over his eyeballs. Sleepy looking.

"It's okay," Doreen doesn't feel offended. "Um, well, I grew up religious but I had a bit of a rebellious period when I was a teenager. Then I found God again."

"Ewww... a rebellious period! Do tell."

Doreen shrugs. "I don't know. I did some bad things."

"What bad things? I like bad things." Miranda laughs, blows a strand of hair out of her face. Cocks her head toward Doreen with eager eyes.

Doreen laughs too. She has never had anyone react so light-heartedly to her past indiscretions.

"I just, oh, I don't know. Normal teenage stuff I guess."

"Did you drink and do drugs? Have premarital sex?"

Doreen feels her face burn. Her ears become a painful red that she can't see but she can feel as definitely as if she were looking in a mirror.

"Oh my God, you DID! Doree-een!"

Doreen looks at Miranda who wears a smile that takes up her entire face. Her teeth are beautiful and gigantic slabs of white. Her face shines.

Doreen feels a smile tug at her own mouth. A sense of pride almost. That long forgotten feeling of what it's like to impress someone by stepping beyond the usual parameters. The bond that solidifies between people when they realize they have both bucked the rules.

Vince laughs on the other side of her. "Enough Ran."

"I knew it," Miranda says, "I could see it buried in there all along. The rebel in you. I can sense these things y'know." She wags a finger at Doreen. "There's a bit of bad girl in all of us."

"A bit?" Vince laughs, "I think in your case, Ran, it's a fuck of a lot more than a bit."

"Piss off Vince." Miranda laughs.

She turns to Doreen, "Okay, well, maybe there's more than a bit in some of us." She winks at Doreen and then goes quietly back to her work. She chews her gum and hums something unfamiliar.

Doreen turns to look at Vince. He looks back at her. Smiles. She notices his eyelashes. Dark and longer than any woman's she's ever seen. They frame his dark eyes so that every other feature on his face is unnecessary.

She lets herself smile back.

She turns again to her work and thinks about perspective. Everything is a matter of perspective. There are people with different views of the world, different lenses through which they examine things. She had forgotten this. For so long she had forgotten but in this moment she knows it to be true. There are different ways to look at things. Different ways to feel about them. Her black and white world turns a very fuzzy grey.

The break bell goes.

And life goes on.

Tom crawls on top of her in the dark and pokes at her briefly with his fingers before pushing himself in and beginning to pump at her in rabbit-like jabs.

She closes her eyes.

She distances herself from the spastic, jerky movements of her husband, and replaces them with something smooth and slow.

She takes herself away from the darkness and into something where she can see and where she is not afraid to look. Dim light.

She retreats to somewhere dark-eyed and olive skinned. Somewhere young and firm and careful. She blankets herself in smoky flannel.

She feels herself opening up. Her neck and back arch. She inhales and exhales fully, deep gusts of air suck into her lungs and seep back out of them, filling her ears with the sounds of her own breath and pulse. Her thighs fall apart.

"What the Hell is wrong with you?"

She opens her eyes. Dark room. Tom's silhouette. His colourless eyes and sad, saggy flesh.

"Stop acting like that. You're a wife and a mother, Doreen and don't forget it."

"Shh." She tells him and closes her eyes against his image.

He tugs her hair and slams into her viciously for the rest of the act. He yanks at her and tries fruitlessly to evoke submission from a body that has already given in.

As he's beginning to soften without yet having been gratified, he wraps his hands around her throat, an obvious final attempt to rouse himself back into stiffness. He only softens further. He falls out and dangles above her like a useless and worn out garden hose. He curses at her for it. It is her fault.

Doreen drifts comfortably into sleep with sticky thighs.

She does not dream.

"Tell me how things have been going?" Lisa Griffin adjusts her body in her chair, lifts a hip, scoots back, straightens. She then crosses one leg over the other and rests her clipboard on her knee, pen poised and eager.

"Pretty good I think." Doreen feels alert. There is energy that has not been spent. There is something coaxing her to stay clear and aware.

"Good. That's good." Smiling. Writing. "Tell me what's been happening. The job, the kids."

"The job is good. The kids are good."

Lisa smiles. She stares. She is waiting for Doreen to continue. Her pen is restless.

"I really like working. I feel so much better actually. You were right. It has made me more patient with the kids. I actually wish I could work more often."

"How often are you working now?"

"Mondays and Wednesdays. And only half days. I wish I could work more."

"Maybe you can eventually."

"Hm."

Lisa writes.

"I used to work you know. Before I re-met Tom. I worked in an office and made okay money. I had thirty thousand dollars saved when we started dating."

"Wow. That's impressive Doreen. Good for you. So you have some financial sense. Some skills with money. That's excellent."

"Well, I lived with my parents. They didn't make me pay anything. I didn't do much or go anywhere. I just worked and saved. I put some food in the cupboards. Bought a car with cash."

"Good for you."

"I guess."

"Did you say you re-met Tom?"

"We knew each other in high school."

Doreen begins to wring her hands. Her ears go pink. She can tell by the degree of the heat in the tips of them that they have begun to colour but have not turned quite red. She wishes she could control it. Such a transparency. Her body betraying her emotions like a catty friend excited to spread gossip. She wishes she were hard to read instead of being see-through and vulnerable the way she is.

"Oh, yes, maybe I knew that." Lisa lifts pages. "Maybe Smiley told me that. Anyway."

"I had a car and a huge chunk of money saved and a job. And I took photography. Some courses in college. A few after I graduated. Just night course type things. Nothing professional. But I had a photograph win third place in a contest once. I got fifty dollars and the picture was in the newspaper. It was of an old lady sitting in front of a church. Black and white."

"Very nice. Do you still take pictures?"

"Tom takes the pictures. He has a pretty expensive camera and I wouldn't want it to get damaged or anything. I don't even know where that picture is now."

Writing Lisa says, "Well, you should look for it. And if you find it, I'd really like to see it."

Doreen smiles.

"Have you ever thought about getting back into photography?"

"No."

"Because?"

"I don't think about things like that. Tom takes pictures of the kids and his golf tournaments. Hunting trips."

Lisa writes some more. Doreen looks around the room. Lisa then stares at her, seemingly waiting to see if there is anything left to be said about the topic of photography. When it becomes clear that there is not, she changes the subject.

"So. The kids. You said you've felt more relaxed with them?"

"I have. Definitely."

"Excellent. So that makes you feel better about yourself, doesn't it? When you are being the mother you want to be."

"I guess, yeah. I'd like to be alone with them though at some point. I mean, not to do anything in particular, I just wonder. Are they going to let me go back to doing it on my own ever? Do you know?"

"Well, of course. You are more than capable of taking care of your own children. I mean, ideally you would be running your own household. Of course. Right now I think everyone is just trying to give you as much support as possible. Until things balance out again."

"I feel like they might never give them back to me. I feel like all my babies have been taken in some way or another."

Lisa writes. Her face twists again into something that looks frightened to Doreen. Concerned maybe. She isn't sure. Reading people has never been one of her skills. She knows very little about emotion. She recognizes rage, but often only when it is too late. She sees arousal in the faces of men, but again, usually only when it is already too late. Other emotions blend into each other for her. Look too much alike.

"No one wants to take the children from you Doreen. In fact, the opposite is true. We want to get you back to being independent and happy and a thriving, effective mother and wife."

"Did you ever have to forgive something that you thought you couldn't?"

"Well. Yes. Why do you ask?"

"I don't know. Do you think smoking marijuana is a sin?"

"Did you smoke drugs, Doreen?"

"No. But some of my friends from work, well, most of them smoke weed." The word 'weed' feels alien coming out of her. Like she is somewhere foreign taking a crack at a language she is completely unfamiliar with. She feels herself blush slightly. She feels foolish for having said it.

"Oh Doreen."

"Is it a sin?"

"Is that what you're trying to forgive someone for?"

"Oh no. That's completely unrelated. I just don't want Vince to go to Hell. And I worry about him. I'd like to see him in Heaven some day. Him and Isaac."

"Is Vince one of your friends from work?"

"He has such a kind spirit. Such a gentleness about him. I can't imagine him ever forcing himself on anyone. I can't imagine that he would be denied Heaven just because he gets stoned." The lingo again makes her feel childish and as if she is trying to force herself into a garment not at all her style.

Lisa writes. Doreen, tired of trying to read her expression, looks elsewhere. Looks at the sick coloured walls. Watered down vomit comes to mind. Gracie's last bout of stomach flu. Orange juice and half digested pancakes mixed with toilet water.

"Well, I don't think anyone would go to Hell simply for smoking drugs. But we must remember that the body is the temple of Christ."

"How could we possibly forget?"

Doreen meets Lisa's eyes, suddenly unafraid of her reaction. She stares at her, willing her to say more, feeling like a challenge, a debate, although having no real clue what the debate would be about or what side she would be on if she were involved in it.

Lisa says nothing.

"I'm wondering then, if the body is the temple of Christ, what happens to a person who violates another person's temple? I mean, if it's such a vile thing to dirty your own soul, what does it mean if you soil someone else's?"

"In what way?"

"In any way."

Lisa runs a hand across her forehead. She appears sweaty. Disoriented almost. This usually poised and immaculate woman now seems a bit flawed to Doreen. Shakable.

"You are asking some very abstract questions today." Lisa laughs.

"Forget it."

"No. No. God does not want us to violate each other, of course. Murder is a sin of the highest degree."

"Right."

"Does this have anything to do with something happening in your life right now?"

"But the Bible tells us that if a woman is raped she is a sinner. And the man who rapes an unwed daughter must repent by marrying her and paying a dowry."

"Doreen? Were you raped?"

"I still dream about it." Doreen looks back to her hands. Her cuticle is bleeding though she has no memory of picking at it just now.

"Oh Doreen." Lisa moves toward her.

"But Vince, he just doesn't seem the type to do that. He seems so gentle."

"Does anyone know about this? How long ago Doreen?"

"Lifetimes ago."

"Did you tell anyone? Does Tom know?"

"Oh, Tom knows."

"And does he help you through this? I mean, if you're still dreaming about it, surely you have rough times. Violence is a very tough thing to recover from."

"Oh he helps me. He's very supportive. You should see it."

Lisa looks at her watch with what appears to be some sort of regret. But then again, maybe it's relief. Doreen can't be sure.

"We are almost out of time Doreen. But I would really like to come back to this at the beginning of our next session if that's alright with you."

Doreen smiles sweetly.

"Is that alright with you?"

"Does it matter? Whether it's alright with me or not. Honestly, does it?"

"Of course it matters."

"Hm."

———————————————

When the door opens there is Tom. He is stock still and fixes his eyes on his wife.

Doreen drops her head, averts her eyes. Looks at the carpet and walks quickly down the corridor.

May, 2001

It is a Wednesday. The work shift has gone by with exceptional sluggish-ness and everyone is irritated and seemingly on the verge of delirium when the buzzer goes at three instead of four.

"Why are we done at three?" Doreen directs her question at Miranda who has already removed her gloves and begun moving toward her locker.

"They do this every other month. Shut down an hour early for maintenance.

"I won't have a ride home. I didn't know."

"Didn't get the memo?" Vince is beside her. "I'll drop you off. No worries." Doreen swallows hard. She sees the faces of her critics. Martha, Tom, God. She clears her throat. "Okay. Thank you Vince." He winks at her.

A small group of maintenance workers shuffle in as Vince, Miranda and Doreen, along with a swarm of sweaty, nameless bodies shuffle out.

Outside it is beautiful. May has given birth to early heat. The sun is still bright in the sky though slipping downward slightly. The air is dry and gathers around them without sticking. Memories of unseen things blow by in the slight breeze. Listening to the Eagles on eight track. The feel of corduroy bellbottoms. The smell of kissing potion and Opium perfume.

"Ah! My GOD." Miranda lifts her arms and hands to the Heavens. "Yes. This weather!" She spins around twice with her hands still uplifted and then stops and tilts her head toward the sun.

Doreen finds Miranda's unabashed joy both embarrassing and enviable. She wishes she could raise her hands to the sky and spin like a child without caring who would see or what they would think. She wishes she could lift her face to the sun with her eyes closed and not worry about the world around her. Bathe without ego, in the heat and the light of the afternoon.

Miranda opens her eyes and looks at Doreen and Vince who have both stopped beside her in order to not leave her behind in her moment of lone ecstasy.

"Let's go DO something!"

"Like what?" Vince asks.

"Just SOMETHING. Come ON you guys!" She speaks as if they have told her no a million times already and she can no longer tolerate their resistance. "Let's go sit on a patio. Have a beer. This weather is too good to be wasted. Come on, Doreen." She grabs Doreen by the arm.

"I'll drive," Vince says and although something turns sour in her guts momentarily, it only takes a second before the bitterness turns sugary and gurgles up into her throat as excitement. Memory stirs. Wind blows. Warm air beckons her body to remember being young.

"I'm gunna blaze before we go. I won't drink much, so I can drive." Vince is rolling up his marijuana cigarette in the driver's seat and Miranda has slipped into the back seat, both of them insisting Doreen ride up front. Shotgun, as they both referred to it in turn.

She can smell Vince and her own nerves. Sweat and stale smoke and terror of the kind that makes one feel dread and exhilaration all at once.

Vince lights the joint and inhales a few times, keeping the smoke in, choking on it slightly. He looks at her and nods with his breath still held. He holds it out toward her, this cigarette he has rolled himself that is turning the car skunky and asphyxiating. Doreen shakes her head no as Vince exhales loudly, finishing his out-breath in a guttural sigh.

"You sure?"

Doreen nods. "No thank you," she tells him.

He shrugs and passes it into the back seat to Miranda who takes it readily and goes through the same inhale, hold breath, sputter and choke before exhaling, routine. It doesn't look or smell very pleasurable to Doreen, but she remembers liking it. She remembers the gratification of the pull, the straining of the lungs. She remembers enjoying the buzz as it set in, although she has no memory of what that buzz actually felt like.

They pass it back and forth between them and Doreen begins to feel strange just being in the car as it all happens. She laughs with them when they laugh, even though she's not really sure what's funny. From the back seat, as she's passing the joint Vince's way, Miranda says, "Dude, I LOVE this song. Turn it up." Before slipping the cigarette between his lips again Vince reaches out and turns the volume of the radio up, filling the car with noise.

"Bush," Miranda says, "I fuckin' love this song." She begins to sing, "Got a machine head, it's better than the rest, green to red, machine head." The music blares its strange lyrics and Miranda sings and Vince smokes and starts the car as he is throwing the last tiny bit of the rolled cigarette out the window.

"Where to, ladies?" His face is flushed and his eyelids have fallen heavy over his eyeballs. His eyes smile without his face having to do so. He looks sleepy and like he's just crawled out of warm blankets. Doreen catches herself staring.

"Go to The Moose," Miranda tells him. "We'll sit outside and get a pitcher."

"Sounds like a plan," Vince says, as he pulls out of his parking spot. They all roll down their windows. They drive with the music blaring and Vince joins Miranda in singing and Doreen feels at the same time so out of place and so at home. She remembers and she forgets all the little things that make up happiness, that create a person, that shape an experience.

She puts her head back on the seat behind her and just listens, breathing in the skunky air.

The air outside is intoxicating after so much cold and gray. The world is a much nicer place when it's alive with heat and light and the promise of summer.

Human energy is everywhere. People are pouring out of cars in groups and making their way toward patio tables and chairs. Traffic is heavy on the street in front of them. Music blares from rolled down car windows. Roller-bladers and bikers and people walking dogs parade down the sidewalk in a steady stream. The weather has brought everyone out of hiding. Everyone wants to feel a little sunshine and move the bodies that have begun to atrophy over the long stretch of time that was winter. This is the first truly nice day they've had all year.

Miranda and Vince are chain smoking cigarettes.

A young waitress comes to the table wearing a black t-shirt and black pants and a fanny pack around her waist that sounds heavy with coins as she walks. She carries no note pad, but has a pencil tucked behind her ear. Doreen thinks about the sensation of pencil on paper. She is reminded of Lisa Griffin.

The girl has auburn hair much the colour of Faith and Gracie's. Doreen sees a quick snippet of the future, looks to the girl's breasts which are pressing and stretching the fabric of the shirt. She takes a panicked inhale and looks down.

"What can I get you guys?"

"We'll get a pitcher," Miranda says, "you guys care?"

"Get Canadian," Vince tells her.

"Aw, Canadian. No Vince. That stuff is shite. We'll take a pitcher of Bud."

The waitress looks at Vince as if to confirm, to get permission to bring back what Miranda has ordered.

Doreen watches the exchange. Vince smiles at the young girl and nods. He says, "Looks like we're drinkin' Bud."

The waitress smiles with young, white teeth and plump lips and pulls some menus from under her arm to present them, "Need these?"

"Do we wanna eat?" Miranda asks them. Without waiting for an answer she says, "Yeah, let's get a couple appetizers. Just leave one of these." She pulls on one of the menus, taking it and opening it in a brash sort of pushy manner. Miranda is an aggressive human. Something Doreen was always warned against being. Be submissive. Give in. Let lie. Be a pretty girl but not too pretty. Be a good girl.

The auburn waitress looks directly at Vince and says, "I'm Holly by the way, I'll be your server today."

Vince smiles at her. Doreen thinks about sitting in his lap. She used to sit in the laps of boys. It was an easy way to show them what you wanted. What you were willing to do. Or, as it often was with her, what you were pretending you'd be willing to do in order to be kissed and validated. In order to be seen.

Vince watches the girl, this Holly, as she walks away.

"Yep nice ass, get over it," Miranda says with her face still in the menu.

Vince laughs. Lights another cigarette.

The beer comes to the table, Miranda orders mozzarella sticks and breaded mushrooms and Vince pours beer into three glasses. Just the smell of the alcohol sets Doreen askew.

She looks at hers while the other two take thirsty gulps.

Miranda puts her feet up on the wrought iron fence they are seated next to. She once again tilts her head toward the sky with closed lids. She makes noises that indicate pleasure. She seems to get lost to the world around her, at will. Doreen wants to live a day in the young girl's skin.

"It is gorgeous out. I can't wait to get back out West," Vince says.

"When are you leaving?" Doreen asks. The thought of his absence kicks her in the ribs.

"When are you taking a drink of your beer?"

At this Miranda snaps out of her intimate moment with the sky and pops her eyes back open.

"Yeah, Dorey. Drink up. Christ."

Doreen raises the glass to her lips tentatively. Her body is meant to be a temple.

The sting of the booze, when it touches her lips, takes her somewhere shadowy. She wants to drink it and be normal and not fear for repercussions. These two in front of her seem to fear nothing. They seem to do whatever they like with only pleasure and abandon. They seem to be indulging in some treat whenever they breathe. With them there appears to be no thought of future, no fear of consequence.

She longs to know that kind of unencumbered joy. But she is not like them. The world has taught her not to be. She has learned too many times the trap of pleasure, the risk of joy. She has learned never to close her eyes to the sun but rather to keep them open at all times. Half open, even in sleep.

She takes a full swallow. "Thatta' girl." Vince winks at her. Her thighs go rubbery against the metal chair.

"Anyway. I'm looking to go back within six months. I don't have a date set or anything. I've got to save some money first. I can't God damn wait to look out my window and see the mountains again. And go mountain biking. Fuck, this city is a drag. The closest thing I have to wilderness here is the fucking sprouts." He laughs, drinks. Miranda laughs too.

"True dat," she says. Doreen has no idea what this means or if it is even English.

"So what do you do for shits, Doreen?"

Doreen stares blankly.

"For fun? What do you do when you're not working?"

Doreen searches her mind for an answer to give the girl. She looks at Vince. He drags on his cigarette and smiles at her with his dark, hooded eyes. She wonders what life consists of for him, to make it so that there is always a smile behind his expression.

"Well. I'm mostly with the kids I guess. We have a prayer group on Friday nights sometimes now."

"La-aame."

Vince says, "Randy!" through a laugh. It's a kind laugh rather than a mocking one. It's a laugh that agrees but sympathizes.

"Well," Miranda says, making no apologies for her rudeness. "I mean, seriously, everybody has to have some fun once in a while.

"Fun means something different to everyone, Ran."

"Suck it, Vince."

"You produce it, I'll seduce it."

Miranda laughs, "Oh my God what grade are you in, eight?" She laughs again. "Besides, don't tease. It's been a long time since I've had my pussy eaten. I might just get drunk and take you up on that."

Doreen feels her ears almost ignite from the heat that barrels from her neck up her face and lands in the tip of them. She takes a few full swallows of beer in a row.

"Aw, really? I'm sad for ya babe. I'd do it. You know, as friends."

"Well, Chloe's with Fuck-nuts 'til Friday." Miranda laughs and closes her eyes to the sun again.

"Might get messy though, just to warn ya. I'm a squirter."

"Really?" Vince's face lights up like he is five and the end of the parade is near. Like any minute now Santa will come around the corner waving.

Miranda laughs. "Wouldn't you like to know."

"Well now I would, yeah."

Doreen can't tell if this is a serious conversation or not and as usual she only knows the full meaning of some of the words being used. Others are left to her interpretation which is often inaccurate. The only thing she knows with certainty is that she feels enormously uncomfortable and is turning purple with shame. She tunes it out. She can't listen anymore. She has an image burned into her imagination of Vince's beautiful head of hair moving back and forth between Miranda's young, splayed legs. It turns the fabric of her underwear warm and moist and at the same time makes her stomach contract with something vile toward her friend. Toward them both.

She drinks a few more hearty gulps and begins to feel it. It comes back to her in a heartbeat, the old familiar feeling. The crawl of alcohol from her guts up the back of her neck and into her skull. The loosening. The giving in. She can't enjoy it. She is terrified.

God comes to her. He whispers and provides white noise. He helps her block out the pornographic things being discussed. He pets her and reminds her and points out the lesson here.

Doreen reprimands herself. She does not belong here. She does not belong amongst heathens nor does she belong beyond the boundaries of her back yard. She belongs at home. With her husband, with her children. She needs to have another baby. She needs to fix this.

Standing up and pushing her chair back in one motion, Doreen says, "I would like to go home now."

Vince and Miranda stare at her.

"We just got here."

"I need to go home."

Vince stands up, "Okay. That's okay. I'll drive you."

"No." Doreen points to his seat, gesturing, with a sense of urgency, that he needs to sit back down, that he needs to not take one more step toward her.

"I told you I'd get you home."

"No. I need to call Martha. I can't go with you. I can't do this."

Vince puts his hands up in front of him, palms facing her, two olive-skinned flags of surrender. "Okay. Sorry."

The girl, this flirty, slutty Holly who wants to have sex with Vince is walking past and Doreen grabs at her like she is a flotation device. "I need a phone."

"Okay." The girl puts the tray of food she is carrying down on a table and takes Doreen by the arm. "There's one inside. I'll take you to it."

"Thank you." Doreen lets herself be led by this big breasted whore toward the wooden door that will lead them inside.

"Is everything okay?" The girl asks. She smells like vagina. Like unwashed, un-cleansed vagina.

"No."

"Is there anything I can do to help?"

"No," Doreen assures her. "You just worry about saving yourself, little girl."

There is a hurricane of ramification for her act of rebellion. She takes it like she should. She shoulders it without complaint. She is put to bed by her husband and told to stay there. He does not want to look at her face. She is disgusting. She is not a mother. She is not a wife. She is the same drunken harlot she has always been. He screams at her and God natters in her ears at the same time. God has harsh words for her. He pushes white noise through one ear drum into her brain cavity and out through the other eardrum as if He is flossing the inside of her skull with it.

Martha is downstairs with the children. Even though Tom does not want to look at her disgusting face he remains in the room to berate her. She deserves it. She knows.

But it is when he begins to remind her of that night in high school, it is when he tells her for what must be the thousandth time since it happened, that she asked for it, that she deserved it, that she was made to reap what she had sewn, it is then that the last tether of anything resembling sanity breaks apart in her. It is in this moment, when her husband is recounting the details of her rape so that she might suffer through it one more agonizing time, that part of her shakes loose permanently.

She is on the bed with her hands over her ears, which does no good because not only are Tom's words too harsh and violent to block out, but an equal amount of noise is coming from inside of her. In cupping her hands over her ears she is only amplifying it. There is no escape.

Tom is yelling and God is yelling and the white noise is reaching painful volumes in her brain when she sits up, takes her hands from her ears and leans forward on the bed toward her standing, pacing husband.

And she says it.

"You. Were. There."

All noise and movement stops and she sees him, young and covered with zits, too much saliva, too much gums. Pinning her, driving into her. Laughing. Pissing on her body.

A little demon she has kept caged for so long in order to protect herself, bursts through the bars of its confinement and scampers into the room. It grins triumphantly at them both.

Tom stares at her. He has finally shut his gross, fucking mouth.

Doreen feels the missed sleep of a thousand nights punch her square in the face with all its force. She collapses on the bed.

There is darkness.

And there is quiet.

Doreen awakens to pitch blackness. A body is snoring beside hers. Her mouth tastes like garbage left out in the sun. She very badly needs water. She goes to the bathroom and without turning on the light she runs the tap and cups her hand underneath it. She brings her cupped hand full of water to her mouth and drinks. She repeats and repeats this motion and still her mouth is dry.

She stands, coming out of the hunched and leaning position she had put herself in, and she vomits down the front of herself. The smell of it creates further waves and contractions. She moves toward the toilet, throws up again. Gets to the toilet. Vomits so many times that she begins to smell the coppery scent of blood mixed with the reek of her stomach contents.

She throws up until she is exhausted once again and has no energy or desire to make her way back into the bedroom. She lies against the cool bathroom tile.

She realizes the gravity of what has been done.

She closes her eyes again.

There will never be any sort of freedom again. No leeway. Tom calls the sprout farm and ends her employment. He calls Lisa Griffin and discontinues her counseling sessions. He puts his mother's house up for sale. Doreen feels everything around her spinning.

She bites her nails down to the quick and then continues to rip flesh until her fingers themselves are being chewed. They bleed, they scab, they bleed again. She eats the scabs. She tastes the blood. She keeps chewing.

She paces through the days and then sometimes through the nights as well. Gets up when Tom has gone to sleep and paces in the living room, chewing her nails bloody as she recaps events in her head. The admittance of what she has always known, the saying it aloud, has set free a lifetime of repressed memories that keep her awake and taunt her until she feels she might not be able to take anymore. She feels the urge to stop existing. She feels so deeply the need for silence that she begins to think about how to make it stop. She imagines all the ways that one might end life.

She thinks about tying a rope tightly around some fixture. She tugs at the ceiling fan in the dining room and wonders how much weight it might be able to hold. She thinks about beams in the unfinished part of the basement, in the attic. Trees. So many of them around the perimeter of the yard.

She wonders could she bring herself to slit her wrists. Could she dig the knife in far enough, and keep going despite the pain. Would she be able to watch herself bleed out without panicking and crying for help? If it would make life stop. If her mind would still itself. If it prevented her from having to wake up one more time to this life of confinement and repentance. If it stopped her from having to remember the details of things that she has spent a lifetime repressing only to let them loose in the end. If it would make it all stop.

She doesn't think she'd be able to get a hold of drugs. She would never be able to get to the Doctor by herself or fill a prescription without supervision. But a bottle of pills would be a good way to go. A sleep she'd never have to wake up from. Oblivion followed by black and eternal nothingness. Because suicide is a sin. And she would not be in Heaven. She would not hold Isaac in her arms. And that might be the very thing that keeps her from doing it. She wonders though, how much longer she can hold on. In the light of reality, in this new string of mornings where all of her nightmares have become real and she has had to face them, she is not sure how much longer she can hold on. She apologizes to God ahead of time. Just in case. She prays for the Rapture to just come now.

Just let it come now before I take matters into my own hands.

Tom doesn't look at her anymore. But she knows he is not ashamed of himself. He is ashamed of her. He is remembering all the reasons for what happened. Her clothes that night. Her drunkenness. Her sitting on the laps of boys who wanted nothing from her but to use her body for pleasure. He is remembering why he needed to teach her what he did. He is ashamed to have married such a vile, un-chaste human-being.

Tom and his mother begin to run the household as if Doreen is not there. They speak to each other and arrange the schedules between themselves. She is another child. One more dependent. They both look at her with resentment filled eyes.

She no longer leaves the house. Not to go to work, not to go to counseling, not to greet the girls at the bus. Not to take Eden to tutoring or the rest of them to swimming. Martha takes Jacob and Faith and Grace Isabella with her to meet Eden and Delilah when the bus pulls in at three thirty. Tom takes the children to appointments and lessons. Doreen stays home with Martha's supervision and whichever children are left behind.

She leaves the house for church and only church.

But it is better this way. It is safer this way. Doreen does not trust herself or the world or God's inclination toward punishment. She is safe inside. Safe with supervision. She never should have trusted that Lisa Griffin and her women's liberation propaganda. The Bible says the man is the head of the household. The man is God. And God is all. Lisa Griffin was sent to test and she did and Doreen failed but at least she didn't let Vince get his hands on her body. At least she passed that test and put herself back where she belongs. Home with her children. Home where it will be safe. Where everyone will be safe from her.

Thank you, oh Heavenly Father, for the safety of my home. Thank you for Tom who takes care of me like a husband should. I am an ingrate of the worst kind and unworthy of love and yet, you love me, Lord. Thank you. Amen.

It is mid May when the maple keys begin to rain down from the sky. Doreen sits in the back yard wrapped in a blanket worn thin by the stream of children who have wrung it through their needy hands. A blanket as tattered as she is from the years of being needed and clung to. It does little to warm her but she keeps it snug around her shoulders nonetheless.

Her shoulders have become boney. The rest of her too. Eating is a task she has been forgetting to carry out. She has to be reminded. Instructed. As with everything. "When is the last time you ate, Doreen?" "Have some lunch, Doreen." "Chew with your mouth closed, Doreen. God is watching."

She startles when Delilah and Eden suddenly bound toward her. Afternoon. Past three thirty. The day half gone with her having no real recollection of it beginning. Of course it had begun but she's been up most of the night for so many nights in a row that the end of one day and the beginning of the next have become impossible to tell apart. Reading. Praying. Listening. Trying not to sleep. Not to dream. The dreams have become unbearable now that the words have been spoken aloud. The details painful and raw. Each scene uncensored and unfathomably sharp. Her own strange version of A Nightmare on Elm Street. The voice in her head warning her, "Whatever you do don't fall asleep."

The girls are showing her art work from school. Painted flowers on pink construction paper. Green leaves. Doreen can smell the paint. She can smell glue. The children have loud voices that irritate her ears. The silence of the back yard violated and shattered by the shrill unceasing voices.

Doreen raises a finger to her lips. "Shhh" she tells them. "Look at the maple keys."

Doreen gestures toward the sky and the girls look up and for the briefest of seconds there is a pause in the noise. The three of them watch the maple keys helicopter down out of the trees and land in the grass.

Then as abruptly as the noise had stopped it begins again. Squeals of excitement, strings of words about the trees and the sky and God. Energy and movement that agitate Doreen. She doesn't want them right beside her. She doesn't want the hot breath of their words in her ears. Where is Martha? Why has she been left unattended with the girls?

"Go see if you can catch one," she tells them. They drop their back packs and their artwork. They run into the depths of the yard with their hands reaching toward the sky and they laugh and twirl and fall. Doreen watches. She feels a chill. She wonders if her legs will hold her when she tries to stand. And for how long. For how many more days will her body carry her through the rooms of her house and in and out of the van on Sundays?

And then the old woman appears, "There they are," she says, looking out into the yard at the spinning figures with the outstretched arms.

Doreen thinks maybe she should respond. But with what? With "Yup"? With, "There they are."? With "Isn't God great?" She has no clue. Maybe with "Quite the son you've got there."

Instead she says, "Don't leave them with me."

Martha looks down at her like Doreen is something parasitic. Something that is draining the life out of the old woman as she stands there. That's exactly what she is, she supposes. A drain on everyone who has to deal with her. Martha expels an exhausted sigh.

"Girls! Eden! Delilah! Come in and have something to eat please, girls!"

Doreen pulls her knees up to her chest and wraps the blankets tighter around herself. There is a wave of noise and movement and then she is alone again in the silence of the yard, watching the maple keys drift down from the tree tops and land at her feet.

She keeps her eyes locked on the ceiling. She can't close them and she can't look. Tom thrusts into her without mercy. As hard as he can. She can feel him hitting her bladder. She pisses a little. Smells it. Gags. His fingers dig into her arms. His weight pins her to the bed. She can hear him laughing but isn't sure if he actually is. Then the white noise takes over and she hears nothing. Stares at the ceiling. Feels nothing.

The Baptism was meant to cleanse her of her sins, to rinse away the past.

She had walked into the lake fully clothed, the water rising around her, her white dress billowing out as she took the slow steps needed to reach Reverend Smiley. He smiled at her like an encouraging parent. Coaxing her forward.

The sun had been shining, creating a harsh reflection off the surface of the water, making it hard for her to see. She squinted into the afternoon light, faces coming in and out of focus. Her father, the sister of Tom, Tom himself, Smiley.

As her head was gently pushed down and then held underwater, she was supposed to feel something undeniable. Some explosive moment of forgiveness and relief and rebirth. Instead she felt panicked. She felt the need to push back, to break the surface and emerge, to fight off the hands that were pressing on the crown of her head, holding her under the cold water of the lake. Every instinct she possessed instructed her against giving in, told her instead to fight. But she didn't. She could not.

It had been meant to create an after that would contradict the before. Before Christ, when she was a heathen and a harlot, when she was unrighteous and soiled and ruined, and after Christ, when all was forgiven. She had expected to emerge from the grungy lake a new person, ripe with purity, one that belonged to the Lord, to a family, amongst the Holy. She had expected to feel saved.

When she came back up she took gulps of air and spat water from her lips, rubbing the water out of her eyes and pushing her drenched black hair from her forehead. There were faces again, faces smiling. She pretended to smile back. She performed in the way she knew she was expected to.

She had wanted to feel different. So badly, to feel like someone new.

She had felt the same.

No wave of relief, no lightening of body and soul. Just the same old rock of dread in her gut and the same memories fighting for air-time in her inadequate brain. The same old thoughts in that stupid head of hers and the same dead heart somehow still beating in her chest.

And life had gone on. Exactly as it had been before. She had repented and been born again. And yet, no matter how hard she prayed to feel the difference, she remained unchanged. Still dirty. Still wrong. The same girl who had done the same wretched things.

She had wanted to feel clean. Like the sins of the past had been washed away and belonged then to the lake and to the rivers it emptied into.

But from the minute she emerged from underwater she had known that the past still belonged to her. That the past would always belong to her and to anyone that came from her.

She knew it again when Isaac was born purple and still. And she knows it now.

She had tarnished not only her own soul, but the souls God sent through her.

The Baptism had not saved her.

There was no hope for any of them.

The days continue and very little is expected of her now. Tom barely looks at her. Martha encourages the children to leave their mother be. Still they try to climb on her and cling to her. They continue to leak and smell.

The days carry on with her as more of an observer now than an actual participant. She watches as it all unfolds. The sun coming up, bodies emerging from rooms, burners turned on, children and dogs and adults eating and shitting and making unnecessary noise. She reads her Bible and chews her nails and has no need for sleep whatsoever. Her eyes sometimes close but only for short intervals of time. Then they open again and it's all the same sights. The same walls, the same faces, the same words across the page.

It feels as if other people are only dusty figments of her imagination. Bruno and Jack and Vince and Miranda. Lisa Griffin. Sometimes she can't decide if they are people that truly continue to exist in the world some-where or if they are simply characters she has made up in her head and has since stopped writing scripts for. Their faces have become fuzzy in her mind. She can't make out their features anymore. Hair colour, bone structure, skin tone, it all blurs and melds until she has trouble telling any of her memories apart. There are a pair of dark eyes surrounded by olive skin that try to look into her while Tom pounds down from above, but she shoos them away. It only makes the task at hand more repulsive, more difficult to endure. That memory only makes Tom's face that much more intolerable.

She asks Martha one day in May, late May maybe, but she isn't sure about the days anymore.

"Lisa Griffin. Is she real?"

Martha is folding laundry, standing next to Doreen and making piles on the couch as she goes. She stops, holding a pink nighty, and stares at her daughter-in-law with that look that tells Doreen that she has once again said something that is, in one way or another, inappropriate.

"I was just wondering."

"She goes to our church, Doreen. You spoke to her on Sunday."

"Ah."

"My brothers?"

"What about them?" Martha has resumed folding but she is doing it in slow motion, clearly distracted.

"I have brothers?"

"Doreen."

Doreen looks out the sliding glass doors. Sees that the wind is gently blowing the trees. Everything is so tiring.

"They call marijuana cigarettes 'weed' and joints and 'blunts'."

Martha stops folding again. "Who does?" Her eyes are wide with something that looks like shock. Doreen feels calm, yet alert. Martha's reaction seems to her, not quite right. Somehow disproportionate.

"Kids."

Martha nods. "Well," she says, "that's nothing we need to concern ourselves with."

"And what about the autism?"

"What do you mean?"

"Eden."

"Doreen, I don't know how much more of this any of us can take. "

"Hm." Doreen looks down into her lap at her hands. They are still. Lifeless birds strangled and left to rot in an abandoned nest.

"Ah well. Should we have some tea then?"

Martha leaves the folding unfinished and moves toward the kitchen. "You sit down. I'll make the tea."

Doreen gnaws at her fingernails, what little of them is left. Draws blood. Swallows a piece of something. Cuticle maybe. Skin from her fingertips.

Martha makes tea noises from the kitchen. The clicking of the stove knobs being turned. Water running. Kettle set down on element. Cupboards opening. Mugs hitting counter. Drawer opening. Spoon hitting counter. Fridge, milk, sugar bowl.

Doreen waits.

Under her breath she begins to sing, *This is the story of a girl*....

June, 2011

June begins much the way that May had ended. With Doreen sleepless and dazed, accomplishing very little beyond reading her Bible and listening to God through the stereo speakers. With Tom and Martha running the household and Doreen's role as mother consisting of taking orders from her mother-in-law about who to wash and what to peel and where to sit and who needs what, and her role as wife consisting of the usual.

Jacob has taken to crawling into her lap in the span of time before Tom gets home and the supper and bedtime rituals commence. He sits quietly on her, sometimes with a book or a toy and talks softly, not seeming to expect any response from her, which suits her perfectly. He smells of lawn; of twigs and rain.

The older girls continue to be mostly obedient and easy while the younger two demand and carry on and throw themselves around. Martha has tried toileting Gracie but has had little success. The toddler seems to like walking around in a diaper full of her own piss and shit. Doreen is grateful not to have to deal with too much of that.

June begins with the stream of maple keys thinning but still spinning down around her in the afternoons. Soon the kids will be done school for the summer and that will make things less taxing in some ways, but more so in others. They will no longer have to worry about the timelines that school demands. No getting the girls to and from the bus. No homework or meetings with teachers. However, this break in routine also means that all day every day the house will contain five children instead of only three, who need and want and eat and make noise. And of course Eden will need lots of extra help all summer. To cure her. To stop her from remaining retarded.

The days go on. Always.

It is a Monday when Gracie comes down with what appears to be the flu. A stomach bug of some sort which the child has seemed prone to since birth. Doreen is convinced that the girl enjoys creating more mess for the adults around her to have to deal with. That she likes making a putrid pile of her own insides in as many places as possible. All over her bed, on the hall carpet. Down the bathroom door. On the floor of the playroom. Just like that fucking dog. Stench and disgust.

The child whines and carries on like it is dying. Clings to its Grandmother, whimpers for its father, creates more chaos in an already chaotic home.

And now Doreen is expected to get up off the couch and do some helping out. Tom explains this before he leaves for work.

"You can get off your ass today and help my mother. Enough is enough of this poor, depressed Doreen bullshit."

Martha looks on from the kitchen while she takes bowls and cups down from the cupboard, an apprehensive but not unpleased expression on her face.

God whispers in Doreen's ear. White noise threatens but subsides before it begins.

"Okay Tom"

Tom has some more things to tell her. He points his finger at her face while he does so. Lazy. Useless. Poor excuse for a mother. Do this. Do that. For the love of Christ.

Doreen nods in compliance. Martha looks on. The dog licks the top of Doreen's bare foot and she reflexively jabs at its face. The animal yelps. Tom looks at Doreen like she has just committed yet one more sin. She shrugs at him. "Slobber."

"Oh, you're a real piece of work."

Tom grabs his briefcase and his travel mug from the counter and kisses his mother on the cheek.

"Make sure she is helping today. You don't need to keep doing this all by yourself. Especially with a sick baby. Have a good day, Mom."

"You too, Tommy."

Doreen is instructed to bring the baby down to the couch and change the pukey bed sheets. She would have felt resentment before. Right now she feels very little of anything. She climbs the stairs hearing the voices of Delilah and Eden and Martha and Jacob. Hearing the dog barking. Hearing Faith crying about something or other. Protesting yet again. Doreen climbs.

When she opens the door to the bedroom the smell in unbearable. It attacks her senses, bile immediately rising in her throat. She throws a hand over her mouth and nose. She runs across the hall and vomits in the bathroom sink. Why? Why this task? Any other task for fuck sake.

As she approaches the bedroom again she hears the baby call out to her. A small voice that doesn't remotely resemble the voice that she has grown to recognize as Grace Isabella's.

Fighting her body's urge to escape and expel, Doreen forces herself into the room, bile stinging and burning at her throat, her hand over her mouth, her stomach clenching and unclenching in relentless waves.

When she reaches the bed she looks down into it and sees piles of vomit that have soaked and stained the bedding and surely the mattress underneath. The child makes a noise again, a word that sounds like mama and Doreen looks down to see a languid and discoloured Gracie reaching a tiny, exhausted arm toward her. Doreen's breath catches in her throat.

The child is gray. Sweat beads gather on her small forehead, the hair soaked, the eyes grave and sallow.

She sees, as she has in the past, God's wrath.

She picks the baby up from the bed and while trying desperately not to be sick again makes soothing sounds. "Hush. Baby. It's okay. Mama's here." She doesn't recognize these words, they are alien but she hears herself utter them anyway. Like something rehearsed. Something she has read and memorized and is now performing. "Shhh," She tells the child. "Mama's here now."

Downstairs the morning is underway and soon the girls need to be waiting for the bus. Jacob and Faith are already in the basement watching cartoons and drinking from sippy cups. Doreen lays the baby on the couch.

"How long has she been throwing up?" she asks Martha.

"Since early this morning. Four o'clock ish."

"Something's not right."

Martha stops and stares as she seems to do every time Doreen utters a word these days. Then she says, "She's sick."

Doreen nods. The baby makes a noise that is indecipherable. Something in Doreen's chest feels as if it is being clenched in a huge invisible fist.

She drops to her knees beside the child and begins to pray.

God, please watch over Gracie. Please protect her, Lord.

But that's as far as she gets. She isn't sure what exactly she should want to happen. For the Lord to make the baby better or for him to take her home. When she thinks of her own life she can't help but acknowledge all of the suffering she would have been spared had it ended sooner.

She gets up and sits next to the gray body. Stops praying. She has no idea what she should be praying for.

As Martha is about to leave to walk the girls out to the bus stop she tells Doreen to get Gracie some water. "We need to replenish her fluids. She's been sick quite a few times."

Doreen nods. Gets up. Pours water into a spill proof sippy cup. Brings it to the child's mouth. Something rips at her insides as the little girl tries with what appears to be great effort, to wrap her small colourless lips around the spout of the cup. Doreen remembers every ounce of resentment Gracie has ever made her feel. Every tantrum. Every single time the child has made a fuss about something stupid and refused to stop until Doreen was red with rage and beyond control. She wants to feel something definite. Something she can recognize without doubt. Instead she feels unsettlingly vague.

The baby seems to want to drink. She looks parched. Dry lips. Dry nose. Even the eyes seem to lack moisture. Fluid-less. If only babies were always like this. Quiet and dry.

Gracie sucks, making very little noise. Breathing seems laboured when she has finished. She opens her eyes slightly to take a look at her mother.

Doreen touches the baby's head. Smiles down at her to the best of her ability.

The child opens its parched lips. "Mama." And Doreen feels fingertips touch the back of her hand, dry too, and much hotter than they should be.

The baby closes her eyes again.

"Sleep baby," Doreen tells her. "God loves you."

But sleep does not descend upon the baby just yet. It is as if the water reaching the stomach causes it to respond, to reject the liquids the body so obviously needs. Gracie rolls onto her side holding her stomach, moaning in what is clearly agony, and vomits again. Down the couch, onto the floor, the front of her pajamas drenched and sour. Doreen runs from the room to deal with her own bodily demands.

The child doesn't cry, simply expels everything within her and then closes her eyes.

"Did she throw up again?" Martha is back from the bus stop.

"She threw up the water."

"Okay." Martha begins to take care of things. Cleans, changes, soothes. Doreen stands back and watches, feeling as if she is watching something not really happening. Something on a screen, a dream perhaps. She begins to see the scene as if she is hovering above it all. She can see herself standing helplessly beside the couch, a strange look on her own face. The limp baby. The old woman fluttering about. The animal coming into the room and lapping at the vomit on the floor.

"We're losing her," She hears herself say it and yet there is no reaction from anyone else. The old lady continues with her efforts to rectify the situation. She puts the dog outside, takes the baby's clothes off, wipes her with a face cloth, puts clean pajamas on her. Doreen tries to speak the words again but finds that her mouth won't move.

God's voice begins to speak to her. His words clear, precise. He tells her what she's always known. What he has been trying to tell her for months. About her life, about Tom, about the fate of these poor, doomed children. Doreen feels herself begin to rock slightly. This has always been inevitable, she tells herself. Hasn't it.

It is when the boy child appears at the top of the stairs that Doreen snaps back into her own body and becomes part of what is happening again. The old woman tells her to get Jacob what he needs. More juice, a clean shirt, apparently there has been a spill.

She does what she is told, knowing there is more talking going on around her, but unable to grasp any of the words. Hearing only meaningless, muffled sounds.

The boy child goes back downstairs. Doreen stares at the small girl, its flesh the colour of chalk. It throws up again.

Doreen stares.

She is sitting on the couch beside the sick baby and she is staring out the glass doors onto a yard full of trees. She hears Tom's voice. The day has passed.

"She's got to go to the hospital. Tommy, she's not keeping anything down. Not even water."

Doreen looks at her husband. He glares at her. If he could slap her he would. She can see that.

"What's this one been doing all day?" He asks his mother, gesturing toward his wife.

"It's been fine, Tom. And really that's not important right now. This little girl needs a doctor."

They are in the van. The baby doesn't cry. They are in a cold waiting room. For hours. Sick people are all around them. Coughing. Crying. Yelling at the nurses, at the receptionist. Insisting they've been waiting too long. Demanding something be done to help them. Doreen watches and listens while Tom holds the baby on his lap. Doreen touches her and is surprised by how hot the body is.

Tom utilizes this time wisely by reminding Doreen of her shortcomings while they wait. Like a stern parent he explains to her how things are going to change and how she needs to pull her weight and how he has no idea what her God damn problem has been these last few weeks.

Yes Tom. Sorry Tom.

She has no idea how long they wait, but it is dark outside when Tom begins to get angry. Tom begins to do what the others have done and raise his voice. He tells the nurse how sick his daughter is. He tells her about the taxes he pays. He says this is ridiculous. Still it feels like a horrible amount of time drags by before they are led out of the waiting room and into a small bright room with a bed.

The doctor is brown and difficult to understand, his thick accent mangling the language so that the words are often impossible to decipher. This irritates Tom further. He snaps at the doctor. He asks him over and over again to repeat himself. He then asks if there isn't someone white who might be able to help.

"How about someone who speaks English, huh? How about that? Can we make that happen? En-*glish*. Understand?"

A nurse comes in, Caucasian and blonde. Round hips. Huge, confined breasts. She speaks in clear English.

"She's been throwing up since four this morning. She's not even keeping water down," Tom tells her.

The doctor says something but Doreen isn't sure what.

After all that time waiting they are sent home. The nurse has given them four children's Gravol and advised them to stop and get more. Tom is furious. The baby is limp and the colour of ash. Doreen bites her fingertips, tears them open. She stares out the window of the van. Tom rages beside her. Spits and sizzles and slams his hands on the steering wheel.

"Shut up Tom."

He stops, his mouth drops, and he takes his eyes from the road for a dangerous amount of time to stare at his wife. "Pardon?"

"Shut. UP."

She looks back at Gracie. There's not much to see.

She looks back out the window. She can't be one hundred percent certain, but she is pretty sure that the van is silent.

It is somewhere around three in the morning when Doreen is all alone and pretty sure that God has said all that he needs to say for the night and she has read so much already that she can feel the blood vessels in her eyes straining and bulging, that she goes upstairs to the bedroom of the younger girls.

When she reaches the doorway it is evident that the child has once again thrown up. Doreen picks her daughter up quickly. Gracie wraps her arms around her mother's neck. Her body radiates heat. Not a dry heat anymore, something sticky and pungent. She is slick with her own perspiration.

Doreen carries her downstairs to the couch, lays her on it, watches her sleep. The breaths are laboured. The child moans and twitches. She thinks to pray again but then remembers that she doesn't know what to ask God for. Praying is what she has always done. It's what you do when anything is wrong, or frightening, or whenever you've screwed up. It's what you do when you burn supper, or your husband is late coming home, or when the children don't get along with their cousins. You pray. When you're locked in a closet. When your brother is being beaten in the next room to the point where you aren't sure he'll survive it this time. When your husband is punishing you again for your indiscretions of a hundred years ago.

It seems like it should be the thing she turns to now. Prayer.

Then they cried to the LORD in their trouble, and he delivered them from their distress. He made the storm be still, and the waves of the sea were hushed. Then they were glad that the waters were quiet, and he brought them to their desired haven

And yet Doreen can't bring herself to do it. She has no words. She has prayed before that the jam would turn out the way Tom liked it, as good as his Mother's, as tasty as his sister's. And yet as her youngest child lies dying on the couch she can find nothing to say to God. Nothing to ask for. No offerings.

Please God let the jam be delicious. If you just let me not screw up the jam I promise I won't zone out during service anymore. I promise to try harder with Tom's sisters. Anything Lord, just let the jam be to Tom's liking.

And now as her daughter's body is deteriorating in front of her, dehydrating and deflating Doreen cannot come up with one single offering.

Tom has gone to work and Doreen is in the upstairs bathroom going through the motions of washing herself because Martha has informed her that she hasn't brushed her teeth in days and Doreen has had to take her word for it, when despite the running water filling the room with noise, Doreen hears Martha yelling. It is a God awful sound. Like an animal wounded and terrified. Doreen should be moving fast. She knows this, and yet she moves slowly to the top of the stairs and even more slowly down them. The screaming continues. The old lady, and she thinks she hears her son crying out, bawling her name, Gracie's name.

It feels like she is walking down the stairs for a very long time and that the yelling is going on for much longer than seems reasonable. She reaches the bottom of the stairs, walks through the kitchen, Martha sees her. She screams at her to call the ambulance, to call 911. Doreen sees the baby. The body is twitching, the head jerking. Froth is spilling from the mouth. Jacob is there crying.

"Yes hello? 911? We need an ambulance."

It is only Doreen who goes with the baby in the helicopter. The first time she has been allowed to be alone with any of her children in as long as she can remember. Of course, she is not alone. There are medical people there too. And a pilot she presumes. Another time on the way there, the body twitches and jerks and froths. People jump up to do things to the body. It's no use. Doreen knows this as she watches. There is no point.

There will be no more worry about diapers. Only Faith's bad temper to deal with. The rest of the children will keep growing and needing less and Jacob will be the youngest. The sweet calm baby.

Doreen is sitting on a plastic chair staring into her lap where her bloody hands are lifeless. The floor is shiny, marble-like, although not real marble, she supposes. Not in a hospital. Although this is the important hospital. McMaster Hospital. Things are serious now.

She hears footsteps on the hard floor. She looks up and sees Tom charging toward her. His hair is a mess, his tie is askew, top buttons of his shirt undone. His face is twisted into something she isn't sure she has ever seen before. His eyes are full of fear. Brimming with a pain she doesn't understand.

He reaches Doreen and bends down and pulls her into his arms and breathes into his wife's neck, "Is she okay?" He looks up at her, kneeling in front of her on the floor. Because they created this child together? Is that why he suddenly feels that there is kinship between them in this moment? She pushes him away gently, but assertively. She doesn't want him to touch her. Their sick child creates no bond between them on her part. He is still Tom. Repulsive and vile.

"She's in a coma."

Tom stands up and runs his hands through his hair a few times, over his face too. He paces in front of her. He says, "Oh God. OH GOD."

Doreen watches him. He looks at her, seems to be searching her face for something she knows he's not finding. She can feel her own ambivalent expression. Is aware of how dead her eyes are in their sockets.

"Who can I talk to?"

Doreen points down the hall to where the nurses' station is. Tom goes, his feet *clack, clack, clacking* down the hard corridor.

Doreen sits. Stares into her lap. Time passes. Tom returns.

He sits down beside her and puts his head into his hands. Does the face and hair rubbing again. He looks at her with tears in his eyes. This seems so uncharacteristic of Tom. She is surprised by the intensity of his reaction. His legs are moving up and down, up and down, in a state of nervous agitation. Like they want to go somewhere but have idea how to begin moving forward.

When Isaac died it was different than this. Tom's reaction. They had held the baby together, the body in Tom's arms, the head cradled in Doreen's hands. Tom's bottom lip had trembled. Tears had threatened but had not over taken him. There was a sadness but no panic. An unspoken resolution. God had wanted his child back. Everything happens for a reason. At home the house had been quiet. Still. Unchanged. The baby had never been there and therefore when they returned home, there was nothing missing. No absence.

Tom looks at her again now, seeming to search for something, some connection between them perhaps. Something to signify that they are the only two people in the world that can understand each other in this moment. She stares back at him.

"Why is this happening?" he asks. She knows he's not expecting her to answer him. She knows that in his mind there is only one answer, and that he is simply uttering words out of desperation, hoping that an explanation spoken out loud might make what's unfolding somehow easier to bear.

"Because of me."

"What?" he breathes the word out in exasperation.

"You heard me."

Tom runs his hands over his face again. Pauses. Gets up. Paces again. Drops to his knees in from of the row of chairs they've been sitting on. There are a few other people in the room. They are looking now.

"Pray with me. Come on, Doreen. We need to pray."

He bows his head, assuming traditional prayer position.

"I'm not praying, Tom."

He looks up at her, dumbfounded. Tears swell up into his eyeballs and spill over the edges and down his flabby cheeks.

"What? Why not?"

"I'm tired of praying, Tom. I have nothing left to pray about."

"Doreen." His tone is pleading. A tone he has not taken with her ever.

Doreen stands up. "You go ahead," she tells him. "I'm going to get a tea." He opens his mouth and sad words come out, desperate and pathetic, that fade into the squeak of her sneakers as she trudges down the hall in search of caffeine.

The baby has been put on life support. A machine helping her breathe. She can remain on life support, but because of the seizures she suffered, the best they can hope for is to be stuck raising a vegetable. The child will never grow up into something independent. Will shit and piss itself until the end of time. No progression, no development, no life. Just a body that continues to do the disgusting things that bodies do, but that cannot become anything other than infantile.

As the doctor, in a voice that is delicate and practiced, explains this and the options available to them, Tom sobs. He sobs like a little boy. Like a small child grounded from the only thing he loves to do and deeply regretful of the actions that caused his punishment. He sobs without apology. For a brief moment Doreen admires him for it. For his unabashed angst. For his ability to, after all that has passed, still feel so deeply.

Doreen stares. She watches the doctor's lips move. Brown lips. Clear English. Tom is oblivious in this moment to race or colour of inflections of voice. She catches certain words, the unfamiliar ones; cerebral, anoxia, palliative. She stops listening long before the lips stop moving. God is there. The white noise is there. Her arms hang limp at her sides, she doesn't move. When the doctor's mouth finally stills itself and he turns and leaves them to each other, his shoes make no sound on the marble floor.

Tom collapses. His body appears to just give out on him, his limbs folding. Doreen looks. Her head is full. She feels herself blinking. Can almost hear the wet click of her eyelids meeting and then pulling apart again.

And again there is movement and chaos and people in scrubs are gathering around Tom. She watches. She hears her own heart beating in her chest, her own lungs pulling in air and expelling it again.

Then there is a hand on her arm. She turns to see a face she doesn't know. A young face. The hair is pulled back, there is too much mascara. The lips are moving. The teeth are white. The breath is coffee and something doughy. Doreen is pulled gently and she feels her feet following without her consent.

She is lowered into a chair. It's all happening at a pace that doesn't seem real. Slowed down and sped up. She has the sensation of being underwater. The young lips move some more, right in her face. Trying to make eye contact. Doreen nods. She sits. She folds her hands in her lap.

And as quickly as the commotion started it recedes and she is alone on a hard chair. Sun is pouring in through a wall of windows. Sun. Daytime. She has no idea how long this has all been going on.

She thinks about thanking God for the glory of this blessed day, for all his gifts, for doing what is right and good, but she doesn't. Instead she sits and stares.

Doreen has a thought somewhere in the folds of her mind, that maybe it should've been just them. Just her and Tom, perhaps Delilah. Maybe even all the kids. That it should've been sacred somehow.

She keeps that thought to herself as Tom's sisters and their spouses pour into the room. She can't help but think of them as voyeurs. Showing up for the spectacle of the thing. She would've hated them before. Now she can't conjure the depth of emotion it would take to do so.

The machines create noise that has become part of the room. The baby is lifeless although no longer gray. The head is bandaged. Tubes come out of the body. Doreen is positioned near the bed. Tom is still overcome by his grief. His face leaks unceasingly. He keeps looking at her with eyes begging for something she can't give. She should feel the same agony. She should look at the state of her husband and have compassion. Empathy. His pain should be hers. But all she can do is watch it. She sees him there in his agony and she recognizes it. She can't feel anything about it but tired. She just wants to go home.

Looking down at the baby, she remembers Isaac in his lifeless perfection. Gracie is like her older brother now. Quiet. Still. The machine breathing for her is calm and rhythmic. The face is dry. She looks pretty in this moment. Except for the ears.

Medical people come in dressed in whites and greens. They hover around the baby. They speak to Tom, and to her, but she lets Tom take care of the responding. She doesn't speak, but feels herself nodding.

It isn't until Reverend Smiley arrives that things can get underway. The room is full of what appears to be anguish, but it is an anguish Doreen doesn't trust. Tom's family is a paparazzi of sorts. Always has been. Looking for something to take pictures of, something to write about. Something sensational that they can make themselves feel a part of, by witnessing and documenting.

When Smiley enters the room it's as if God himself has arrived. The family gathers around him, their sobs become louder, some dropping to their knees and wailing. Doreen watches them. Tom joins in the gaggle. They all hug and rock and sob. Doreen stands beside the body which is about to be pulled from everything that is keeping it alive. Her hands are folded in front of her, hanging in front of her crotch.

When the family gathers in prayer, Doreen holds Tom's hand in one of hers and Martha's in the other to help create a circle. She boughs her head as ordered, and closes her eyes. Smiley rattles on about Gracie returning home in peace, about the strength and importance of family in this time of grief and loss. Doreen wonders where the children are but then remembers. Ronald McDonald house. It feels like she hasn't seen any of them in days. Maybe she hasn't.

When the prayers are finished and everyone has hugged again, after Doreen has been taken unwittingly into too many sets of arms, the procedure begins. Needles in, tubes out, Tom's family in a huddle around the baby. A woman in a white uniform begins to hand the body to Doreen, seeming to want to lay it in her lap.

Tom's voice, something about wanting to be the last person to hold her. Words that he hiccups out, barely discernable. Doreen doesn't argue. Looks down at the face. Yellow striped pajamas with buttons. Rusty hair.

The body suddenly gasps a few times and Tom begins to weep openly once more. Noisily.

God has left her alone to endure this. To observe. To understand.

The room fills with the performance of the behaviors that grief commands; tears, noise, people falling against other people. People gripping themselves, their own temples, their own chests.

Finally the breath slows and stops. And it's done. The nurse's hand on Doreen's shoulder. Tom's face buried in the baby's hair.

Grace Isabella. God bless you and keep you.

The doctors had offered her some drugs, something to sedate her, to help her get some sleep. Something to take the edge off of something that never seemed to manifest. Doreen had made peace with Gracie's passing before it took place. It had been God's will.

Tom had been offered the same drugs and frankly Doreen thinks he should have considered accepting the help. She can tell that her husband is feeling something acute and debilitating. His face appears battered and discoloured in the days following Gracie's death. It seems perpetually on the verge of giving in to collapse. The lips tremble, the eyes twitch, the skin seems to have given up, sagging more visibly than it had only days before.

Doreen finds herself wanting to feel sorry for him, digs into herself for some crumb of compassion that she might be able to offer up. The man has lost his daughter, after all. He had loved the child to the best of his ability, she is sure. In his own imperfect way. Love, as far as she can tell, is such a flawed thing anyway, and she cannot fault Tom for not knowing exactly how to love his children. She is sure he has tried. Lord knows he's done a better job than she has at it. Especially with the girls. Especially with Gracie and Faith.

But when he tries to curl his body into hers in the night, she pulls away from him. His body trembles and his face leaks and he rocks himself, curled into the fetal position in some attempt at comfort, she supposes. He reaches for her body and she pushes his hands from her. He utters her name into the darkness in a way that pleads. But it is too late. She rolls over and faces the wall and lets the white noise fill up every cranny of her skull so that she won't hear him begging for respite.

It has been too late for too long.

The days that follow the death are wrought with busy-ness and it is evident that no one can decide how much responsibility can safely be placed on Doreen. Not only has she just lost another child, but she has been emotionally fragile for some time now, walking a tight rope of sanity just to get through each day. Delicately the sisters tell her what she might help them do. It is a gentleness she is unaccustomed to.

She does what needs to be done, which is made easier by the fact that she does not sleep. She makes arrangements; flowers, guest books, child care. She tends the children minimally. She does what needs to be done. She tries to cry. She can't. She doesn't.

During the service a fire truck passes and Jacob runs to the window of the church in excitement. He points and calls out, "Fire truck!" and Faith joins him, standing on tippy toes to see. An uncomfortable wave of quiet noise moves across the church as mourners turn to look. She should rally them but she doesn't. They don't understand. Let them marvel over the lights and sounds of the fire engine. Let them remain untouched by the grief that sits heavy in every pew of the church but theirs.

Tom just looks over at them helplessly and cries. This is when she realizes with clarity the depth of her husband's current grief. When he passes up the opportunity to be the boss. Regular Tom would see this as a teachable moment. Would wrangle his offspring into shame and submission. This version of Tom, this small and sad version of her husband, only watches helplessly, his features crumbling and melting as he does. Martha puts a reassuring hand on his thigh. The older girls sit beside their father, hands in laps, letting silent tears stream down their cheeks.

During the reception the children run around and eat desserts and drink cups of pink punch. Doreen becomes agitated with the hugging. Everyone wants to hug her despite her aversion to being touched. Too many smells, too much sweat. Tears smudged against her cheeks and in her hair. It is almost too much for her to endure. She has to go somewhere else in her mind. Back to the closet of her childhood. Where it is dark and she is alone.

Bruno doesn't come. Jack and his wife show up and so do her parents. They are just more people to her now. Just more arms and tears and body heat. She thanks them for coming. She thanks every one for coming.

When finally she has a chance to sit, Delilah comes to sit beside her on the burgundy couch of the reception room. Her daughter knows not to touch her, not to speak. She sits beside her mother in silence.

A young cousin comes up. The granddaughter of one of the sisters. Its name is something with an L. It bounces on the couch next to Delilah. Her daughter smiles down at it. The child is wearing pink. There is food on the face.

"Stop bouncing okay," Delilah says.

"Why?"

"My mom doesn't like it." Doreen looks to her daughter. Forces a smile. Delilah's eyes are puffy and red. Her hands are in her lap. Folded. Her fingers tucked up into the palms of her hands.

"Why she doesn't like it?"

"Because it's annoying. Just please stop bouncing okay."

The child has already stopped. She just wants an explanation as to why she had to.

"Where's Gracie?"

Doreen looks the child in the face. The eyes are brown, the hair auburn. The nose puggy and freckled. Cheezies. It is Cheezie residue smudged on the face.

"Gracie is in heaven," Delilah says. "She doesn't want to come home anymore."

Doreen stares down at her daughter.

"She *can't* come home anymore," she corrects. It's how they had broken it to the children. *Gracie has gone to live with God, she can't come home anymore.*

"She *can't* come home anymore." Delilah repeats her mother's words directly to the child.

"Why she can't come home?"

Delilah lets out an irritated sigh. "Because she can't okay. God took her back. Now please go find your Mommy, okay?"

Doreen looks down at her eldest daughter again. Long hair, tired eyes. And as Delilah opens and closes her fingers in a clear showing of agitation, Doreen notices that the nails are gone. The skin is scabbed. There is a tiny balloon of blood near one of the cuticles.

Doreen looks at her daughter's face again. Feels her own eyeballs darting frantically over the features and then back to the bitten bleeding fingers.

"Why she can't?"

"Because she can't, I told you."

It is then than Doreen wonders if perhaps Delilah was correct the first time. Look at this life. Look at these daughters slowly but steadily becoming their mother. Perhaps it's not at all that Gracie *can't* come home. Maybe it really is that she doesn't *want* to.

With that God's voice is in her ears, and she is confident in her revelation.

It is on the way home in the van that what's missing becomes palpable, that the void becomes an entity in and of itself. The space where Gracie should be. An emptiness that is stark and undeniable.

Tom is driving. The children are quiet in the back. All but Faith who has asked for her sister several times. The children had lined up at the coffin before the ceremony and had placed a picture of themselves inside, to be buried with their sister.

"Where do we put it Daddy?" Faith had asked. "Put it on her heart sweetie, that's where she remembers you." One of the older cousins had burst into tears at this point, burying her head into her mother's shoulder. She had a baby the same age as Gracie. A blonde son. And some older children too. Her face was red and blotchy.

Clearly Faith doesn't get it. Children handle death in their own way, Smiley had assured them. And now it was their job to help the children grieve. One more job. An exhaustive list of jobs.

Each time she asks either Doreen or Delilah provide her with a similar version of the same answer. *She's gone to Heaven. She lives with God now. She's in Gods arms. She's with Grandpa in Heaven.*

The child whimpers and fidgets and asks, *but when is she coming home, Mommy?*

Doreen can hear Delilah beginning to sniffle once again. Tom beside her driving, is doing what he can not to break in front of his children. Doreen can see it. His face doing the same thing it's been doing for days. Aching to dissolve. His eyes are wet.

She stops looking at him.

"I'm ready for the Rapture."

She turns toward him once again.

He takes his eyes off the road briefly to look at his wife. "I mean it. Let it come down upon us now." Tom looks up to the ceiling of the van then. "Come on Lord, I'm ready for it. Please get us out of here."

Doreen nods. Turns. Looks out the window at darkness.

———————————————

The June sun creeps slowly into the back yard and awakens the world. All but Doreen who is already awake. Bible in lap, tea in hand, radio off now so that no one will know what she's been up to.

Life continues. Even when babies are taken from their mothers. Even when families and lives are permanently changed, the days go on. Mortgages have to be paid, children need to be fed. Dog shit has to be cleaned up from the grass in the yard. It just keeps happening. The sun rises, things are done, the sun sets again. There isn't even a pause in the cycle. No time to readjust.

Martha gets up and begins to clean the already clean kitchen. She puts the kettle on. She does this with nothing hindering her. With no baby in tow.

Gracie's bed has already been taken down. Remnants of her, stored away. Photos removed from the fridge. This is how Tom wants it. He doesn't want to be reminded. He wants to carry on. He goes back to work the day after the funeral. The children are to return to school. Business as usual. His anguish spent.

They will have to wait for the autopsy report. Indefinitely it seems. Until.

Doreen had been surprised that Tom had allowed it. The temple being violated in such a way, the brain cut into, the chest split open. Tissue removed and analyzed. Doreen was surprised. But Tom wanted to know. Said he *needed* to know. It seems he isn't trusting God on this one. For some reason Tom is unable to just accept this as part of God's plan. Interesting that Tom gets to pick and choose when to do so. When to accept and when not to. He has always had that option, has always granted himself leniencies.

He appears in the kitchen like it is any other day. Clean. Bright eyed. Straight tie. Combed hair.

The dog, the children, they all emerge. All but Gracie.

Breakfast, clothes, out to the bus, pick up from the bus, and what feels like a whole lot of empty space and silence in between.

A supper of pasta, and garlic bread, and Caesar salad, and Coke-a-Cola.

Vacant space. Quiet air.

"I want Gracie to come back. I'm scared in bed alone."

"I know, Honey. Soon."

"She'll be back soon?"

Doreen nods. "We will see her again. In Heaven. When the Rapture comes."

"And Isaac too?"

"And Isaac too. Now be a good girl and go to sleep."

The child whimpers. It whimpers as if someone has jabbed it in the ribs whenever it is told that the sister will not be coming home. Doreen can see the physical discomfort this information causes her daughter. She can tell that Faith is waiting, still, for the time when someone will say, "She's coming home tonight." For the time when Gracie will appear beside her in the playroom, in the bathtub, outside in the yard.

"Can we go to Heaven soon?"

"We'll see," Doreen tells her. As if the child has asked for an afternoon at the carnival or a new kitten.

"Goodnight, Faith."

The child says nothing.

———————————————

It is the silence, she thinks, that causes God to become irritated with her. The baby gone, the older girls in school, and so much nothingness. Martha tending to Jacob and Faith. God becomes very insistent during these long hours. He reprimands her. He reminds her repeatedly of things she already knows and understands. He points to what has happened and again and again makes it clear to her why. She knows, she knows, she knows.

———————————————

"Doreen? Doreen!"

The old woman has caught her with her hands over her ears trying to block Him out. She shouldn't try to block him out, she should listen. She knows. But she can't take anymore. She can't remember what it feels like to sleep. She is sitting on the floor in front of the couch with her hands crammed over her ears, she can feel herself rocking. The old woman's voice snaps her back.

"Doreen, what's wrong?"

Doreen looks up, stares at the old woman, blinks her eyes.

Slowly she takes her hands from her ears. God's voice finally gone for a moment.

"What's wrong?" Martha asks. Her voice ginger and light.

"It's my fault. You know that right. These kids didn't have a prayer."

"Oh Doreen," the woman's voice has a kindness in it that had disappeared in the weeks before the baby died. She reaches for her daughter-in-law but Doreen is so fucking sick of being touched.

"Don't." She recoils.

Martha pulls her hands back. "I'm sorry."

A surge of some sort of power runs through her. The word *don't* tastes like candy. Sweet and addictive.

"I know how hard this has been. Tell me what I can do for you."

"It's too late."

The old woman pauses, looks at Doreen, her expression confused.

"I'm here to help. You know that, Doreen. For as long as you need."

Doreen shakes her head. She is exhausted, yet wired. Her body has to be on the verge of just shutting down from deprivation and yet her mind is jumpy and spastic. Her mind is insisting that sleep isn't unnecessary. That it is time to be wild and lucid.

She shakes her head, tries to shake away the energy in her brain.

"It's too late, it's too late, it's too late." She says this while still shaking her head.

"I can call Smiley if you want. Or do you want to see a doctor? I can get you in for tomorrow if I call now."

"Aren't you sick of this, Martha? Aren't you fucking TIRED?"

The old woman pulls herself away and stands up.

"Doreen." There is unease in her voice. She backs away further.

"Where's my daughter?"

At this, the old woman clearly becomes frightened. She is rendered speechless while she tries to grasp what is happening. While she appears to be trying to figure out what she should do.

"Sweetie, what do you mean?" The voice is so cautious. So timid. No one has ever called her Sweetie before.

"Grace Isabella. Why are all the pictures gone?"

"It's just how Tommy's coping. You can …"

"Tommy." The name drops from her lips like something she took one bite of and couldn't stomach.

"Doreen. Please"

"Fucking Tommy!"

Doreen gets up. The old woman braces herself. Backs up. Lifts her arms as if to ward off a blow.

"Where are they?"

"Where are what?" She looks near tears, her worn out face contorted into something that makes Doreen feel sorry for her, although she is beyond being able to stop herself from continuing.

"The pictures. Of Gracie. Where are the pictures of my daughter?!" Her voice is so strained from exertion that the last word comes out gravelly and raw, tearing her throat.

"They're in a box. Just tucked away. I'll get them for you. It's okay."

Doreen paces the room just as Tom had paced the hospital hallways. Frantic. Panicked. More energy coursing through her than she's felt in weeks. Months perhaps. Ever. She wants to see her baby. She needs to know. Tom can't just tuck things away whenever he's done with them. Just hide things whenever he doesn't want to face them. He can't just pretend that they never happened, that they don't exist.

Tom isn't the boss.

Martha comes back into the room with a cardboard box. Not even a Rubbermaid tote. Just a degradable box, susceptible to mould and vermin.

Martha sets the box on the floor. "They're all still here," she says. "It's okay."

"It's okay." Doreen repeats her mother in-laws words. "It's okay." She scoffs at this. Shakes her head at it.

She kneels down, opens the box.

Portraits taken at Sears. Gracie in an embroidered dress. A bonnet hiding her ears.

Doreen holds the photograph in her hands. Stares at it. "People don't dress like this, you know."

Martha blinks, clearly perplexed. Clearly reaching the point where she wishes there was something she could say to make this stop, to calm the situation, but where she has had to give in to the fact that there just isn't.

"Seriously. People dress babies in jeans and hooded sweatshirts. Look at this dress. Fuckin' Laura Ingles Wilder." Doreen isn't thinking. Just talking. Nothing is running through her head to guide her words, she is just saying them. Just letting whatever pops into her mind spill out into the room.

She laughs. Tosses the picture to the side. Rummages through the box. She finds some snap shots. Gracie and Jacob on a slide, the sun shining through the cartilage of her daughter's oversized ears. Doreen reaches up, touches her own ear with one hand while holding the photo in the other. She shakes her head. Laughs. "Yoda."

"Doreen. Please."

Doreen grabs a pile of snapshots and frantically flips through them; Gracie in front of a cake, Gracie in nothing but a diaper. Gracie smiling in the stroller with a Popsicle in her mouth, red food dye number forty running down her chin and neck.

She stops flipping through the pictures and looks up at her mother-in-law.

"Where is Isaac?"

"Doreen..."

"Pictures of the baby. I know we took pictures. Where are they?"

Martha bites on her lip. She is about to cry, Doreen can tell.

"Where are the pictures of Isaac?" Again the words come out raspy and painful.

"Okay." The old lady leaves the room again and Doreen gets up to move around it, the energy in her brain buzzing and spitting, not letting her stay still even though her body is begging to die.

She feels like she has been conspired against. Like everyone has been hiding something from her. For how long? For what amount of time have these people been controlling her memories with what they allow her to see and what they don't? How long have they been tucking things away in boxes in hopes that she'll forget? She becomes frenzied with this thought. Are there more children? Are there other things she doesn't know?

Martha returns with a small envelope this time. Doreen glares at her. How dare they. She reaches out and snatches the envelope from her mother-in-law, then glares at her some more before opening it. She has been wronged in some way.

She pulls a thin pile of photographs from the envelope and her breath snags in her chest as she looks upon the first one. Discoloured baby. Someone's arms. White blanket. Black hair. Her hand flies up and covers her mouth. She has an intense urge to swallow but her throat closes over and disallows it.

She stares at the photo.

After a few long seconds she drops the pile into the box of Gracie. She looks up at Martha, points to the box. "This can be the dead baby box."

Martha begins to cry.

"They were all doomed," Doreen tells her. "You do see that don't you?"

Martha says nothing. Just looks at her daughter-in-law with an expression that begs her to stop. That tells her to keep back. Not to come any closer to anything.

"They were all doomed." This comes out of Doreen's mouth softly. Quietly. She looks down at the box of photos and then lets her body slink to the ground beside it. She lays out the pictures of Isaac. Five of them. She touches them all. She takes out some of the snapshots of Gracie and lines them up underneath. Touches those. Lets her head hang a little.

Poor things.

There is movement and Martha has lowered herself to the ground too. Beside her. She reaches out and fingers the pictures, pulling one of Isaac out of its spot in the row to look at it a little closer. Tears are fresh on the leather of her face.

"Children must be beloved," Doreen hears herself say, and then Martha's arms are around her, her frail old bones heaving with sobs, shaking Doreen with their strength.

Doreen gives in and lays her head on the old woman's shoulder.

"I'm so sorry, Martha."

"It's okay." The old woman gasps for breath. "You've been through so much."

For the first time in her adult life she believes that someone in this universe is sorry for the things that have happened to her. The apology is both fresh and ancient. It is an apology that is as much for what is happening to them right now, as it is for what a fifteen year old girl endured one hundred lifetimes ago as a result of her quest to be seen.

Doreen pulls away from her mother-in-law. Looks at her. "I'm so tired Martha," she tells her.

Martha wipes her eyes with her fingers. Uses her sleeve to stop her nose. Sits up straight.

"We'll get you something."

Doreen raises her head. Looks into Martha's eyes.

"We'll go to the doctor. We'll get you something. Tommy doesn't need to know." She wipes at her nose again. Looks Doreen in the eye. "You need some sleep."

Doreen has no idea what to say. She does not remember how to genuinely thank another human being for kindness.

So even though she feels it, true gratitude for this offering, she has no words.

She says nothing. Just nods. A strange feeling creeping into her chest. One she doesn't recognize and cannot name.

There will be sleep.

No break in routine. Tom reaches for her in bed. Crawls on top of her, pulls at pieces of her.

She flinches and squirms beneath him, moving away as best she can with his weight pinning her to the mattress. He keeps going despite this. Despite his wife's obvious feelings of repugnance toward the act he is about to force her to participate in, yet again.

But this time when he stiffens, when she feels that vile part of him poking into the flesh of her inner thigh, she knows she can't do this anymore. Not for one more night. She puts her hands against his chest, pushes him up and over, and wiggles out from underneath him. Tom is seemingly too much in shock to even make a grab at her.

She pulls free and sits as far away from him on the bed as she possibly can.

"Doreen." He says her name sternly. A father who is not quite angry but is letting her know he is unimpressed.

"No more."

"Pardon me?"

"No more, Tom. Enough."

"Doreen…"

"It's not up for discussion. I'm done."

Again, "Doreen…" as if in repeating her name he can make her relent.

"Hasn't it been enough? Don't you get it? How many babies does God need to take from us before you understand?"

She pulls her robe off the back of the bedroom door in the darkness and tightens it around herself. She reaches out and grabs a pillow from the bed and then pulls it to her chest. "I'll be sleeping on the couch from now on."

She can hear his mouth drop open. She can hear strings of thick saliva clinging between the hinges of his jaw. Can smell his breath.

She closes the door behind her. Closes the door on a part of her life that should've ended long ago. That should've never begun. Something large and cumbersome slides from her shoulders and is gone.

———————————

Getting the sleeping pills turns out to be an incredibly easy thing to do.

When the girls are at school, Martha takes Doreen into the city to see the doctor, who nods a sympathetic head and bats sad eyes in the few seconds it takes to write a prescription.

"It's understandable that you would be having trouble sleeping." The physician is skinny and middle aged so that the skin appears to no longer fit the face. A garment that probably looked nice at one time, but has long since needed to be traded in for something less baggy and more up to date. "Get some rest."

She tears the prescription from its pad and hands it over to Doreen. And that's all there is to it. No need for permission or her husband's signature. In fact, Tom's name is not once mentioned during the entire interaction. Before she leaves the office the doctor tells Doreen to call in to her nurse if she finds she needs a refill.

Martha drives her to the pharmacy and they head back to the house with a bottle of pills and a secret between them. It feels like a connection, this secret. Like she is on the inside of something instead of standing outside of it wondering exactly what it is.

Doreen is to keep the pills somewhere safe where she knows her husband will never look. She has no real idea where her husband looks. What corners and closets he crawls around in when she isn't in the room. She isn't sure if anywhere is safe from Tom's greedy reach.

She spends a large part of the day prowling the house, looking into empty spaces and trying to imagine whether or not Tom would ever have occasion to frequent them. Would he ever venture into her things under this sink? Where Tampons might fall out of bags? Where there are tubes and bottles of ointments he might find repulsive or unnecessary. She doesn't think so, but she can't be sure.

What if he needed something and for some reason started rummaging through her feminine things? What would her husband's reaction be, to a bottle of white pills boasting her name in clear print? To the violation of the temple? To her clear betrayal of his and Smiley's rules? How would dear Tommy react if, Heaven help them, he realized that his own mother was in on the deception? Doreen feels a smile creep over her face, a much too satisfied grin considering everything her husband has just gone through. What with losing his daughter and all.

She wanders and peers into dark corners and thinks and imagines outcomes. In the end she decides that the safest place for her pills is in the box with her dead children. In the very place Tom has purposely made secret. A spot where he has chosen to put the things he can't face. The box is on a shelf in the basement, a tidbit of information Martha has let her in on so that she can visit it when she wants to look at Gracie, to remember Isaac. She pulls the box, marked PRIVATE in thick black marker, from its spot on the shelf and tucks away her tiny, amber bottle.

God is there while she does this and He is once again, as He has been in recent days, loud and persistent. He gives her ideas about the amber bottle. About the little white globes inside of it. She listens, for she is terrified not to. She listens and nods and agrees. But she doesn't pray. She doesn't thank Him. And once again His voice becomes so shrill and unrelenting that she finds herself trying to shake it away after a time. Aggressively shaking her own head back and forth hoping to dislodge the string of words that shows no sign of tapering off.

She finds herself feeling nagged rather than guided. He is becoming one of them. A father, a husband. One more man nattering in her ear the same tired commands over and over again until she can feel herself going mad. She shakes her head. She begs out loud, "Just stop for now. I will listen later. Please." No one hears her this time. No one sees. The voice quiets but remains. A steady whisper. Something she is constantly aware of.

Doreen goes about her day, which consists of not much more than trying to make it pass. She is once again struck by the feeling of being on the sidelines of her own life. A spectator. Nothing much expected of her except that she will watch, enraptured, and cheer when things go right, boo perhaps, when they do not. But with no real control over how things are played out.

The afternoon and evening pass with excruciating slowness. Tom is more aloof with her than he's ever been, if that's possible. Martha seems not to notice any difference. The children play as if Gracie had never been a part of them. As if her absence is as normal and natural as her presence had been before. "Children handle death very differently than adults," she had been told a million times in the previous days. "They can't fully understand." Even Faith has already begun to adjust, only seeming to notice her sister's absence when she is being tucked into bed in a bedroom that she no longer has to share. Soon this will become their normal. Soon all of them will be more used to a life without Gracie, than they ever were, of a life with her.

Doreen sits on the couch with her Bible in her lap and listens and watches without moving anything. She blinks. Once in a while she does that. She breathes. Her chest rising and falling ever so slightly.

A vein in her wrist twitches. Blue, stringy. She remembers the veins in her grandmother's hands. Thick and alive under the thin, worn skin. She didn't want to hold the hand but she had to. To cross the street when they would walk to the store. She would close her eyes and try not to think of those snakelike capillaries touching up against her own thick palm. She had to close her eyes and pretend she didn't know what the hand she was holding looked like, or that there was blood pumping and gurgling through the veins underneath.

"Can you possibly get up and do something other than stare at the walls?"

Doreen looks up. This act of tilting her head slightly, the most movement she has executed in what feels like hours.

Slowly she brings her eyes to meet her husband's. "Why yes Tom," she says, "What is it you would like me to do?"

He snickers at her, sensing something in her tone that he does not appreciate.

"How about helping with the kids? Remember that? Mothering?"

Doreen blinks slowly. Smiles a bit. "Ah yes," she says. "The delight of mothering."

"Get up."

She sets her Bible down on the cushion beside her and unfolds her legs which had been tucked up underneath her, *criss-cross applesauce*, like she was a preschooler at carpet time. She places her feet on the floor and her hands on either side of her, then pushes herself off of the couch and into a standing position. She is face to face with her husband.

She looks him in the eye. "Yes?"

His eyes squint in anger. In frustration.

"You'd like to slap my face wouldn't you, Tom?"

She sees his fists clench at his sides. Martha is nowhere. There are bath noises and stifled voices coming from upstairs. Television noises from the basement.

Tom takes a deep and very intentional breath. An agitated smirk plays on his lips.

"I don't hit women."

"That's right." She stares at him without blinking. "You hold yourself to a very high standard. I forgot."

He holds her stare, his eyes full of something sadistic, yet helpless.

He makes a noise something like a frustrated laugh that stalls out before it reaches maturity.

She continues to hold his glare.

"I won't live like this."

She nods.

"I mean it, Doreen."

"Okay Tom."

For so long they have been master and servant. In this moment they are opponents, neither one of them willing to back down. Doreen has no idea where this has come from, why she is suddenly unafraid and so free of guilt. Or where that sad sniveling man in anguish over his dead daughter has gone. She keeps her eyes locked on his, not even blinking now.

"You're not foolish enough to think this is it are you?" She says this unflinchingly.

"What the Hell are you talking about now?"

"He's picking them off one by one. It's not over. Be fruitful and multiply? You foolish, foolish man."

Tom folds. He steps back, averts his eyes, submits.

Then looks into her eyes again. "You are crazy, Doreen. You're truly, fucking nuts."

"Am I, Tom? Well, I wonder why that would be."

He shakes his head, attempting to clear it, to refocus.

"We have a family to raise."

"Yes we do."

"So whatever this is, you need to knock it off. Gracie is gone. We can't bring her back. We need to raise these kids together the best we can. Do you understand me?"

"Well I do speak English, Tom."

"Doreen!" he points a finger into her face. She is sure he would like to jab it into her forehead. She imagines reaching out and slapping that finger away. She imagines punching him square in the nose and watching shock and blood cover his face.

"Doreen." He says her name now like a parent trying desperately to keep his cool. Using everything in him not to reach out and shake the shit out of the crying infant, out of the insolent teen.

"We need to raise these kids do you hear me? You and me. And clearly, my mother."

Doreen watches his mouth move. Wet and sloppy. Gums so slick she can smell them. The distinct smell of mouth. Lips moving over gums. Skin friction. Bile rises in her throat.

"We have a lot of years left of this and we owe it to these kids. So you need to pull it together. When they're gone, Hell, when Jacob is sixteen, we can go our separate ways. But that's a long time from now."

"And Isaac."

"What?" his face twists into something that tells her she is retarded. She can almost hear him saying in his head, what the fuck is this retard talking about now?

"You said you were sorry that Gracie died, but you forgot about Isaac."

"For the love of Christ, Doreen!"

"And..."

"Stop!" he points that finger in her face again. Jabs it at her nose as close as is possible without making contact.

"Just. Stop. NOW."

She shrugs. Looks down at the carpet. Tom is in charge once again.

"Go help my mother with the baths. And this is enough. Do you understand me? We are done with the bullshit, Doreen. Done with it."

Doreen looks at her husband. Stares into those colourless eyes. Sees him.

She takes a deep breath and then looks at her husband and smiles. "Yes Tom." And she leaves the room. Up the stairs to help her mother-in-law, with whom she shares a secret, bathe and put her children to bed.

She is delirious with the need for rest. And drunk on the idea of it.

Martha and Tom have both retired by ten o'clock and it is suddenly no longer a secret that Doreen spends her nights alone on the couch. The dog has slept with Tom for the last two nights. This is a bonus for Doreen. No more mutt stench while she tries to concentrate.

She creeps down into the basement to pull the PRIVATE box from the shelf, her heart thumping in her chest while she does. She is terrified he'll come up from behind her. Scared to death he will snatch this opportunity out of her hands before she has the chance to really have it. She so badly wants oblivion.

She is only supposed to take one, or start with half a dose if she wants to, the doctor had said. See how that affects her. She puts two into her palm. Then, after she has put the lid on the bottle and placed it back into the cardboard box, she pulls it out again and shakes a third pill out. Just in case. Just in case two isn't enough and she can't fall asleep.

Still nervous and shaky from her rebellion, she climbs the stairs and sits down on the couch. A full glass of water sits on the end table. She looks down at the three round tablets in her hand. She is well aware of her church's interpretation of the Bible concerning this issue, but she doesn't know how God actually feels about her ingesting the pills. She isn't sure of His take on her desecrating Christ's temple. She only knows that He has other ideas. Other things He thinks could benefit her more. Could benefit them all.

She worries for a moment, about this act. About the lie. About intention-ally going against Tom and Smiley and the Word. She worries that even though God hasn't personally forbid her from taking them, He might get angry. He might punish her again. She has spent her entire adult life trying to avoid God's wrath. Trying not to anger Him. Knowing she had failed Him before. Not wanting to relive anything close to what had happened in the past. Her father had warned her. Had told her. You reap what you sow, little girl.

She had lived in that terror, day in and day out, for so long that it had become part of who she is. Part of her days, her nights, her physical self. And now here she is on the threshold of throwing it all away. And that part of her that has always lived in fear, kicks and screams and begs her not to take the pills. It quickens her pulse and makes her sweaty. It steals breaths from her. Her hand quivers a bit, the pills vibrating in her palm.

But what can He do? What could He possibly do now? What could be worse than taking a mother's children? Than allowing a woman to be violated brutally once and then night after night for eternity? There's nothing else. She already knows the worst pain, and she is suddenly, in an instant, no longer afraid to feel it again. So what? So. What.

She takes two. Swallows them both at the same time with a swig of warm water.

Ten minutes later, when she isn't sleepy yet, she takes the third. She reads the Bible. She waits.

When the letters on the page begin to swim, she puts the Bible down. Words try to jump out before she closes it. She sees them flying off the page attempting to come with her, to not be left behind.

She lies down and closes her eyes and there are daisies. In a circle. Like necklaces against a black background. She feels as if she is reaching out to touch them. And then there is dark.

She dreams that there is gum in her hair. Tom is cutting it out. He is trying to do this without her knowing. He doesn't want her to know that, somehow, he has gotten gum in her hair.

"Wake up. Doreen. For Christ's sake, wake up!"

Someone is shaking her body. She wants it to stop. She pulls herself from the grip, she slaps at the hands.

"Doreen! Wake UP!"

She tries desperately to pry her eyelids apart, uses all her strength to do so, but they only want to snap closed as soon as she parts them slightly. Her eyelids are fighting with her.

The voice in her face is Tom's. Of course. Tom's hands shaking her. Tom's saliva stinking up the room. His feet. His ball sack.

She rolls onto her side. She feels queasy. Her brain is thick. Her hands shaky. Tom commands her sit up, to hurry up, to get it together, for the love of Christ.

It is Saturday.

Once Tom has lectured her to his satisfaction about her ridiculousness and Doreen has stood in the shower for a long enough time to become somewhat alert, able to stand erect unassisted at the very least, nothing else is said directly to her about her difficulty waking. She can hear Martha and Tom having private conversations, hears her name in their hushed tones, but she doesn't concern herself with it.

The day is difficult. Thick and heavy. She has trouble understanding and her small periods of alertness are overshadowed by large portions of the day that drag her back down onto the couch. Her knees long to fold. Her neck gives very little effort to the task of holding up her head. God's voice is garbled and sluggish. The children grate on her as if they are filing away at her nerve endings with something dull and abrasive.

Despite sleeping for way too long, according to Tom, she is exhausted. More tired than she can ever remember being. Twice she falls back to sleep and twice Tom shakes her to wake her up. She nods at him a very slow nod. One that takes concerning amounts of effort.

Martha comes to her quietly in the afternoon to inquire about her dosage. Asks her if she started with half a pill like the doctor had told her to do. Tells her she needs to cut back on whatever she took. Doreen continues to nod the slow, difficult nod. She agrees with Martha. Thanks her.

She has a coffee at supper time which prompts Tom to ask, "What's up with drinking coffee? You've been drinking tea as long as I've known you."

There is a pissed off edge to his voice. She has irritated him, yet again. This time by choosing coffee over tea. By making a decision she failed to debrief him about first.

She thinks to say, *I'm sorry, I must have forgotten to ask your permission.* But it would take too much effort. She just looks at him briefly and then looks away, down into her steaming cup of caffeine.

The coffee gives her what she needs to get through the rest of the evening. Supper clean up, baths, stories, bed, dog. She manages to assist Martha with a lot of it. She manages to make it through most of what she needs to do.

There is a slight glitch when she goes into the bedroom of the youngest two girls and is startled momentarily by Gracie's absence. By the missing crib. The vastness of the room. Her immediate reaction is to panic. To call out. To yell to the other adults in the house that something is wrong. To please help her find the baby.

As quickly as this feeling washes over her it recedes and is replaced by her remembrance of the truth. The baby is gone.

Her heart turns to cement in her chest. Hard and too heavy. Painful to carry.

Faith calls out to her. Says, "Mommy" in a whine. Makes wet noises with her face. Doreen doesn't see her. She only sees the absence. She cannot see what's in front of her. She is only aware of what's missing.

As she leaves the room she hears the child begin to whimper, calling out to her repeatedly now, but Doreen can't force herself to remain in that room. She can't look at Faith and see the common features between her and her sister who is gone. She should. She should be trying to make everything as normal and comfortable for her remaining children as she can. She should put them first.

And so train the young women to love their husbands and their children.

Instead she turns away. From the voice of her daughter, from the emptiness of the bedroom. From what she doesn't have the strength to look at.

She practically bumps into the old lady as she is leaving the bedroom.

"Go rest," Martha tells her. Doreen doesn't even bother with the slow motion nod this time. She goes to her own bedroom and shuts the door. Pulls her Bible from the bedside drawer and reads. The words swim and blur but she presses on. She closes her eyes tightly and then opens them wide. She does this repeatedly, whenever necessary, in attempt to un-fog her vision. She reads and reads and reads until she hears Tom's footsteps on the stairs.

She closes the Bible and gets up. They don't speak as they pass each other in the doorway. She thinks he looks at her but she only sees it from her peripherals and can't be certain. Still, her skin rashes over at just the idea of it. With the thought that he is sizing her up, thinking about her holes. She moves quickly to the stairs and descends.

Downstairs she reads some more. She reads until there is no question that the house is long asleep and then she once again creeps to the basement for the secret box. She won't take as many tonight. The brain fog has been a double edged sword. Being numbed out, being slow and lacking in alertness has its sweetness. Half oblivion. Dulled senses. The inability to feel or understand anything too fully. The appeal is there.

But Tom is aggravating in his demands. Trying all day to snap her out of it. She can't handle another day of his questions and insistence. She will only take one tonight. She shakes a pill out onto her palm, not nearly as nervous as she had been the night before. Incapable of it perhaps.

Upstairs to swallow the pill.

She sits on the couch reading the Bible, waiting for it to kick in.

When reading becomes too much for her eyes she quietly turns on the stereo. She plays with the dial. She listens for God so she can tune Him in but he isn't there. She listens to the news instead. It's a horrible thing. This might be why Tom has worked so hard to protect her from it. Car accidents and home invasions and sexual assaults. Politicians lying. Movie stars committing suicide. Rock stars overdosing on drugs.

She listens to as much of is as she can, hoping God will show up and interrupt. She wants to turn the dial away from it but can't bring herself to. She hopes God isn't angry. She has violated the temple after all. She hasn't prayed in longer than she can remember.

Despite the sedative, she begins to feel anxious. She is worried. She wants to pray, knows she should, but when she goes to fold her hands in front of her chest she sees Gracie's lifeless body. She hears the maniacal laughter of drunken teenage boys. She can't pray just now. She can't.

Eventually the worry overtakes her and she begins to pace the floor. She can't pin exactly what she is nervous about but an unmistakable sense of doom has gripped her, draped itself around her shoulders and is clinging to her.

She paces and tries in vain to still her thoughts. She wrings her hands. She bites her nails until they barely resemble anything human. She spits the pieces of nail and skin out onto the carpet. Pacing, pacing, pacing.

She goes back down to the secret box and gets another pill.

Sometime later, she has no idea how much, there is rest. A period of black and thoughtlessness. And then Tom's ugly face is in hers again. Tom's clammy hands on her shoulders shaking her. Tom's extensive amount of gums wet and stringy as he demands, once again, that she get up.

Church today. Wear nice clothes. Stop acting like a retard. Look alive.

Yes Tom. Okay Tom. Good morning Tom.

"How're you holding up?"

Doreen tosses these words around in her head. What does that mean? Holding up? Holding up what? No matter how hard she tries, she can't wrap her brain around these words that have been spoken by the sister Gwen. Doreen looks at her own hands. The only thing she is holding is a child's sweater.

Martha speaks. "We're managing the best we can."

Doreen nods. That seems right.

There is a hand on her arm, rubbing. People are tender and concerned. Nobody demands anything of her. Instead they do it all for her. Other people gather the children from the nursery and load them into the van and bring plates of cold cuts and bags of buns and cases of pop to the house. Potato salad and cold pasta and cut up vegetables with dip. It all appears without Doreen having to do anything.

There is a disorder where mothers make their own children sick on purpose. Doreen watched a TV movie about it many moons ago. Back when she wasn't this version of herself that she is now. Mothers make their children sick by injecting them with Windex or water from the fish tank. Doreen thinks maybe she understands this now. Nobody asks too much of a mother with a sick child. Or of a dead one.

She doesn't bother to fight off their hugs. No energy for it. Even though the warm flesh pressed up against her and the smell of human makes her want to pull away, she can't. Her body is heavy and slow. She stands docile and blank faced as everyone touches and squeezes her body.

She hears herself telling them goodbye as they leave. The June heat is sticky today and she wants nothing more than for the house to stay shaded and cool. But so many people coming and going makes things warm and moist. The backs of her knees are slick and this repulses her. Her own pores excrete things. She can feel chemicals coming out of her. Can taste them on her tongue and at the back of her throat. She has a strong urge for hygiene but can't muster what it would take to attain it, nor think of a reason to excuse herself in the middle of the day for a shower.

"Oh, Honey. Oh my goodness, what happened?" The sister called Suzie is the last one to leave and she is holding Doreen's hands in hers looking down at them, her face aghast.

Doreen looks down and sees her own hands being held in the palms of the sister Suzie. The sister's hands are white and clean. There are rings on the fingers. A few of the fingers are folded over her own and she can see that the nails have been painted with something colourless. Something shiny and protective.

Her own nails are mangled. Her fingertips are discoloured and ragged. Scabbed over in places, freshly bleeding in others. A piece of torn skin has not quite let go of one of her ring fingers.

The sister looks close to tears. She is staring at Doreen trying to get her to keep eye contact. She is mocking her in some way. She is going to tell everyone about this. Doreen wants to pull her hands away but they remain lifeless, refusing to do anything but be held and stared at.

Doreen feels like she should answer but there is nothing to say. There is no explanation.

The sister drops Doreen's hands and pulls her in for yet another unsolicited embrace. The sister is crying now, her body rattling, her face beginning to leak. She smells like garlic and fabric softener. Doreen waits for the hugging and the crying to end.

After what is too long a span of time the sister finally lets go and stands back from Doreen with a wet and blotchy face. She shows no sign of being able to calm herself. The crying has taken her over. It appears to be unstoppable. Doreen watches her, waiting for her cue that she can walk away. Go back to the couch and find her Bible.

The sister is rubbing her eyes. She is apologizing. She is sorry for crying, sorry she can't stop. She is saying Gracie's name. Her body is trembling. Doreen thinks that she should say something but she doesn't know what it would be. She isn't sure what exactly is happening. Just that the sister is very sad and that this state of grief seems to be preventing her from leaving.

The husband of the sister Suzie, in this moment Doreen has no idea of his name, comes to put an arm around his wife. There are some children. Small versions of the dad. Faces that look exactly like smaller versions of his even though she isn't even sure if they are boys or girls. The husband pulls the sister into an embrace. He apologizes to Doreen too. His eyes are wet and green. They remind of her of walking out to the yard in the morning while the grass is still wet with dew.

Martha comes into the room and there is more hugging and crying.

"Martha," Doreen finally brings her mouth to say, "can I be dismissed?"

Martha also appears to be crying. "Of course. Go sit. I will come back and make us a tea."

Doreen should say thank you but she doesn't. She's just glad to escape the blubbering and the touching.

The children are in the basement and Tom is in the yard with the dog. She watches him out the glass doors of the living room. He is doing something with machinery. A lawn mower perhaps. Something green and mechanical.

She listens for God's voice but it isn't there. She can't decide how she feels about this. He has been so demanding lately. So irritated with her. She had been begging him to stop. To just stop talking. But now the silence is like another missing thing. Something else she had gotten used to that has now been taken away. Another absence. She's thinking about this and then suddenly she isn't. Suddenly there are faces against a black background. There is fruit on a table with a black table cloth. There is nothing.

Once again she is being shaken awake. Not by Tom, but by Martha's gentle hand on her shoulder. Martha's raspy voice repeating her name.

"I made you a coffee instead," she asks Doreen to sit up and take the mug. Doreen feels her own face slick with drool.

Finally she has been sleeping and yet she has never been more exhausted in her life. The pills aren't helping anything.

Nothing helps anything.

She doesn't take another pill that night. Leaves the amber bottle with her name on it in the secret box. Next to Gracie and Isaac.

She has decided that she prefers sleeplessness to sedation. She will take the wired exhaustion that comes from going days without sleep over the groggy and incapacitated exhaustion created by the pills. She will stop violating the temple. She will prepare for the end.

She stays up and listens to the radio. She listens to the news again. More horrific tales of humanity. More to worry about and fear. Perhaps the Rapture has begun. Perhaps this is the beginning of God's wrath, this world they already live in. This world they've brought their children forth into. She listens to it endlessly, absorbing the horrors. Contemplating the atrocities. Maybe the Rapture is already upon them and no one has figured it out yet.

This worries her. She knows their fate. She does not want the children left behind.

Sleep comes to her in waves, residue from the sleeping pills knocking her out and its effects wearing off and rousing her back into consciousness. She dreams about nothing of substance. Objects. Food. A field of yellow flowers with a tractor, seemingly abandoned, in the middle of it.

She doesn't need to be shaken awake on Monday morning. She is once again awake before anyone else. She waits to hear the baby but then remembers that she won't. This will take some getting used to.

The conciliation is in the fact that Gracie is safe from Hell on Earth. She'd like to think the baby is safe in the arms of Jesus, nestled next to her infant brother. She tells herself perhaps that's true. She tells herself what she needs to sometimes in order to make it through another day. She supposes that's what they all do. Martha pretending she raised a decent son. Tom telling himself he has repented well enough to no longer be considered a sinner. It seems to be what humans do. Tell themselves a better story than the truth.

It is Monday morning and June is half over. Soon school will be finished and the children will be home all day for two months. They will attend day camps. Tom will take vacation and Doreen will be blessed with his presence, all day, every day, for a full four weeks. They will go somewhere. To a beach. Somewhere where the children can be outside all day. Martha will be with them this year, she guesses. Martha is a permanent fixture now for an indefinite amount of time. A guardian. A sitter. Someone to make sure Doreen doesn't keep fucking it all up.

"Wow, you don't look like a complete invalid today."

"Good morning Tom."

"Make coffee"

"Yes Tom."

And the day begins. But still Doreen can't bring herself to thank God for His blessings. She should pray, but she does not.

Sometime in the afternoon God begins to talk to her again. The grogginess from the pills remains but has eased considerably. He begins with soft sentences and becomes louder and more persistent as the afternoon fades into evening. He wants her to be mindful of the signs. He points out the same things over and over again. She knows. She tells Him this but He keeps repeating. She must need the lesson reiterated. She must still need to learn. She must not be doing something that she needs to do. She tries very hard to listen without fighting Him off.

"Heavenly Father, we thank you for the food in front of us. We thank you for family and friends and for keeping Isaac and Gracie safe. Forgive us our trespasses, Lord and lead us to salvation. Amen."

Doreen opens her eyes and looks up at her husband as he is finishing Grace. His skin is freckled. He has moisture on his lips. She has to look away.

The children chat with their father and their grandmother. Delilah asks if they can have pickles. Doreen looks down into her food and notices a piece of cartilage on the end of her chicken leg. Rubbery and slick with grease. She can smell it. Dead flesh. Rotting animal body. She gags violently and has to jump from the table to make it to the bathroom on time.

Hugging the toilet she knows. She knows instinctively and without a doubt. It has been forever since she's bled. It was too late. When she finally told her husband that her body could take no more. When she finally pushed him off and removed herself from his bed. It had already been too late.

She would like to scream NO! to the sky but there is nothing left in her. All she can do is remain on the cold tile of the bathroom floor and stare into the sickening water of the toilet bowl.

She stays up all night and reads and listens and God natters at her for hours upon hours about His intentions. About her responsibilities. About everything that needs to be taken care of. She paces and chews and stays awake.

She stays awake until it is Tuesday morning.

Another day of all the same things as the day before. Another day of Tom's demands and Martha's instructions and the four walls of the house. Of children who require varying degrees of maintenance. Of putting food into her mouth without desire. Of remembering a little girl who was once there and is now gone. Of remembering an infant boy who never got the chance to do anything. Never took a breath. Of remembering a group of boys who forever changed who she was. Of knowing one of those boys has been sleeping beside her for a lifetime. And now, of knowing, she is once again harbouring his seed. She hopes it is a boy. Another son for Tom.

She reads the Bible, chews her fingers, paces the floor. She tries to have conversations with the people around her but finds ideas very fleeting; difficult to follow and hold on to. One thought and then another and then another with nothing binding them together. Martha looks at her often with a confused and sad expression. Something helpless.

Tom is home for supper at a decent time. Martha had made lasagna and hadn't asked Doreen for help. Doreen had paced around behind her mother-in-law, chomping on herself until finally Martha had given her the task of washing and chopping romaine lettuce and putting it in the salad spinner. Doreen had managed.

Now everyone is at the table. Except Gracie. The high chair has been stowed away. They will need it again soon enough.

"I was thinking it might be nice to plant a tree for Gracie." She had heard about this on the news. A little boy had been shot at a school somewhere in the States and his class had planted a tree in his honour, in the woods behind the school yard.

Tom puts his fork down, wipes his ugly face with a napkin and stares at his wife, as he has a thousand times before, like she is the town idiot. Like she could not be more wrong and more ridiculous if she put great effort in to doing so.

"A tree?"

Doreen nods. Puts her own fork down, relieved to have a break from the task of eating. The tomato sauce is so strong in her mouth she can feel it burning canker sores into her tongue and the soft flesh of her cheeks. The pasta is slippery and feels like warm rubber.

"To commemorate her death. Or, her life, I guess."

"What would be the point? Really?"

"A place in our yard to visit. For the kids. Would you like that Dee? A place to visit with Gracie whenever you wanted?"

Delilah nods but with apprehension. The girl is too smart to directly contradict her father.

Martha pipes up, Doreen having forgotten for a moment that the old woman was even there. "I think it's a lovely idea, Tommy. Karen Gaudet planted a tree for her husband when he died last year. It's something people do now."

Tom picks his fork back up and stabs a piece of Romaine lettuce. Nods at his mother. "Sure. Alright. We'll plant a tree."

He stuffs Caesar salad into his mouth, an oversized portion of it, and looks back at Doreen. White salad dressing oozes out around the outline of his mouth as he chews.

"Excuse me." Doreen quickly wipes her face with a napkin and is back on the bathroom floor again just in time. She is sweaty and exhausted when she has finished.

She stays still and quiet next to the toilet in case there is more to come.

She begins to make a list in her head.

Infertility.

Still birth.

Autism.

Gracie.

She gathers herself when she is sure that her stomach has expelled everything in it and some of itself too and that there is nothing more to come for now. She splashes cold water on her face and dries it with a towel.

She returns to the table, gathers up her own plate and dumps her remaining food into the garbage.

"What are you doing Doreen? You need to eat."

"I'm pregnant Tom."

She doesn't wait for his response. Doesn't turn to see the smug look she knows he'll be wearing. His gloating colourless eyes. She leaves the kitchen before any of them can say anything.

She remembers a woman called Lisa who told her not to have any more babies. Who pleaded with her to hear just this one word of advice. Who told her there would be consequences not only for her, but for the children she already has.

Didn't Lisa know that there had always been consequences? That the sins of the mother have, all along, been visited upon by the children. What difference did it make now? None at all.

She waits for the house to fall asleep once more and spends the entire night awake again. Reading her bible. Absorbing. Listening to God. Swinging back and forth in her mind between complete and utter resignation and the need for escape. Again ideas seem elusive. They flutter around her and then fly away. She reaches out and tries to grab hold of them but there is no use. Her mind reels around and around and disorients her. She needs to sleep. She thinks about having a few hours of respite from thought. But then of course she must be wary of her dreams. Asleep or awake there is no relief. No break from her mind. No respite from memory.

By the time Wednesday night arrives, she has been so many hours without sleep that she can't remember it. Her brain is wired and thoughts whip around and scatter like fall leaves in the wind.

Martha has asked her if she's sleeping. Has whispered to her in private about the sleeping pills. Is she using them. Are they helping. Doreen assures the old woman that she is indeed using the pills and that they are a wonderful aide. The woman nods looking unconvinced. Doreen then begins talking to her about yard work and a hummingbird feeder and how much Gracie liked peanut butter and jam. The old lady pats her hand. Says in an exhausted and shaky voice, "This too shall pass."

And they carry on.

As always, life goes on.

A woman on the news has drowned her children. In birth order, no less. She will go to prison now where everything will be done for her. Where meals will be made and brought to her in her solitary cell. Where her husband will no longer be able to take jabs at her body and impregnate her. Where she can read and sleep.

An elderly woman has been raped in her bed in the middle of the night by a teenage boy. He had repeated the words, "I hate grandmothers," in her eighty-nine year old ears while he sodomized her.

Somewhere in the States there has been another school shooting. Some killed, many wounded. Everyone traumatized.

Gas prices continue to inflate.

The news is a horrible, horrible thing.

The Rapture is upon them.

Doreen listens and listens and while she does He whispers in her ear, commentates, explains. He points out to her the things she should be noticing. The themes and the mood and the tone of the world into which she has brought forth life. He speaks softly to her at times but easily becomes

harsh and demanding. Fluctuates between soothing and command-
ing. Whispers and then screams. It begins, once more, to drive her to
madness.

Watch therefore: for ye know not what hour your Lord doth come.

She gets up and paces the room, eats her fingers, sits back down, opens
the Bible, closes the Bible, stands back up, paces again.

She wishes for something to do other than this. She wishes that sleep were
a possibility. She wishes for whatever it is that makes a person normal.
That makes a person able to lie down at night on a soft pillow and fall into
a state of unconsciousness that lasts a span of uninterrupted hours and
allows her to rise refreshed and capable.

She pictures the child growing in her womb. Sees her body, once again,
stretching and tearing. The marks on her belly that have finally begun to
fade into something slightly pink, turning purple and angry once again.
Her breasts leaking milk, hard and hot and pained as she feeds her infant
formula from a rubber nipple.

She pictures sleepless nights and spit-up and the thick mustard-y shit of a
newborn. She continues to pace, to chew, to turn the dial on the radio,
to turn the pages in the Book hoping that something definitive will jump
out of the pages and turn her life into something other than what it is.

**And if I go and prepare a place for you, I will come again, and
receive you into myself; that where I am, there ye may be also.**

The sun comes up and fills the yard as well as the living room with soft
pink light.

Doreen is exhausted but knows she will never sleep again. Knows she
will be stuck in this horrific state of perpetual wakefulness for eternity. So
that she might keep reliving the past. So that she can hurt continuously

without the respite of unconsciousness. It is part of her punishment. The uninterrupted agony of living.

When Martha and Faith come downstairs with sleepy eyes and wrinkled nightgowns Doreen can barely see straight. She can feel the veins in her eyeballs strained and burning from reading the tiny print of the Bible for an undetermined number of hours. She barely recognizes the two people in front of her. Is confused, momentarily, about who they actually are.

The little girl comes to her and raises the arms like it wants to be picked up. It seems too large to be carried. Too long. Doreen sits down on the couch and lets the child curl up beside her. She can smell something that she wants to recoil from. The smell of unwashed human. Of sweat that has spent hours gathering in the creases of the body and stagnating there.

She stares down at the child and tries to make sense of it sitting beside her. She thinks of the dead one. She waits for the boy. The boy has always been the easy one, hasn't he. She has never had much trouble feeling affection for the boy.

More children begin to emerge and soon the old lady begins speaking. Doreen can hear the voice but cannot make sense of the words, nor decide who they are directed at. Is the old woman speaking to the children or is she demanding something of Doreen, herself? Doreen watches the lips move, sees the eyeballs staring. The older girl is staring at her too. Her lips opening and closing very prettily. No saliva. Nothing wet. Just sweet, dry lips that move without expelling anything but noise.

The girl's face looks upset. It changes as she moves her mouth. Becomes twisted and worried. The eyes look misty. Doreen watches.

Eventually the old woman puts her hands on the shoulders of the eldest girl and steers her away from her mother. Doreen watches. Wonders how long it has been since she has blinked.

She wants to get up but can't. Her body says no. Her body remains on the couch like a block of cement. Like something that has been planted and has deep roots anchoring it in place.

She watches as more of the morning unfolds. Faces spring up in front of her and talk but she doesn't bother to respond. She can't. She thinks of words momentarily but they leave her brain before she can bring her lips to utter them. Her lips won't move anyway. She can feel them drying and cracking as she sits there.

Even Tom gives up. He shakes her shoulders a bit, makes angry faces and froths at the mouth as he speaks. Still, no matter how angry Tom appears to become, Doreen cannot react to it. She can't bring herself to speak or move and nor can she bring herself to care that she is incapable of either.

She sits on the couch for what she thinks is hours. Some of the children leave, the man leaves, the old woman and the dog and the boy child flit in and out of the room. The other girl too. The one that smells like fish. Doreen just sits. She stares. She listens to God because she has no choice. He doesn't stop. He nags and natters and insists and Doreen can't fight it off so she has no other choice but to give in. To let it take her over. He speaks vile words. Frightening words. She lets them stream into her head and dissolve.

The old lady brings things to her. A glass of water, a sandwich on a plate. Doreen takes bites of the food that she doesn't taste. Chokes as she swallows them down. She can't remember the last time she went to the bathroom or had a shower or was able to hold onto a thought or a sentence for long enough to make sense of it.

She goes back to reading. It is the only thing she can do that makes any sense. She reads the words, one at a time, holding onto their meaning for the briefest of moments before the meaning is lost and she is piecing the vowels and the consonants of the next word together.

The older girls return home and the house fills with cooking smells and the sun begins to fall behind the trees and Doreen has barely moved since it came up. Has not spoken.

She looks down into the thin pages of the good Book and sees something red smudging the words and sticking the pages together. It is blood. Her blood, she realizes, from what's left of her fingertips. She has no recollection of chewing her nails throughout the day, but clearly she has been doing so ravenously. She has mutilated herself. Her fingers may never resemble the fully developed fingers of an adult woman again. Instead they will look like something stunted. Something that failed to thrive.

There was a world once that she thought was different than this one. One where there were possibilities. A time when she had known, with every fiber of her core, that she would escape the confines of her mother's closet, the torment of the threatened leather belt. A place where she had been pretty and young with tight skin that fit her bones, and breasts that stood at attention on her chest instead of pointing sad brown nipples to the ground. A time before.

Now there is nothing. She is nothing but an overburdened body worn ragged by the years. There is no promise. No hope. Different confines but with the same result. A woman stuck in a space too small, not knowing what's worse, remaining tightly enclosed, or facing what is on the other side of the door.

Martha comes to sit beside her and she is speaking but again Doreen has trouble hearing the words let alone making sense of them. It's as if she is watching television with the mute button on. All the necessary parts of conversation are present except the sound. And her participation.

And then, slowly, she begins to hear something. The raspy voice of her mother-in-law becomes somewhat audible. She can make sense of some of the words. Sleep. Pills. Tommy. Doctor. The movement of the lips matches the sounds. Matches the words coming out of the mouth and into the room.

And all at once she finds her own voice. Hears it say, "I can't do it again Martha. I can't have another baby."

Martha stops moving her lips and stares at her daughter-in-law for a few seconds before beginning to rub Doreen's shoulder firmly. Back and forth, back and forth, the old leathery hand across the bones of Doreen's back. An apparent attempt to soothe. Something compulsive and desperate.

The old lady speaks quietly. She says, "The Lord giveth and He taketh away." This Doreen hears with clarity.

She nods. And then as the old lady says something else her voice becomes again just a garble of sounds until it fades into nothing. The lips moving without sound once more.

Doreen stares into the darkness of the yard and eventually isn't sure if Martha is still beside her or not.

All night she reads the Bible. Feverishly. Reads until she can almost feel her eyeballs begin to bleed.

She comes to from something she isn't sure was sleep but thinks might have been. She may have drifted off. She may have fallen into slumber for a period of time. She has no idea how much time has passed or if she was even asleep. She may have been awake the whole time but drawing a blank. Sitting with her eyes staring straight ahead and nothing happening otherwise. No thoughts in her brain, no awareness of the world around her or of the ticking of the clock. Oblivious to the passing of time.

She comes to and she is sure there is a way that she can give herself an abortion with a coat hanger. She would just have to untwist it with a pair of pliers from Tom's tool box. Straighten it and poke it up into herself. Twist it around.

She reads the Bible and barely notices now when droplets of blood spatter and smudge the words. It seems to be happening on every third turn of the page. She sucks on her fingers to stop the bleeding, but without even knowing it she only ends up chewing them open again.

> **For the life of the flesh is in the blood: and I have given it to you upon the altar to make an atonement for your souls.**

Morning comes and she has no idea what day of the week it is. She only knows that although she has not seen the sun make its entrance, the sky has gone from black to whitish gray. She only knows that it is wet outside. She can feel the dampness in her bones. Summer rain. Dank and sorrowful.

When Tom puts his face in hers in another futile attempt to bring her back to the land of the living, to the world of the functional, she takes in his features. She looks into his colourless eyes and notices the structure of the nose and the cheekbones. She thinks about things. Imagines them. She sees the flapping lips and wants nothing more than to make them be still. She can make out some of his sentences. He is yammering at her about taking care of herself while she is pregnant. He is talking about his unborn son. She stares.

He scolds her about her fingers. Points his own finger into her face and reprimands.

God begins to natter over top of Tom.

She can't decide what would be worse. Burning in the fires of Hell or living this Hell on Earth with Tom for one more day. For one more night.

She sees the dog come into the room and watches Tom let it out into the yard.

She glares at it as it comes back in. The smell of it, like the inside of a body, like something that has been cut open and left splayed on a butcher's block. She throws up in the kitchen sink and believes Tom is scolding her for this as well. But he is all lips and no sound. Thankfully the mute button is on once more and Tom is nothing but a presence in the room for her to maneuver around on her way back to her spot on the couch.

She reads, she reads, she reads.

> *And the fifth angel sounded, and I saw a star fall from heaven unto the earth; and to him was given the key to the bottomless pit.*

She finds herself in that state of coming to, several times again that day. Coming to. Awakening from something she isn't sure is sleep. She finds herself rocking. She rocks like the little girl in the closet once did. Back and forth back and forth to stave off the agony of remaining still.

Martha rubs her back a lot. Rubs her shoulders. Tries to feed her. Gives her water. Gives her tea. Sets things beside her only to come and take them away again.

Doreen looks down and sees the little boy beside her. The dark brown eyes stare up. He seems much too little to have such worry in his eyes. She touches the brown hair. Folds and unfolds the small fingers. The old lady pulls the boy away.

She sees the old lady crying in the kitchen. Sees the face wet with tears. Watches the body tremble.

She reads her Bible. Chews herself to pieces. Reads her Bible.

> **And in those days shall men seek death, and shall not find it; and shall desire to die, and death shall flee from them.**

Light turns to dark again.

And then again, dark turns to light.

The same thing. Over and over and over again.

Saturday June 23, 2001

Doreen is awake still, unable now to remember what sleep feels like, what it is, what it does for the body, when the people again come out of bedrooms and fill the house with sounds and smells and movement.

She can no longer sit. She has to move around. Her eyes are half blind with the strain of reading and exhaustion. The faces in front of her are fuzzy. She rubs and rubs her eyes hoping to somehow wipe away the film that is adhering itself to her eyeballs, but it is of no use. She can feel it, something thick and opaque mildly obscuring her vision.

The voices come in and out. The people around her speak to her and to each other and she hears certain sentences but not others. She catches random words but many more escape her. She tries to do some of the things that need to be done. Moves silently around the kitchen, her body seemingly fighting her. Her arms heavy and lazy. Her legs holding her up reluctantly, lording over her the fact that they could, at any given moment, fold up underneath her and send her crashing to the floor.

And wouldn't that upset Tom. If her legs gave out from underneath her and she was to collapse on the floor from the pure exhaustion of her life, there would be no sympathy. There would be no comfort. No help up. No guidance into a softer spot where she could rest.

Instead there would be ridicule and reprimand and irritation. As it had always been. As she had shamed and burdened her father by having the audacity to be attacked by six teenage boys drunk out of their minds and blind with violence, so has she embarrassed and inconvenienced Tom one thousand times since. By needing. By being flawed. By doing all those human things that her husband finds so utterly distasteful.

No, she mustn't fall. She mustn't collapse. Not now, not ever. She mustn't draw attention to herself and her shortcomings.

She pours coffee and dresses it. She takes tentative bites of a banana, desperately trying to keep it down, not to choke it back up onto the counter.

The white noise fills her brain and sloshes around in her skull, annihilating every other sound in the universe. Again lips move and eyes stare but she hears nothing.

The banana is mush in her mouth, clammy and sticky and leaving a slimy film in its wake. It is no use. She runs to the bathroom. Coffee and undigested banana. The smell makes her heave again. She wishes she could puke up what's growing inside of her. Vomit Tom's seed up into the toilet and flush it into the sewer system. Instead it feeds off of her and burrows into the lining of her body. There is no way to stop it. Nothing she can do. As always. Nothing she can possibly do. The desperation within her becomes something solid and alive. As parasitic as the fetus itself.

Her stomach aches and cramps as she leaves the bathroom and returns to the couch.

God's voice is in her ears. Loud. Angry. He has had enough.

Doreen, too, has had enough.

She has spent forever hoping, praying, that someone would show up and save her. That somehow she could save her children. She has prayed for understanding, for forgiveness, for love. From a father. From a brother. A husband. She has wanted something to take the edge off, something to numb, if only for a short span of time, the pain of memory. To dull the grief. She has wanted to sleep without dreaming.

And yet all the praying and the hoping in the world have done her absolutely no good. Have done nothing to bring peace or earn her anything close to resembling love. Have done nothing to make her a better person. Have done nothing to save her children. And she knows now, she knows that there is no use in any of it. The children will stumble over and over again. The children will stumble because they came from sin. From evil. They came from the nothing that she is.

It is when Martha comes to her with coffee on her breath and the smell of age leaking from her pores and tells her she is going into town for the afternoon that Doreen knows. God nods his head. He smiles into her eardrums.

The sister Mary has had a problem with her health. Doreen tries desperately to tune in to what the old woman is telling her. She catches as many words as she can, holds on to them. Digests what is happening. A few hours. Martha will be gone for just a few hours. She needs not worry about much. Tom is there with the kids. Supper. Warm up the pot of homemade soup. There is a loaf of bread. There is chocolate milk.

"Okay, Doreen? Alright?" The eyes are pleading. The expression wants desperately to believe that Doreen can handle the task at hand. That this near catatonic woman can cook soup and not hurt anyone for a few hours. The eyes beg to see something that is no longer there.

Doreen nods her head. She tries to say yes, okay, but nothing happens. Her head just nods until the old woman pats her knee and rises to leave.

The smell of the soup simmering on the stovetop makes Doreen's stomach contract into something rock-like and painful. She can smell the spices. Basil. Thyme. Cinnamon. Vegetables float at the top of the pot, bringing to mind something regurgitated. Doreen remembers the sharp jabs of forced sex. She remembers her body being torn. Remembers her asshole bleeding for weeks. Remembers Tom.

The children come in and out of the room. The oldest girl gets bread ready. She puts glasses on the table. She talks to her mother gingerly.

"Stir the soup my love," Doreen tells Delilah. It is one of the only sentences she has managed all day. The first thing she has said since she admitted out loud that she didn't have it in her to birth and raise another one of Tom's children.

She leaves the girl with the soup and she goes to the basement to the box of hidden photographs. To where Gracie and Isaac will always be. To where smiles are worn on faces in snapshots. Eternal smiles. To where Isaac will always be peaceful and blue. To the box of dead babies.

She pulls the box from the shelf and rummages through the photos without looking at any of them. She slips the pill bottle into the pocket of her jeans and places the box back on the shelf.

"Thank you, Dee." She takes the spoon from the girl's hand and stirs. "Now go back downstairs until I call you up."

The girl obeys.

"Lord bless this food we are about to eat. Thank you, Lord for my mother's help. I don't know where we'd be without it."

Doreen stares at her husband as he says Grace. He has a blemish. Something raised and puss-filled just below his nostril. The children have all bowed their heads in prayer. Doreen is sitting upright watching her husband's eyeballs move underneath his lids. Watching the gummy mouth move. Listening to his words. Even in prayer he finds a way to dig into her. To make her aware of her constant state of failure.

"Lord, keep Isaac and Gracie, and Lord, please bless the new baby on the way. Thank you for your gifts. Gracious, Lord. Amen."

Doreen is still staring at her husband as he lifts his head and opens his eyes. He meets her eyes and looks, of course, perturbed.

The children too lift their heads and open their eyes.

Doreen ladles soup into all of their bowls. She pours them chocolate milk while Delilah passes the bread basket around and Tom begins to spread butter with a knife from their wedding set.

Martha's cooking is so wonderful. Thank goodness for Martha. Doreen watches as her husband and her children take enthusiastic mouthfuls of hot soup. As they use thick slices of homemade bread to sop up broth. As they slurp and gulp and sigh.

"You need to get your vegetables. Probably what happened with this one." Tom gestures toward their defective child. Pretty little Eden. Blonde hair, blue eyes. It is Doreen's fault. She didn't eat enough vegetables to properly grow the child's brain, leaving it stunted and inadequate.

Doreen tears off small pieces of bread, doughy and moist, and puts them to her lips. "This is all I can stomach right now," she tells her husband. "A few more weeks and I'll have my appetite back." She chews the bread. Swallows it. Takes sips of tap water from her glass.

The meal concludes and bodies leave the table. The dog scrounges around the floor, lapping up any crumb that has been dropped, making disgusting sounds with its oversized pink tongue. Doreen wants to kick it in the face but Tom is nearby. He is in the living room with his stinky feet up on her coffee table. He is watching the baseball game and grunting, his hand tucked into the crotch of his pants.

The children are in the basement and it isn't long before their voices taper off into nothing. It isn't long until there is quiet.

Doreen tidies the kitchen. She pours the leftover soup into the dog dish. She rinses bowls and puts them in the dishwasher. Her body is moving now. Moving fluidly and without resistance. Her limbs are picking up speed. Despite the condition of her fingers, they are working aptly and with precision. She cleans.

She looks in on her husband. He his holding the television remote with a limp wrist, the device slowly falling from his grasp. His eyes are heavy, dropping closed and then popping back open and blinking. He sees her. Turns to look at her.

"What?"

She shakes her head. "Nothing."

She goes back to the kitchen, wipes the counters, sweeps the floors. She returns the placemats to their places on the table.

She wrings out the dishcloth and folds it in half. Drapes it over the faucet so that it can dry. Tom hates nothing more than a smelly dish rag.

Tom passes through the kitchen on his way upstairs. He is colourless. She smiles at him as he passes by. He does not return the gesture. He simply walks past her and continues his journey up the stairs.

Doreen is sitting on the couch in the living room when she hears Martha come in the door. It is dark outside. The house is quiet. Doreen has a mug of tea in her hands that has long gone cold. She takes a deep full breath.

The old woman makes a sound that is unlike anything Doreen can recall hearing in her forty years on earth. The noise is indescribable.

Doreen looks up.

Martha has dropped her purse and her hands have flown to her face. To her mouth. Her eyes are wide with horror. Doreen understands.

The sight of the dog would be upsetting to anyone, she supposes. His throat and belly bleeding. The innards spilled onto the carpet. The smell of it had been vile. Martha is likely smelling it now and fighting off the urge to retch. Doreen however, stopped smelling it a while ago.

To her mother-in-law she says, "You might want to call the police."

The old woman begins to scream. The scream is gut-curdling. Doreen wonders if the old lady's heart will survive the scene upstairs. She thinks to tell her not to go up there but knows it is no use.

The old lady is saying *no, no, no,* and making her way toward the stairs.

Doreen remembers that there was a lot of blood. Tom's hunting knife is somewhere in the debris. She remembers that she has left Jacob in the bathtub. He had to go first. After Tom of course. Jacob was the most difficult one for her. He was the closest thing to love she could remember since Bruno. He is angelic now. Sweet floating angel.

Martha's noises become too painful for Doreen to tolerate. The anguish is gargantuan. But it was inevitable. Surely, in time, Martha will understand.

God pets her, fills her head with the white noise that blocks out her mother-in-law's horrific noises.

Doreen places a hand over her stomach and begins to pray.

Thank you, Lord for the life that is growing inside of me. You are a gracious and giving Father and I am not worthy of your gifts. Forgive me my trespasses, Lord and keep this unborn child safe. Thank you for the blessings of this day.

Amen.